Another woman senator in a long red sweater and black miniskirt came to St. Clair.

"It happened so fast, there was nothing you could do. I'm Renata Glover. Did Irene choke on something? Can choking cause convulsions like that?"

"Not usually," said St. Clair. "Was she ill?"

Senator Rubenstock shook her head. "Strong as an ox. She could handle a breakfast meeting, sit on committee all morning, do a fund-raiser at noon, and raise hell on the senate floor in the afternoon. Then give a talk before some citizen group in the evening."

"She was also strong enough to go to the mat with the male opposition in the senate," sighed Senator Glover. "I don't know what the women in the legislature will do without her."

Senator Rubenstock flashed Senator Glover a warning look. "Watch it. People are listening."

"Listening for what?" asked Karen Wolfson.

"For nothing," said Senator Rubenstock.

By Janet McGiffin
*Published by Fawcett Books:*

EMERGENCY MURDER
PRESCRIPTION FOR DEATH
ELECTIVE MURDER

# ELECTIVE MURDER

## Janet McGiffin

FAWCETT GOLD MEDAL • NEW YORK

A Fawcett Gold Medal Book
Published by Ballantine Books
Copyright © 1995 by Janet McGiffin

All rights reserved under International and Pan-American Copyright Conventions. Published in the United States by Ballantine Books, a division of Random House, Inc., New York, and simultaneously in Canada by Random House of Canada Limited, Toronto.

Library of Congress Catalog Card Number: 94-90856

ISBN 0-449-14925-0

Manufactured in the United States of America

First Edition: May 1995

10  9  8  7  6  5  4  3  2  1

# CHAPTER

# 1

DR. MAXENE ST. CLAIR peered around the crowded Senate Hearing Room in Madison, Wisconsin, looking for an empty chair. Her red hair had frizzed thanks to the tight wool cap she had put on to combat the driving snow in the walk from her car to the senate building. The few moments in the ladies' room smoothing her hair and repairing her makeup didn't seem to have had much effect. She had driven from Milwaukee through near blizzard conditions to testify before the Senate Health Care Committee, and she was amazed at the number of people who had done the same.

A few months before, Senator Irene Wisnewski, a Democrat from Milwaukee, had appeared at St. Agnes' ER during Dr. St. Clair's shift. She wanted to see how state welfare money for medical care in emergency rooms was being spent. St. Clair had always voted for Senator Irene and she was glad to explain the problems with the state system.

During the hours Senator Irene was at the emergency room, two pregnant women had come in during the last stage of labor and delivered tiny, sick babies before the women could be transferred to Maternity. St. Clair had gone into a tirade about how emergency rooms are misused by pregnant women living at poverty level, and that state-funded neighborhood prenatal clinics would keep them from delivering in emergency rooms.

So when Senator Wisnewski phoned months later, asking

St. Clair to testify for her proposed bill giving state funds for prenatal clinics, St. Clair was happy to help.

St. Clair's feet were numb. Morning fog had made visibility near zero, turning the drive into an ordeal. The Madison streets were sheet ice and snowdrifts and jammed with parked cars. She ended up parking six blocks from the Capitol building. After wading through salt-melted slush, St. Clair's only decent pair of comfortable pumps were ruined.

Across the packed hearing room, she spotted an excited blond woman in a bright pink suit waving at her. St. Clair pushed down the crowded row to the empty seat the woman had been guarding. The woman stuffed St. Clair's heavy wool coat under the seat and stuck out a hand.

"Karen Wolfson. Remember me? I was with Senator Irene when she came to St. Agnes' ER last fall. I'm a lobbyist for the State Nurses' Association and I'm testifying for the senator's health care bill, like you. Senator Irene said you were coming, so I saved you a seat."

Senator Wisnewski was standing at the front of the room talking to several other senators near the raised dais that filled the end of the room. The senator was wearing a brilliant blue wool suit with a chartreuse blouse. The bright colors made her tall beehive hairstyle seem even whiter.

Other senators began taking their seats, pouring themselves glasses of water, flipping through papers. Senator Wisnewski disappeared out a side entrance, then reappeared eating something. She said something to the security guard, who laughed, then she sat down in the center of the middle row. She leaned forward and tapped sharply on the shoulder of the small, stout man sitting in front of her. His thin gray hair was plastered over the top of his head. He jumped, startled, then picked up the gavel and pounded the audience into silence.

"The Senate Health Care Committee is now in session," he announced in a reedy voice. "I hereby turn the hearing over to Senator Wisnewski."

Senator Wisnewski's raspy cigarette voice silenced the last of the whisperers.

"A few months ago I visited St. Agnes Hospital Emergency Room in Milwaukee to see for myself why emergency rooms use up so much of our state welfare dollar. What I saw at St. Agnes' ER caused me to write my health care bill, which cuts state money for expensive emergency room procedures. I replaced these cuts with money for preventative care clinics, such as prenatal clinics. Dr. Maxene St. Clair, who works at St. Agnes Emergency Room, is here today to explain why much of her work is unnecessary and overexpensive, and why emergency room doctors can be replaced by more cost-effective people such as public health nurses."

Maxene listened with amazement. This was not what the senator had explained over the phone. She stood and walked forward to the witness chair, collecting her thoughts.

"Mr. Chairman and members of the Health Care Committee," she began, "can I plead the Fifth Amendment to keep from testifying myself out of a job?"

She waited for the chuckles to subside. "I came here to explain why we need state-funded prenatal clinics for poverty-level pregnant women who use emergency rooms to deliver their babies. Giving birth is not an emergency, but it has become one for women who cannot afford prenatal care. It is unhealthy for babies to come into the world in the same room with gunshot victims or people with heart attacks. Many poor women, including those on welfare, are so afraid of being turned away from a hospital that they come to the ER at the last moment of labor and we don't even have time to transfer them to Maternity."

St. Clair paused to check her note card. "Because of budget cuts in federal- and state-funded prenatal programs, I see more women with no prenatal care who arrive at the ER hoping for the best. For pregnant teenagers and women with medical problems, Senators, our best is not enough. They often suffer serious complications and deliver tiny babies who stay in the hospital long after the mother has gone home. These women need a neighborhood state-funded prenatal clinic to spot complications early, and to help them have a healthy pregnancy."

She glanced at her watch to see if she had passed the three-minute limit. "While I agree with Senator Wisnewski that many people come to the ER with imagined or minor illnesses and waste money by receiving expensive diagnostic procedures, I cannot agree that emergency rooms can be replaced. Modern life is precarious, and even the most cautious individual can need immediate and drastic medical care. Senators, don't cost-contain emergency rooms out of existence."

She looked up at Senator Wisnewski. The senator was staring at her with her mouth open. She half rose, waved her hands, and opened and closed her mouth several times. Then she pitched forward onto the long table. One flailing arm hit a coffee cup and a pitcher of water, splattering the senators in the front row. Then she slid sideways off her chair and disappeared behind the table.

Someone in the audience screamed.

St. Clair ran up the stairs of the dais and pushed aside the knot of senators bending over Senator Wisnewski. The senator's body was jerking, knocking against the chairs. Her feet banged against the long table. St. Clair put her hands on either side of the senator's head to prevent injury. A woman senator with dark hair pulled into a bun and wearing a navy-blue suit had knelt next to her and was holding her legs. Karen Wolfson arrived, flung herself on her knees, and took the senator's hands.

The convulsions began to diminish, but so did the breathing. St. Clair put her ear against the senator's heavy chest. No pulse, no respirations. She felt for a carotid pulse on her neck. No pulse. She felt for the sternum, and raised her fist, then smashed it down over the heart, trying to repolarize the electrical activity. No resulting pulse on her neck.

The woman senator was pushing the chairs out of the way. She knelt by Senator Wisnewski's head and tilted her chin upward.

"Start ventilations?" she asked St. Clair in a calm voice.

"Yes," said St. Clair. She looked up at the committee chairman, who was standing, jaw agape, eyes bulging. "Call an ambulance," she ordered, and placed her hands over Senator Wisnewski's heart. She began pushing down rhythmically with all her weight.

Because of the icy streets, the ambulance took fifteen minutes to arrive. St. Clair, the woman senator, and Karen Wolfson kept working, trading off when one of them tired. When the ambulance attendants arrived, they quickly transferred the senator to a respirator and continued CPR, but after another fifteen minutes it was clear that they could do nothing more there in the committee room. The senator needed more drastic care if her heart was to start beating by itself.

"We can do a temporary pacemaker in the ambulance," one medic murmured to St. Clair.

"No other solution," she said.

After a brief word with the two uniformed policemen who had arrived at the same time as the ambulance, the medics got ready to move her out. The policemen cleared people away from the side entrance and opened the doors.

St. Clair and the senator in the navy-blue suit sat in the back row watching the ambulance attendants quickly wheel the senator's blanketed body out the staff entrance. They continued breathing for her by pumping in air with a hand-held ambu bag.

The packed room had been quiet, but as they left, the whispers became loud voices. One of the senators, a man in his thirties in a rumpled shirt and loosened tie, walked over to the security guard standing by the public entrance. He spoke for a moment, then the security guard raised his hands.

"Ladies and gentlemen, Senator McNulty has just suggested that these two policemen and I stand here at the door and write down your names, addresses, and telephone numbers. As soon as we have this, you can leave."

"McNulty thinks he's still prosecuting attorney," muttered a senator in front of St. Clair. He was wearing a gray tweed jacket with blue pin-striped shirt and burgundy tie.

"McNulty knows what he's doing," snapped the senator with the gavel.

Maxene turned her attention to the senator sitting beside her on the floor. "Good job with the CPR."

The senator stuck out a hand. "Beverly Rubenstock. I had Red Cross training but never thought I'd use it." Now that the flush of exertion was fading, her face had paled and her hands trembled.

Karen Wolfson grabbed St. Clair's arm, but before she could speak, another woman senator in a long red sweater and black miniskirt came over to St. Clair.

"It happened so fast, there was nothing you could do. I'm Renata Glover. Did Irene choke on something? Can choking cause convulsions like that?"

"Not usually," said St. Clair. "Was she ill?"

Senator Rubenstock shook her head. "Strong as a ox. She could handle a breakfast meeting, sit on committee all morning, do a fund-raiser at noon, and raise hell on the senate floor in the afternoon, then give a talk before some citizen group in the evening."

"She was also strong enough to go to the mat with the male opposition in the senate," sighed Senator Glover. "I don't know what the women in the legislature will do without her."

Senator Rubenstock flashed Senator Glover a warning look. "Watch it. People are listening."

"Listening for what?" asked Karen Wolfson.

"Never mind," said Rubenstock.

# CHAPTER

## 2

JACKSON MAYERLING, MADISON police chief, slammed down the phone and reached for his quart bottle of antacid tablets. He shoved three into his mouth.

"Senator Irene Wisnewski fell over dead half an hour ago at the Capitol building and the damned senators want me up there," he scowled.

Detective Joseph Grabowski stopped trying to drink his acrid coffee. "That sweet old lady from Milwaukee? What happened?" He rubbed his hands together. Despite his burgundy wool pullover and heavy corduroy slacks, he was still cold.

"Collapsed during a senate committee hearing in front of six other senators and a packed audience. Some doctor there giving testimony tried to revive her, with no luck. I sent a couple of cops down with the ambulance, but the senators want the police chief himself."

"They want to be on TV with the top brass." Grabowski poured sugar into the coffee sludge and stirred it with a pencil.

Mayerling groaned. "Save my ass, will you? Whenever there's a problem at the Capitol, the politicians holler for the best police in the state, and by lucky accident here you are, famous detective from Milwaukee, even from Wisnewski's district. You're hereby an honorary Madison detective."

"You joking?"

"Come on, help me out. Put on your coat." He heaved his big belly out of the creaking swivel chair.

Grabowski pushed away the brown liquid in his chipped mug and considered the idea. He hadn't finished what he came to Madison to do, and maybe this was another chance. Assemblyman Mark Birnbaum from Milwaukee had called the chief of police because someone was vandalizing his district headquarters in Milwaukee—smelly garbage thrown against the door, toilet paper glued to the door handle—annoying enough to call the police. Technically, it wasn't a job for the Milwaukee Detective Division, but whenever public officials called, they got an upper-level detective, whatever the problem.

Birnbaum was in Madison most of the time, now that the legislature was in session, so Grabowski had made the two-hour drive, but so far today Birnbaum's secretary had delayed the meeting twice. When she asked him to come back later a third time, Grabowski gave up waiting and drove to police headquarters to visit his old friend before the snowy drive home.

Grabowski reached for his brown leather jacket. "Sure, why not? Maybe I can catch Birnbaum before he goes into another meeting."

Mayerling turned on the siren and skidded out of the police parking lot. Grabowski put on his seat belt.

"Senator Wisnewski was in her mid-fifties, wasn't she?" he asked. "Isn't it unusual for a woman that age to just collapse?"

Mayerling skidded through a snowy intersection. "Nothing Senator Wisnewski did was usual. She was a one-woman sideshow—got more press coverage than the other senators put together. In politics that's enough for murder."

Grabowski smiled, cheerful despite the frustrating day. He liked Madison, even in winter. Despite suburban sprawl at the fringes, the state capital still felt like a small town nestled by a lake in rolling Wisconsin countryside. The recent January snowfall had blanketed the city, and the enormous maples and elms sparkled in winter sunlight. The white Capitol building rising at the opposite end of State Street from the imposing University of Wisconsin campus lifted Grabowski's spirits, dragging from months of overtime homicide duty in Milwaukee.

At the Capitol building, Mayerling flashed his badge at a nervous parking attendant and pulled up behind an ambulance parked at the side entrance. The open ambulance door was guarded by two Capitol security guards and a uniformed policeman. Ambulance attendants were just lifting a blanketed body into the back.

As Mayerling and Grabowski got out, a television van screeched to a halt and the crew leaped out, dragging their gear toward the ambulance. A cameraman pointed his shoulder camera at Mayerling.

"Hey, Chief," a reporter shouted. "Is it true Senator Wisnewski was poisoned?"

"Damn press!" Mayerling threw his body in front of the ambulance long enough for the driver to slam the door and run to the front. Then, dodging microphones, he and Grabowski hurried inside the Capitol.

The lobby was jammed with people shouting questions at a flush-faced guard blocking the corridor. Grabowski and Mayerling shouldered past them, Mayerling promising reinforcements to the harassed guard.

Ahead of them, a group of people were facing a security guard who was standing arms crossed, back to a large wooden door. The scowl on his face lifted when he saw Mayerling. He pushed open the door.

Inside was hot and noisy. People were milling around the door pushing pieces of paper at a policeman. The senators were sitting in three groups on a three-tiered platform at the end of the room, watching the confusion. Long tables in front of them were scattered with pencils, coffee mugs, water glasses, legal pads, and wadded-up papers.

In the highest tier, four women were talking. One was wearing a slim, navy-blue skirt with a short green-striped jacket. As Grabowski watched, she ran a restless hand through her curly red hair.

Grabowski smiled. She was Dr. Maxene St. Clair, the only woman he had been taking out seriously in the past

year. They had met two years before when a stab wound
brought him to St. Agnes' ER, where she covered the evening emergency room shift. Dr. St. Clair had sewed him up
and then become caught up in a homicide investigation, in
fact, had ended up being chief suspect. At the time, she had
just been divorced, and they recognized in each other a mu-
tual need for companionship. Since then they'd seen a lot
of each other; in fact, Grabowski had no desire to see anyone else.

Grabowski left Mayerling talking to his police officer
and walked over to the raised platform. Maxene hurried
down the steps.

"Grabowski! Are you working on this case?" She lowered her voice. "It was the strangest thing. One minute Senator Wisnewski was fine, and the next, she was having
convulsions."

"I'm a spectator. Dropped in to see Chief Mayerling and
he dragged me along. What are you doing here?" But
Maxene had been called back by a young-looking senator
who was writing on a legal pad.

As Grabowski looked around the room, a stout man with
thin gray hair pasted across his head hurried down the
steps.

"Are you the chief of police? Where have you been? I
called at least six minutes ago."

Grabowski flashed his badge. "City of Milwaukee Police, Detective Division, Joseph Grabowski. Who are you?"

The man's frown smoothed away and his hand swung
forward. "Senator William Wilk, committee chair, from up
around Okonomowash."

The handshake was firm but wet. Grabowski dried his
hand on the inside of his pants pocket. "Are you the
spokesman here?"

"Spokesperson. I also speak for senators of the female
persuasion." Wilk's smile was unctuous.

Grabowski heard one of the women laugh, but Mayerling
prevented him from hearing her comment. Mayerling

gripped Grabowski by the elbow, turning him away from the spectators.

"Wouldn't you know, there's something funny," he muttered. "Senator McNulty says that Senator Wisnewski had been perfectly healthy until she took a drink of coffee. Then she went straight into convulsions. Senator Rubenstock and Dr. St. Clair started CPR, but when the medics took over from them, there was no response."

"So?"

"The medic told McNulty that this isn't anything ordinary, especially considering Senator Irene was healthy as a horse. Irene gave convulsions, she didn't get them, according to Senator McNulty. The medic thinks we should request an autopsy."

Senator Wilk was overhearing. "Autopsy? Is that necessary? Irene had a heart attack. One minute she was sitting up, the next she was on the floor. I've seen it before. I got the Purple Cross for my heroic work as army medic during World War Two."

Mayerling ignored him. He clapped his hands to get the attention of the senators. "I'm gonna ask you folks to stay right here under the protection of this policeman, while Detective Grabowski and I talk to a couple of you. I'll start with the person who was sitting on Senator Wisnewski's right. Detective Grabowski will talk to Senator Wilk."

The woman in the navy-blue suit and man's tie stepped forward. "I was sitting on Irene's right: I'm Beverly Rubenstock." She led Mayerling out the side door.

Wilk mopped his shining forehead with a red checkered handkerchief and motioned for Grabowski to follow him. "I was sitting below her. Fortunately I've some witness experience as citizen volunteer for the National Guard."

Grabowski followed Senator Wilk out the side door, through a small room with desks and computers, then down several hallways and up a flight of stairs. At his office, a secretary in the anteroom hung up the phone quickly as they passed through into a sunny corner room. Wilk dropped into a high-backed leather chair behind a mahogany desk and rubbed a hand over his strings of gray hair. As an afterthought he gestured Grabowski to a chair. The diamond in his gold pinkie ring glinted in the afternoon sun.

"I was looking straight at her when she keeled over," he said. "Dr. St. Clair had just said something about her health care bill that I knew would piss her off, so I turned around to see if she was going to explode. She opened her mouth and dropped straight forward. Knocked over her coffee cup and splattered my jacket. Plain heart attack; I don't know why you're talking autopsy."

"Did you do anything?" Grabowski made a note.

"Jumped up and tried to stop her from hitting the floor too hard, like I was trained in the army. Beverly, that's Senator Rubenstock, helped. Then Beverly and Dr. St. Clair started CPR."

"Had Senator Irene been feeling ill, or did she look any different from usual?"

"To tell you the truth, I looked at her as little as possible. She reminded me of my fourth grade teacher." Wilk took a silver flask and a shot glass from his desk drawer and poured out a finger. He tossed it back, stiff-wristed.

Grabowski pushed over a diagram he had drawn of the tiers of seats where the senators had been sitting. Three long rectangles represented the rows of tables, and small squares represented chairs.

"Write everyone's name where they were sitting," he ordered.

Wilk carefully wrote his name in all caps in the first row, then, in lowercase, added "Renata Glover (D)" and "Buford Chadwick (R)." In the row behind went "Mark McNulty (D)," "Albert Clark (R)," "Irene Wisnewski (D)," and "Beverly Rubenstock (D)."

"We don't have assigned seats, except for the committee chair, who sits front center—that's me—and Irene, who only sat in the center of the middle row because she said there's a draft everywhere else that gives her arthritis of the neck."

"What did the other senators say about that?"

"A few said she gave them arthritis of the ass."

"Mind telling me who those people were?"

Wilk sat back in his swivel chair and looked hard at Grabowski. "Why?"

"Because, Senator, we have a sudden, unexplained death and six nearby witnesses. If Chief Mayerling or I decide this death wasn't natural, we open a full-scale investigation."

Wilk poured himself another shot. "We're halfway through session, deadlocked on every bill, half of us are up for reelection, and here's a police investigation staring us in the face."

"Take it easy," Grabowski said. "I'm following standard procedure. Tell me in general about Senator Irene's relationships with other senators—no names."

Wilk pulled out his handkerchief and wiped his lips. "Irene represented her district, meaning she voted how the people who elected her wanted, according to her. Off the record, her ideas were loco. She was stubborn, wouldn't compromise an inch, and a real wild card. After hours sitting in caucus with her, I'd think she'd vote one way. Then, by golly, on the senate floor, she'd vote opposite. Once I almost choked her."

"Did other people feel the same as you?"

"Plenty. She was around long enough to make a passel of enemies." Wilk forced a smile. "The lady was a character."

"Would you be surprised if you found out she was murdered?"

Wilk wiped his hands on the handkerchief. "In all honesty, I'm not sure. My feelings could go either way. She had opponents, but murder? We're politicians, not killers."

"Was it you who wanted to call Chief Mayerling?"

"Well, yes and no. We all thought it would be better to avoid bad publicity, many of us being up for reelection."

"Why? What are you afraid of?"

"Look here, Detective, politicians are fair game for the

press. Once something happens that involves us, the damn reporters dredge up every move we ever made. A police investigation will put every traffic ticket smack-dab on the front page."

Grabowski followed him back down the long hall and into the hearing room. Most of the spectators had gone and the senators were huddled in one group. Grabowski consulted his diagram.

"Senator Clark?" he called.

A small, dapper man stood up. He was wearing a houndstooth suit with pale yellow shirt and striped tie, and his shoes had a high polish. He was a foot shorter than Grabowski, with a high, light voice.

"Senator Albert Clark, Republican from Oshkosh," he mumbled as they walked back to Wilk's office. "I can't imagine how I could help you. I was paying no attention whatsoever to Senator Wisnewski. I never pay attention to her."

"Do you work with her much?"

Clark sighed. "As little as possible. Unfortunately, Health Care Committee members are supposed to work together, so, despite the fact that she was a Democrat and a difficult woman, Irene and I backed some of the same bills. I even signed onto her idiotic health care bill."

"What do you mean, 'signed onto'?"

"A technical term. It means I added my name to her proposed legislation to indicate that I supported it to the point of virtually adopting it as my own. Irene's bill said the state will pay prenatal clinic expenses for all women without health insurance. She was crazy: The cost is enormous, every pregnant welfare woman in the country would move here, and her program would be impossible to administer fairly. I'm up for reelection and my Democrat opponent is actually spreading 'tax and spend' posters in my district. That's hard for a Republican to swallow." He unwrapped a hard candy and popped it into his mouth.

"Why did you sign onto her bill if you didn't like it and

it might hurt your reelection?" Grabowski was honestly curious.

"Because Irene promised to sign onto a labor union restriction bill of mine that normally she wouldn't touch with a ten-foot pole. Now it's too late." He crunched the hard candy.

It took half an hour for Grabowski to learn that Clark had paid no attention to Senator Wisnewski in the hearing and had not spoken to her in days. He sent him back to the hearing room while he glanced over his notes.

Mayerling appeared in the doorway, his thick gray hair standing up. He tossed his notebook onto the desk and collapsed on the leather couch.

"The female senators are yours from now on, starting with Rubenstock. She's wacko. Women are wacko anyway, and in politics they're astronauts. If I hear 'my dear policeman' one more time, I'm throwing Senator Rubenstock in jail. She never answered a question directly, and I couldn't tell from the tone of her voice when she talked about Wisnewski whether she hated her or was pissed off about the coffee on her suit."

"Who else did you talk to?"

"The female doctor, St. Clair, who was here to testify. She said she thought the senator may have been dead when the convulsions stopped, but couldn't say for sure. She holds some hope that autopsy will show something. Then I talked to one little short male named Chadwick who said he was a Republican and that Senator Irene wasn't bad for a Democrat. Otherwise, he didn't remember a thing and smiled the whole time. I think he's been in politics so long, his face froze like that."

Grabowski sighed and propped his feet on the desk. "The way politicians carry on, we could be here all night. We won't know anything anyway until we get the autopsy, assuming you ordered one."

Mayerling nodded. "I put a rush order on it, but it could take overnight. I suggest we compare notes, find out if our stories are similar, then I'll read off a description to the sen-

ators. If everybody agrees, I'll let them go, and if the autopsy comes back funny, we'll catch up with them tomorrow."

"Politicians can agree on something?" But Grabowski
nodded agreement.

Mayerling propped his notebook on his stomach as he
lay on the couch. "According to my witnesses, the Senate
Health Care Committee was starting to hear Dr. St. Clair's
testimony on Senator Wisnewski's health care bill. Senator
Wisnewski opened her mouth to comment, then fell forward, splattering coffee and water all over the senators in
front of her."

He turned over a few pages. "The coffee came from the
pot at the end of the room, which everybody drank out of,
and the water from the cooler in the room behind the hearing room. Senator Rubenstock, Dr. St. Clair, and a lobbyist
named Karen Wolfson did CPR until the medics got there.
Senator McNulty, who used to be public prosecutor in
Green Bay, told everyone not to move anything and made
them all sit still while the audience left."

Grabowski nodded. "I got the same. But if we let the
senators leave, won't they compare notes and change their
stories if the autopsy comes back positive?"

"Can't be helped. Politicians always change their stories."

The room was empty of spectators and Senators Wilk
and Chadwick were smoking by an open window when
Grabowski and Mayerling returned. Chief Mayerling raised
his hand for attention.

"Please sit where you were when Senator Wisnewski
died," he ordered.

He waited until the senators had settled on the dais and
until Maxene St. Clair and Karen Wolfson had seated themselves together in the audience. The security guard stood by
the door. Mayerling held up Grabowski's seating chart.

"Put a star by your name if you moved at all during the
hearing," he ordered. "That includes the entire hearing, not
just the few minutes before she died. While you are doing

that, I'll read you a statement of what happened. If I left anything out, write it on your pad, put your name on the top, and hand it to me on your way out."

"What are you looking for?" demanded Senator Rubenstock.

Grabowski answered. "Did you see anybody give Senator Wisnewski anything to eat or drink, or did you see anyone say something to her that disturbed her?"

The room quieted, and everyone looked at Beverly Rubenstock. She frowned at her pad of paper, then began to write. She was still writing when Mayerling started to read:

"At approximately twelve forty-five, during a Senate Health Care Committee hearing, Senator Wisnewski collapsed forward onto the table, spilling her coffee and water, some of which splattered onto the clothing of people around her. Prior to this time she had not complained of feeling ill. Senator Wilk and Senator Rubenstock helped her to the floor. Senator Rubenstock, Dr. St. Clair, and Miss Karen Wolfson started CPR while Senator Wilk instructed a secretary to call an ambulance. Senator McNulty instructed all senators not to touch anything on the tables. After approximately fifteen minutes, the ambulance medics arrived, began a life-support system, and, fifteen minutes later, took her to the ambulance. Senator Wilk called the chief of police. During this time no one moved anything on the table, including the coffee cups. The Madison police instructed the audience to give their names and leave, but everyone else remained in the hearing room until the police arrived."

Mayerling looked around the room. A few people were writing on their notepads. He waited until they had finished. "If everyone generally agrees with this statement, given the changes you are writing on this pad, you are free to go."

The room emptied out quickly. Maxene St. Clair and Karen Wolfson handed their papers to Mayerling, then followed Grabowski into the hall.

"Bizarre," Maxene said to Grabowski, "but not impossible. I'll be interested to see what condition her heart was in."

"If I hear, I'll let you know. Dinner Wednesday night?" he said.

"You know each other?" Karen inquired.

"A few years," St. Clair answered.

Mayerling had collected the papers and came hurrying out to the hall. "I sealed Senator Irene's office, which is the best I can do until we hear from the coroner if we have a case. I'll call the office, then we're out of here." He went down the hall towards Wilk's office.

Grabowski waved good-bye to Maxene and wandered through the halls around the hearing room, glancing into the offices. Secretaries were sitting at reception desks piled with papers and crowded with computer terminals. He found Senator Wisnewski's office by the brass nameplate on the door. An overweight woman smoking a cigarette was talking on the phone.

"She's only been dead an hour and my phone is ringing off the hook," she was saying. "I want you to tell the switchboard that Senator Wisnewski's office isn't taking any more calls until tomorrow, at least."

She slammed down the phone and spotted Grabowski standing in the doorway. "This office is closed," she snapped. She grabbed her coat off a rack and stomped out into the hall, locking the door behind her.

In the next office, a young woman was watching papers come off a printer. The room was so crammed with desks and partitions that it looked like a rabbit warren. The woman herself resembled a small bunny, with her round face, large brown eyes, and small nose and mouth. The eyes, however, were sharp.

"Detective Grabowski, Milwaukee police," she called out. "I am delighted that someone of your caliber is helping clear up this situation. Senator Rubenstock is up for reelection and we can't let this drag on too long. Bad press."

Grabowski felt he had missed something. "How do you know about me?"

"I saw you go into the Senate Hearing Room. Besides, our Communications people found out all about you as soon as you showed up. They did a general press release for senate Democratic leadership, then one for each senator. Here."

She handed him a sheet of embossed senate letterhead with Senator Rubenstock's name at the top. Grabowski read aloud:

" 'For Immediate Release. Senator Irene Wisnewski (D-Milwaukee) died unexpectedly at twelve forty-five P.M. today during a meeting of the Senate Health Care Committee. "She was a real warhorse," said Senator Beverly Rubenstock (D-Waukesha). "She had strong principles and she never gave up on her goals. Her death will leave a big hole in the state Democratic party." Funeral services are at Jesu Parish in Milwaukee. Send condolences to her office at the Capitol building in Madison.' "

"Doesn't say anything about a police investigation."

"They're preserving the reputation of the senators."

Grabowski wondered if she was joking, but her round face remained serious. She waved him to a hard-backed chair and pointed at a small microwave in the corner with glass mugs and a tea canister stacked on top.

"Tea? Coffee? Sorry, there's no beer."

"Has my beer-drinking reputation preceded me or was that a shot in the dark?"

She smiled. "Information is currency here; we trade it. I heard you're forty-two, unmarried, you've lived in Milwaukee all your life, and you're the best detective on the Milwaukee police force. A few women here are planning to know you better."

Grabowski smiled. "And who are you?"

She blushed. "Kay Landau, legislative aide for Senator Rubenstock and Senator McNulty. Did you know that Beverly did CPR on Senator Wisnewski until the medics got there?"

Grabowski nodded. "Tell me, Miss Landau, did you know Senator Wisnewski well?"

She poured him tea from a thermos. "Well enough to know that what happened to her couldn't have been an accident."

"What are you saying?"

"I'm saying there are plenty of males here who will be glad she's dead. This may be the end of the twentieth century, but politics is still a big men's club. Women only got the vote two generations ago, and most male politicians wish women were dishing up chicken à la king at a fundraiser, not holding a gavel at a committee hearing."

Chief Mayerling came down the hall at that moment and beckoned to Grabowski. They went out to the parking lot where the lot attendant was hovering over the squad car. Mayerling skidded through the slick streets to an Italian restaurant on State Street.

"Thanks for the help, Grabowski," he said, wiping beer foam off his lip. "Somehow you kept those senators from screaming about special services they should get because they're senators. You haven't seen anything till you've seen a riled-up senator."

"Let's hope the autopsy comes back with nothing special on it," Grabowski commented. "I got a funny feeling in there that politicians like creating their own truth, and it might be hard for them to face facts staring them in the face."

"Don't make politicians more complicated than they are," said Mayerling, draining his beer. "Half a politician is full of shit and the other half is full of hot air."

# CHAPTER

## 3

GRABOWSKI WAS SLEEPING so heavily that he slept through his ringing phone and awakened to Chief Mayerling shouting through the answering machine.

"Pick up the phone, Grabowski! Your switchboard said you were home because the only woman you go out with is working in the emergency room tonight."

Grabowski fumbled at the receiver and dragged it under the covers. He had been out late drinking beer with friends and had gone straight to bed without turning up the heat. The house was icy. "I'm here," he mumbled.

Mayerling lowered his voice a trifle. "Another one of them got it, goddamn it! They can't quit with just one; no, they have to keep on destroying our peace of mind by knocking each other off. Let them continue, I say, let them all kill each other. Then we can elect a better bunch."

"What are you talking about?" Grabowski peered at the luminous hands of his clock. Three A.M.?

"The night sergeant got a call from a bar off State Street. An ambulance left there fifteen minutes ago with another senator. The bartender isn't sure she'll make it to the hospital."

"She?" Grabowski turned on the bedside lamp. The clock still said three A.M.

"Senator Rubenstock."

"She's dead?" The shock woke him totally.

"Don't know yet. The hospital will call me after they've worked on her. I'm going to the bar to find out what happened."

21

"Senator Rubenstock was in a bar at three in the morning?"

"Grabowski, you wouldn't believe this town when the legislature is in session: drunk driving, disturbing the peace, wild parties at rental apartments. We get calls in the night from angry wives all over the state wanting to know what their husbands are up to." Mayerling stopped to catch his breath.

"What happened to Senator Rubenstock?"

"Same damned thing as the Wisnewski woman. She took a sip of her drink and fell face forward on the bar. The bartender did CPR until the ambulance got there."

"Have you heard anything from the medical examiner's office about Senator Irene?" Grabowski sat up, pulling the covers up to his chin.

"They woke me up two hours ago with some weird lab result—something in the blood that shouldn't be there."

"So Senator Irene was poisoned?" Grabowski rubbed his eyes.

"We won't know until we speak with her doctor and compare the results to blood tests she's had under normal conditions. In the meantime, I sent some uniforms over to the Capitol building to seal Rubenstock's office as well as Senator Wisnewski's. They'll both stay sealed until you get there in the morning."

"Me?" Grabowski had a sinking feeling.

"The head honcho, Senator Wilk, called me twice. Wants you on the case, especially now with Rubenstock gone to the hospital. Senators think only big-city detectives can handle crime. Fine with me, pal. The senators are all yours. I already cleared it with the Milwaukee chief of police."

Grabowski winced, imagining the middle-of-the-night conversation with his testy superior. "What time do you want me in Madison?"

"Seven o'clock. My office."

Grabowski hung up and lay thinking about Senator Rubenstock. He had spoken to her for only a few minutes, but he had liked her—a straightforward, plain-speaking woman. Mayerling called her wacko, but Mayerling called all women wacko, starting with his wife. Grabowski reset his alarm for five A.M. and went back to sleep.

The Madison Police Department was quiet compared to Milwaukee's busy four-story headquarters with its crush of police, prisoners, and people needing assistance. Mayerling was at his desk, slurping coffee. When Grabowski arrived, he shouted at his secretary for coffee, and washed some aspirin down with a slug of Maalox from a large bottle. He shoved several stacks of stapled papers across the desk at Grabowski along with a purse sealed inside a plastic bag.

"The complete autopsy isn't back yet, but we opened the case anyway. Here's what my people took from Senator Irene's office and her car. We sent the candy and medicines from her purse to the lab. The lab found nothing unusual in the water cooler or the coffee the senators were drinking yesterday, including the few drops left in the senator's cup after she knocked it over. My fingerprint squad dusted her office for prints. It's sealed up again, waiting for you to look it over. I've got a uniform on her door and on Rubenstock's." He picked up his ringing phone.

Grabowski took a sip of what passed for coffee and skimmed the list of items found in Senator Irene Wisnewski's desk and purse. In her desk, besides the usual letters, reports, and other documents, there had been bags of candy, bottles of aspirin, cough medicine, and mouthwash.

He dumped out the purse. Lipsticks, face powder, perfume, wallet with ID, credit cards, and fifty-five dollars in small bills. There was also a pocket notebook with scrawled notes.

"Okay if I take this?" Grabowski held up the notebook.

Mayerling was hanging up the phone. He nodded. "That was the hospital about Rubenstock. Alive but sick. They pumped out her stomach, stuck IVs into both arms, and put her on a respirator. She can't talk until she's off the respirator."

"Does the hospital know what happened?"

"All the blood tests aren't in yet and the doctors aren't

committing themselves. All we've got are statements from the bartender and people in the bar about what she ate and who she was talking to before she passed out. You've got those in front of you."

"Could they actually remember?"

"Not really. The place was crawling with political types. It's a hot spot for wheeling and dealing, and politicians buzz around there like flies. That's why Rubenstock went, according to her secretary. She wanted to get into the old boys' network, as the secretary called it. Incidentally, the secretary has gone wacko. She claims the male senators conspired to poison Rubenstock and Wisnewski, and she's ready to gun down all of them. She has a handgun permit, but I told her I'd confiscate the gun and lock her up too if she didn't stop with the threats."

"Did she accuse any particular male?" Grabowski made a note to talk to Senator Rubenstock's secretary again.

"Not yet. Maybe she'll tell you; you have a way with women. My fingerprint squad is at her office now."

Mayerling handed Grabowski a folder with all the papers turned in the day before by the senators. The label had Senator Wisnewski's address. It was a South Side working-class neighborhood of Eastern European descendants with a sprinkling of Mexicans who had ventured out of the port district.

There wasn't much crime in those neighborhoods: residents enforced their own peace.

Grabowski added the reports from the fingerprint squad to the folder, as well as the reports of the interviews with the bartender and people in the bar. He stuffed Senator Wisnewski's small notebook on top.

The Madison streets were crowded with students and their half-repaired cars. Winter semester at the university was midsession and students were jaywalking everywhere, an arrestable offense in Milwaukee. At the senate parking lot, the attendant took a few nervous minutes to scrutinize Grabowski's ID and his dented blue Plymouth.

"What's going on?" He rested his hand on the windowsill. "I heard a rumor that Senator Rubenstock was poisoned last night just like Senator Irene."

"We can't speculate at this time." Grabowski eased his foot down on the accelerator. Barely eight in the morning and even the parking attendants were spreading rumors.

The Capitol building halls were quiet. Grabowski watched the fingerprint crew at work in Senator Rubenstock's office and decided they knew their job and he could come back later. Rubenstock's secretary had gone out for coffee, at the request of the fingerprint squad. He continued down the hall to Senator Wisnewski's office, where a uniformed policeman stood guard.

The office of the late Senator Irene Wisnewski sat on the east side of the Capitol building and was splashed with morning sunlight. It was also heavy with cigarette smoke, which hung in a blue haze around the desiccated plants on the windowsill. An overweight woman in her mid-fifties with a pale, fleshy face sat at a desk eating potato chips. As Grabowski walked into the room, she emptied the last of the chips into her mouth and mashed the bag into the overflowing wastebasket. When she caught sight of Grabowski, she jumped and shrieked.

"Don't scare me like that," she panted. "It's bad enough with a cop outside the door; I can't handle people walking in unannounced. Don't you know two women senators were poisoned?"

"Sorry," said Grabowski, "I'm looking for Rhonda Schmidt, Senator Wisnewski's legislative aide."

"That's me except that I'm out of a job since she's dead, but maybe they'll keep me awhile to clear out the rubble. There isn't much since I worked overtime last week to get ready for the health care committee hearing. Not that I got paid for overtime, but Irene used to let me leave early sometimes if she couldn't think of any reason to keep me here."

Rhonda Schmidt's mouth quivered, then she pulled another bag of potato chips out of her drawer, slashed it open with large scissors, and held out the bag to Grabowski.

Grabowski took a handful and sat down at the adjoining desk. "I'm Detective Joseph Grabowski."

"I know." Rhonda shoved a handful of chips into her mouth. "I saw you yesterday. You're a hotshot Milwaukee detective from Irene's district. I heard a rumor Irene was poisoned."

"I heard that, too."

Rhonda opened a tiny refrigerator under her desk and pulled out a cola, which she handed to Grabowski. She cracked one open for herself. "What have you heard about Beverly Rubenstock?"

"Nothing. What have you heard?"

"Still on the respirator, but her vital signs are stable." She drained half the cola.

"What was Senator Wisnewski like to work for?" Grabowski tried to get control of the interview.

Rhonda stuffed another chip into her mouth and began searching through the papers on her desk for cigarettes and lighter. She stopped chewing long enough to light the cigarette.

"She was terrible. I kept threatening to quit. I applied for other senate jobs, but Irene liked browbeating me too much to write me a decent recommendation."

She took a drag on her cigarette and rubbed a swollen ankle. "On the other hand, she was reasonable when I needed time off. I got pneumonia last winter and my legs swelled up like sausages and now my circulation won't work right. I have to drive to Milwaukee for treatments once a week or so, and Senator Irene let me do it. Of course, she always made me pick up some document from her Milwaukee district headquarters, which meant a big detour for me."

"You live in Madison?"

"That's right. The senator's Milwaukee district office was staffed by volunteers. I did all the paperwork out of this office."

She offered the cigarettes to Grabowski, who shook his head and reached for more chips. He nodded at the closed door to the senator's office, sealed with red tape. "I'll need to check in there now."

Rhonda picked up the ringing phone and gestured for Grabowski to go in. "He's here," she said into the phone, "but he doesn't know anything we don't."

Grabowski ripped the seal off the door and stood looking at dirty ashtrays and crumpled candy wrappers on a round conference table. A computer sat on an executive desk by the window. The smell of stale cigarette smoke was overpowering. Grabowski made a note to ask if the fingerprint crew had taken away the ashes and butts for analysis. Then he turned around and found Rhonda standing behind him, lighted cigarette in hand.

She pointed with her cigarette to an uneven stack of papers next to the computer terminal. "You might start by looking through her calendar and papers. I need the calendar back soon so I can call people who had meetings scheduled with her. There are also letters in here I have to answer."

Rhonda stuck the cigarette in her mouth and dragged a spiral notebook calendar from underneath the papers.

"This is my copy of her calendar. I wrote all her appointments and speaking engagements here, then I phoned her every morning at eight o'clock and she updated her own calendar. Sometimes. Mostly she forgot or got it wrong."

"Where is her calendar?"

"Could be in her briefcase. She stuffed everything in there she wanted me to do, then she'd toss the whole briefcase onto my desk and I'd spend an hour looking for something she put in her purse by mistake. The briefcase and purse looked exactly alike."

"Where's the briefcase?"

Rhonda shrugged. She took a heavy drag on her cigarette and propped the cigarette in the ashtray. Grabowski handed it back to her.

"Let's not disturb the evidence," he suggested.

She held the cigarette over her cupped hand. "Maybe her briefcase is at her house. She didn't bring it to work yester-

day, even though it was full of papers I needed." She left
the room and returned with another ashtray.

Grabowski had quit smoking fifteen years before, and
now the smell of it choked him. He opened the window a
crack to let in some clean winter air, and sat down at the
desk chair. The height of the chair seat suited his long legs.

"Was Senator Irene tall?" he asked, opening the drawer.
The knobs were thick with fingerprint dust.

"Big. Big voice, big hair, big clothes." Rhonda dropped
into the chair as if the thought of all that bigness tired her.
The phone in the other room rang and she answered it on
the senator's desk phone. "He's here, going through her
desk," she reported into the phone. "He doesn't know anything we don't."

Grabowski took out of the folder the list of objects the
Madison detectives had removed from Senator Wisnewski's
desk and opened the drawers to get an idea of where they
had been. The large bottom drawer had held mouthwash
and Vitamin C tablets, as well as the red high-heeled shoes
that were still there. The soles were nearly new. The second
drawer had held Christmas candy, aspirin, and throat loz-
enges. The third drawer had held the purse and now had
only potato chip crumbs.

Grabowski glanced through the papers. "Any chance for
coffee?" he asked. He watched the trail of cigarette smoke
leave the room behind Rhonda Schmidt.

He let the smoke dissipate out the window, then closed
it. The morning sun warmed his back as he started through
the papers. There wasn't much: a folder of correspondence
from the Senate Democratic Caucus with caucus meeting
dates and discussion topics. Across several topics, someone
had scrawled, "Bullshit" or "BS!!!" Grabowski set those
aside to ask Rhonda to identify the handwriting. The second folder held two letters thanking her for helping with
problems or for speaking at their clubs. Across one of them
was scrawled, "I did this?"

Rhonda appeared in the door with two cups of coffee.
Grabowski gestured at the folders.

"Is everything you put here still here?"

She set the coffee on the desk, then brought over small pots of sugar and cream. She settled in the chair, lit a cigarette, and started going through the papers one by one.

"These are Irene's notations," she confirmed. "Her caucus correspondence is all here. Irene said it was political and that I didn't need to concern myself with it, which meant I had to keep track of it and pretend I don't know anything. She thought everyone had the same selective memory she did."

Grabowski continued his search through the desk. The top middle drawer held two personal letters, both from women, both with photographs of children. Under the letters was a small pink piece of paper with MARK written on it and "Tuesday, 15th, 9 P.M." The night before she died.

Grabowski checked her calendar: nothing about Mark. He held the note by the corner. "Know anything about this?"

Rhonda frowned, shook her head, then rechecked the calendar. "I don't recognize the paper or the handwriting. I wonder what she was up to."

"Did she make appointments without telling you?"

"Hardly ever, and when she did, she blabbed so loud on the phone, I knew exactly what she was doing. But I never heard a word about Mark. I suppose he could be a lobbyist or someone on staff."

"Do you have lists of those people?"

"You betcha." She heaved herself out of the chair and left the room. The phone rang. Grabowski read through the senate Democratic schedule again until she returned with a thick manual of lobbyists' names and a staff directory from the senate and state assembly. The phone rang again and she went back to her desk.

The lobbyist book was an education. He hadn't realized how many lobbyists worked for hospitals, health care groups, educational organizations. Even universities had lobbyists. After half an hour he found two lobbyists and two senate staffers named Mark. One staffer was listed as

Administrative, the other as Research. He pulled an evidence bag from his pocket and stuffed all the correspondence into it, including the small note, and waited in the outer office for Rhonda to get off the phone.

Senator Wilk came down the hall and paused in the doorway. He slid on a smile and slapped Grabowski on the back.

"Heard anything about cause of death?" Senator Wilk glanced at the evidence bag in Grabowski's hand.

Grabowski ignored the question. "You know who Mark is?" He held out the small pink note.

Wilk peered at it as if he had never noticed the bag. "Never heard of him." He clapped Grabowski on the back again and strode down the hall.

"Did Senator Irene use her computer?" he asked Rhonda.

"She couldn't remember how to read her electronic mail, even how to print something. But not many senators use E-mail. They're worried someone might read what they're telling each other."

"Can I see her E-mail?"

"If I remember her secret password." She heaved her heavy thighs into the executive chair and typed a few commands into the senator's terminal.

"Whoa!" she said. "The last time she checked was six months ago. I bet she has five hundred messages."

Two hours later, Grabowski rose to ease the crick in his neck from staring at the senator's E-mail. Aside from sports bulletins, most messages were from senators asking for support on specific bills. Grabowski called in Rhonda.

"Is this sports news legitimate or are these code words for certain bills?"

Rhonda leaned over the machine. "All legit, except that these senators are using state equipment to bet on professional sports."

"Point me in the direction of Administrative Staff offices," Grabowski said, and followed her thick legs through the long hallways.

The desk of Mark in Administration was one of six that

were crammed into space intended for three. The room was empty. Grabowski waited until Rhonda had waved good-bye, then looked around. No pink notepads. He looked into the drawers without touching anything inside and continued to Senator Rubenstock's office.

# CHAPTER

## 4

KAY LANDAU, THE aide for Senator Rubenstock and Senator McNulty, was sitting behind a mound of papers with the telephone receiver propped between shoulder and ear. Her round face was pale, her lips tight, and her eyes red and swollen. When Grabowski walked into her office, she slammed down the receiver.

"Well?" she demanded. "When are you going to arrest the bastards?"

"Which bastards?"

"The ones who poisoned Beverly and Irene. You're not going to tell me you don't know exactly what happened."

Grabowski removed a box of brochures from a chair and sat down. "Maybe you could tell me what you know, Miss Landau."

"Kay. Beverly had enemies, male chauvinist pigs who want her out of the senate so they can screw over the women of Wisconsin like they're screwing poorly paid call girls at their Madison apartments every night."

"There are call girls in Madison?"

"That's right, you're the police; you don't know about the real crimes happening to women in this state." She put her head down and burst into tears.

"Miss Landau." Grabowski went around the desk and gingerly patted her on the shoulder. "Please don't think I'm insensitive to the plight of women in Wisconsin. And"—he took a wild guess—"I know you and Senator Rubenstock were doing whatever could be done politically to help women. The senator is very ill, but if she were here, she would want you to remain clearheaded and help find out what happened."

He returned to his chair and waited for the sobs to subside. It didn't take long. Kay Landau mopped her face with a handful of tissues, and blew her nose.

"You're right," she said. "What do you want to know?"

"You have some suspicion about what happened?"

"Damn right I do. After Irene was poisoned, it's plain as the nose on your face. Someone is attempting to break up the Feminist Political Strike Force by using violence. No matter how high women climb in business, industry, or politics, we're still victims of violence."

"The Feminist Political Strike Force?"

"Women legislators who are trying to pass feminist legislation."

"And who are these people who are breaking up this Political Strike Force?"

"The male senators. They're in it together."

"All of them?" Grabowski's voice remained calm.

Kay Landau blew her nose again and flung the tissue at the wastebasket. "Oh, I guess not. McNulty liked working with Beverly and sometimes even with Irene. But you can book the rest of the male senators on a conspiracy charge."

"Do you have any evidence to substantiate these charges?"

"You betcha, and I've kept it for this kind of emergency. Letters, Detective, threatening letters."

She reached into the back of her desk drawer and pulled out a plain business envelope. Grabowski pulled out the single sheet by one corner. The page held one line: "Politics isn't for females. Go back to the classroom where you belong."

Grabowski carefully put the note back into the envelope. He tucked it into his jacket pocket. "This the only one?"

"That I know about. Beverly is a brave woman and she probably threw the others away. Now we may never find out." Her eyes filled with tears again.

"You think this was written by a senator?"

"Absolutely. They don't have the courage to tell her straight to her face."

"Which senator do you have in mind?"

"William Wilk, the wuss. Plays both ends against the middle—try to get a straight answer out of him on anything. Irene and Beverly had him by the short hairs because Beverly can deliver a solid woman's vote on the senate floor and blast his male locker-room pacts straight to hell. With Irene and Beverly out of the way, Wilk-the-Wuss can line up the male caucus like the little tin soldiers that they are."

"You're saying Senator Wilk would poison two women just to control the vote?"

"He's such a sniveling weakling, he can't do it any other way. Now, Mark McNulty could build a solid Democratic coalition. He's got brains, energy, and a sense of priorities—a real statesman. McNulty should watch what he puts in his mouth. Wilk will poison him next."

"Wilk doesn't like McNulty?"

"Power, Detective. Wilk likes being Democratic Caucus chair—perks, you know: name in the paper, ball game tickets, even though lobbyists are supposed to keep their dirty fingers out of their checkbooks. But to stay head Democrat, Wilk has to build a strong state Democratic party headed by him, and Wilk doesn't have the character."

"Miss Landau, you're suggesting that Senator Wilk will poison every potential threat in the Senate."

"Stick around, Detective; you'll see more bizarre behavior than that."

Grabowski left Kay Landau dialing the hospital for a progress report on her employer, and went down the hall to Senator Wilk's office. Wilk was on the phone but hung up midsentence when his secretary waved Grabowski through. Wilk's gray hairs were plastered crookedly across his head.

"Where have you been!" Wilk snapped. "You're on this case because I told Chief Mayerling to put you here, and that means you report to me where you are and what you're doing."

Grabowski took a chair. "Chief Mayerling assigned me to the case, that's correct," he agreed.

Wilk ignored the distinction. "Reporters call here for updates every two minutes, and when they hang up, the senators and assembly members call. I want up-to-date information, and I want it from you."

"I sympathize with your predicament," Grabowski said, "but Chief Mayerling is in charge of information released to the public. Talk to him."

"I'm not the public, damn it, I'm a senator!"

"In the meantime," continued Grabowski, "I need an office with a desk and a phone."

Wilk's face flushed. "Now, look here," he said. "One of my senators is dead and another is comatose. Staff are panicking. The coffee shop is deserted, employees are going home sick, nobody even drinks from the bubblers. I want to know what's going on."

"I wish I could help you," said Grabowski, "but until the lab tells us exactly what the two women ate, and until Senator Rubenstock is well enough to talk, all I can do is gather background information on the two senators and hope for a lead."

"Background information. You sound like a damn pestering newspaper reporter. Which brings me to another problem I want you to handle. I told the aides for Senator Wisnewski and Senator Rubenstock to let our Communications people handle the press, but that young woman who works for Rubenstock is telling them about the male chauvinism she claims controls the senate. I've had it with her. I want you to keep her quiet."

The phone rang and Wilk snatched it up. "I don't know a goddamn thing about how those two biddies got poisoned," he shouted into the receiver, "and don't get past my secretary again unless you have information I don't."

Grabowski glanced over the papers on Wilk's desk, which included photocopies of several newspaper articles with Wilk's name highlighted in green. Wilk slammed down the phone.

"Talk to Diana Ringer, Director of Communications. She's efficient and politically astute for a woman. If anybody has background information, she does." He escorted Grabowski to the door.

"Get Communications on the phone, then find Detective Grabowski an office," he ordered the secretary, and hurried back to his ringing phone.

The secretary already had the Communications Department on the line. She held out the phone to Grabowski.

"Diana Ringer," said a pleasant, cheerful voice.

"Detective Grabowski. Can we meet somewhere to chat?"

"Coffee shop," she suggested immediately. "It's deserted and I'm ready for lunch."

The director of Communications was a tall blond woman, cheerful and self-possessed. She ordered a Greek salad and a sesame roll.

"Don't worry about poison in here except salmonella. Senator Wisnewski always ate in the Senate private dining room."

Grabowski selected an undefinable plastic-wrapped sandwich and followed her to a table where he unwrapped it with caution: dry roast beef with a scant dollop of mustard.

"I'm gathering information to see which direction it takes me," he began. "What can you tell me about Senator Wilk?"

Diana eased a limp cucumber to the side of her plate. "Wilk wants to look like he's in control. I just sent out a press release: 'Wilk proactive; calls in Milwaukee Detective Division.' Proactive is his political buzzword this year."

"Proactive?" Grabowski wasn't sure what that meant.

Diana smirked. "As opposed to inactive. My job is perception. In politics, reality is as it is perceived. Not that reality doesn't exist—some of us even know what it is occasionally. But politicians make reality to be what they want. Not so surprising. The American myth is that we are free to create our own reality. Politicians are quintessential Americans."

"What's reality anyway?" Grabowski agreed, thinking of Milwaukee's inner city and the rich suburbs.

"Exactly. And in politics, reality changes depending on who's cooking up what. Take Senator Irene's health care bill that cuts state funds for emergency rooms and opens inner-city prenatal clinics. Everybody wants healthy babies, right? And statistics show that good prenatal care reduces complications, so the plan really would save Wisconsin state money. Her bill would be easy to administer too: health departments used to have state-funded prenatal clinics and can open them up again. They'll even hire inner-city people as clerks, so we solve an unemployment problem. But Irene's bill was doomed."

"Why?"

"This innocent bill will become barter fodder to bargain through, or bargain out, some other senator's tougher legislation, like clean-air regulations or housing development restrictions. Or her bill will die because Assemblyman Birnbaum from Milwaukee will kill it in the Assembly since Irene killed his auto emissions bill last year and he swore revenge."

Grabowski stopped taking notes to digest this. "I heard her bill wasn't good."

"From Senator Clark, I bet. True, there are better bills, but mostly there are better senators. Irene was rhinocerotic: head down, horn pointed. Her idea of negotiation was 'Do this and I won't assault you in the newspapers or kill your bills in committee.' "

"How did she deal with staff?"

Diana sighed. "Abusive people and submissive people find each other, especially in politics. Many submissive people work for the senate because they feel powerful being close to power. They take verbal abuse in exchange for being privy to information, but there are limits to what anyone can take. My problem as Communications director is preventing my staff from being demoralized by senators' unrelenting rejection."

"Did Senator Wisnewski know she had this reputation as staff abuser?"

"Hell, no. She thought she was beloved because she always got elected by a big majority. But who could beat her? She represented her district, and that included heavy-metal factories who paid for her campaigns. Irene fought every environmental protection bill, from auto-emission controls to smokestack filters. She gave Milwaukee a bad name."

Grabowski frowned. "Would someone in Milwaukee take that bad name seriously enough to kill her?"

Diana laughed. "Normally someone would run against a senator whose voting records were harmful. Or they might try impeachment. But Irene drove people crazy. I've seen senators shaking with fury during shouting matches with her in caucus."

"Any particular senator that she drove crazy?"

"The assemblyman from Milwaukee I mentioned—Mark Birnbaum—who wants to be Senator Birnbaum and who is probably throwing a party this very minute. Irene told a reporter once that she continues running for senator just to keep Mark Birnbaum out of the senate."

"Any special reason?"

"Pure politics. He's Super-Democrat: votes left of center on everything. She voted right of an Idaho Republican except on feminist issues."

"Does he get the seat automatically now that she's dead?"

Diana separated some wilted lettuce from the heap of greens. "Depends on Wilk. As Senate Democratic Caucus chair, he can pressure the Milwaukee Democrats to give Birnbaum the seat. Or he may choose an interim person to hold the seat until the next election. Then Birnbaum would have to campaign. It depends on Wilk's agenda for the Democratic Caucus: proenvironment or progrowth. Irene blocked every environmental bill; Birnbaum was a raving Green."

"So environmentalists in the Senate would want him in."

Grabowski was beginning to understand the lure of politics for people who liked playing mental games.

"Not entirely," Diana corrected. "With Irene blocking environmental bills, other Democrats could propose any wild scheme to pull votes from their proecology voters without worrying about their schemes becoming law. Like requiring only wastewater for watering lawns, expanding bird sanctuaries during duck-hunting season, prohibiting sonar fishing in Lake Michigan. If Mark Birnbaum gets into the senate, other Democratic senators will have to revise their strategy."

Grabowski took out his notebook. "Who might the Democrats choose instead of Birnbaum?"

Diana thought that over. "Let me sniff around for rumors. In the meantime, I brought you a list of the senators' office numbers and the names of their aides."

The clerk behind the cash register shouted at Grabowski that he was wanted in Senator Wilk's office—pronto—and Grabowski realized what it would be like to be at the beck and call of politicians.

"I need to make a private phone call," he told Diana.

"Use the pay phone in the hall. It's the only private phone in the building."

Grabowski had to wait his turn at the pay phone. "Wilk is nervous as an alley cat," he said. "I've been summoned to his office. Got any news about Wisnewski or Rubenstock?"

"Probable poisoning," said Mayerling. "We still don't know what kind or even how it got inside them. It's not typical food poisoning and it entered the bloodstream somehow, is all the lab will tell me. Tell Wilk to call me if he has questions, but you're in charge. Need reinforcements?"

"Not yet."

Wilk still sat behind his highly polished desk, but two other men occupied the chairs and couch. Wilk waved an introductory hand. "You know these folks: Senator McNulty, Democratic Majority Whip; Senator Clark, Republican Caucus Chair. We need the status of your investigation, Detective."

Albert Clark explained in his high, apologetic voice. "If these, uh, incidents involving Senator Wisnewski and Senator Rubenstock were not accidents, if a senator were the cause, and this senator were later apprehended, tried, and convicted, then that senator is a convicted felon, and a felon cannot be a senator. Any votes taken would be votes of a felon, and there will be later debates as to their validity."

McNulty added, "In other words, should we go into temporary recess?"

"I can tell you this much," Grabowski answered. "Both senators were poisoned, but we don't know how or with what. All I care is that every senator who was in that room remains in Madison."

Wilk's secretary handed Grabowski a slip of paper and a key as he was walking out the door. "We found you an office next to the furnace room. It's nice and warm."

Grabowski took the stairs down. The room was a windowless cement cell with chair, desk, and dangling bare bulb. A maintenance man arrived carrying a phone. He plugged it in and wished Grabowski a nice day.

Grabowski closed the door and spread the contents of the folder Chief Mayerling had given him out on the desk. What was the best approach? Find out the rumors about each senator before interviewing them, or interview first and meet the gossips later?

He first read the report from the police who came to the bar with the ambulance to get Senator Rubenstock. Then he read the notes that the senators and Dr. St. Clair and Karen Wolfson had jotted down and given to Chief Mayerling at the hearing room. Then he read the senator's insurance physical report. Then he called Maxene in Milwaukee. It was after two. She should still be home getting ready for her afternoon shift at St. Agnes Hospital Emergency Room.

Dr. St. Clair answered on the fifth ring. He could hear her smile when she spoke.

"Grabowski! The article in this morning's *Journal* said

Senator Rubenstock was poisoned last night and that you had been temporarily assigned to the Madison police. What's the matter, is crime moving to Madison?"

"The criminals were already here." He spent the next minutes describing the situation. "Her insurance physical said she had high blood pressure and stomach ulcers, thanks to cigarettes, alcohol, and coffee. Her nicotine level was near medical record. She and her aide kept the tobacco industry alive. The state crime lab is working on possible leads now. I haven't talked to them yet. You got any ideas?"

"Bizarre," said St. Clair. "That's what I thought at the senate hearing and that's what I still think. I'll ask around if you want. I know some research medical types who might come up with an idea the state crime lab hasn't."

Grabowski hung up feeling reassured. Before she went to work at St. Agnes' ER, Maxene St. Clair had been an M.D., Ph.D., who taught and did research in immunology and biochemistry at the Medical College of Wisconsin in Milwaukee. She had colleagues with medically inquisitive minds. She might come up with some ideas.

Next, he found the number of Diana Ringer in Communications.

"I've been looking over your list of senators and staff," he said. "Can you tell me more?"

"You're located next to the furnace room, aren't you?" she answered. "I'll be right over."

A few minutes later, the efficient Miss Ringer glanced into Grabowski's office, saw he lacked a second chair, and left to find one. She settled herself with a sigh.

"Nice room," she pronounced. "I'll take it over when you leave. I need a place to change into my aerobics clothes. The males get a locker room—showers, towels, soap, shampoo. Women get the women's bathroom. Ever put on nylon stockings in a toilet stall?"

"Not recently." Grabowski glanced at one sheet that read "Senate Democratic Caucus." "Are these all senators?" he asked. "I'm trying to get a handle on who works here."

"One list is Democratic senators—but Democrats in name only. Some vote a Republican ticket under the guise of representing a conservative district—Irene, for example."

"I could call in reinforcements to interview all the people who were in the room when Senator Wisnewski died, but I hope we'll get to the truth by talking to the senators who were in the room and to the other legislators she worked with. Give me an idea of who to talk to first."

Diana Ringer pulled over the list of senators and began making small checks. "These are Democratic senators who signed onto bills with her. I'm not saying they worked with her—they just put up with her long enough to get her support for their legislation."

She then marked the Democratic senators who voted against her routinely, and made similar marks on the list of Republicans.

She moved to the staff members. "This year I wrote for Senator Wisnewski since she has publicly humiliated everyone on my staff. However, in Research, the lawyers are assigned to senators according to issue, regardless of what the senator or staff member wants. Irene's big bill this year was her health care bill, so she got Mark Lewis."

Grabowski noticed that on the list of senators who voted opposite Wisnewski, the first check was Mark McNulty. Diana was on her feet, looking at her watch.

"Come find my office later; I may have thought of something. And give me the key to this room when your investigation is over. Here, possession is one hundred percent of the law."

It was nearly three o'clock. Grabowski went back to the coffee shop for a take-out coffee, then spent an hour in his room rereading the senators' comments about what happened when Senator Wisnewski died. He read Senator Rubenstock's first and set it thoughtfully aside. He then carefully read the comments of Mark McNulty, who had talked with Senator Wisnewski several times before the hearing started.

He spent another half hour reading through the information that Diana brought about how legislation is passed into law. Then he picked up the phone and started down the list of senators, making interview appointments. Senator Renata Glover was in conference, but Senator McNulty was available, according to Kay Landau, who was aide for both Rubenstock and McNulty. Their offices adjoined.

When Grabowski appeared, Kay rose and poured a cup of coffee from a thermos.

"You have twenty minutes before his next meeting." She carried the coffee inside, then waved Grabowski in.

The senator was asleep on the couch. He sat up and rubbed his eyes.

"What a life. When I need a nap, I sleep; it's how I keep my wits hour after hour. Irene slept during committee hearings. In front of hundreds of people. Lately, though, she was jumpy as a cat."

Grabowski looked at his watch. Four precious minutes gone. He pulled out the paper McNulty had handed him in the hearing room after Senator Wisnewski died and read aloud:

" 'Not really watching, but quite a few people spoke to her before the hearing. Chadwick, Wilk, Glover, me. Birnbaum phoned and she took it in the staff room. Came back scowling. Whispered a lot to Rubenstock.' "

McNulty pulled a paper napkin from his pocket and slid it across the coffee table. "Here are more people I thought of later who talked to her before the hearing."

Grabowski read aloud. " 'Rhonda Schmidt, Diana Ringer, and the security guard.' Does that much talking go on normally?"

"It was her damned health care bill. Neither Democrats nor Republicans liked it, and everyone on the committee was trying to get her to change it before we had to vote. It was full of holes, unbelievable. She had the same staff as the rest of us, but she wouldn't let them write decent legislation. Mark Lewis would give her something good; she'd rewrite it until it wasn't worth the paper it was word-processed on."

"But if I understand the system, her bill had been passed by the Democrats through to the health care committee. Why?"

"There's a better bill coming from Mark Birnbaum in the assembly that will knock this one out in the next round of committee hearings."

"So why did she look so happy?"

"I never figured out whether Irene understood the political system or just busted her way through year after year. Not many of her bills passed, but few of us have bills that actually become law. Every bill is a fight and a compromise, and more often than not, they end up written into somebody else's bill."

"Is that what happened to Senator Irene's bills?"

"Yes, but she took maximum credit for everything she signed her name to, like most of us. Diana Ringer is a wizard at convincing local papers in sixteen different counties that their senator was totally responsible for a bill."

Grabowski tried to remember how much he had seen Senator Irene's name in the Milwaukee papers. He made a note to ask Diana.

"Did that work for Senator Irene?"

"Do me a favor and stop calling her Senator Irene. It makes her sound like a folksy old lady, and she wasn't. She had the disposition of a swamp adder. She wore the sweetest smile you ever saw, but say something bad about her legislation and she'd go after your balls with a straight razor."

"Seriously, what kind of a person was she?"

McNulty smiled. "If wishes came true, she would have been dead years ago. She was demanding, overbearing, and verbally punitive—an emotional assault weapon. She assumed everyone lived to serve her and she had sympathy for no one. She represented her district as a tough, uncompromising labor Democrat, not an environmental Democrat. She even drove an old gas-guzzler."

"If her district liked her, what about the drive-by shooting that took out her front window last year?"

"If you remember, she had badgered the police into allowing her and some local rednecks to form a special citizen antidrug force. She personally targeted a nest of drug dealers to make an example of. They probably shot up her window before she and her citizen vigilantes burned them out. Remember the fire?"

"Despite that reputation, she had plenty of people coming up to her in committee to talk about her bill."

"She was using her bill as barter, which worked for her last year. Even I voted for last year's version, stupid as it was."

"Why did you vote for it if it was stupid?"

"Because it kept the senate Republican bill out and it didn't have a prayer of passing the senate and getting to the assembly. I could vote for it and stay on Wisnewski's good side. Even if it had passed, Birnbaum was going to sink it. He had a better bill. Neither passed, so they both started over again this year."

"Did you sign onto Senator Wisnewski's bill this year?" Grabowski was trying out the vocabulary.

"Not on your life. That would put my name on record as sponsor, which would bite me in the butt next election. She didn't play well in my district."

"Did you know Senator Rubenstock is in the hospital?"

"I heard. I was surprised Mayerling hadn't put more people on this until I heard your reputation."

Grabowski shrugged. "Who do you think poisoned these two women, Senator McNulty?"

McNulty smiled. "It wasn't me. You probably heard that Irene and I had our differences. Once, she said on the senate floor that auto-emission controls would come to Milwaukee over her dead body, and I said, 'That can be arranged.' The newspapers took it as the joke I intended."

"One last question." Grabowski checked his notes. "What do you know about a 'Feminist Political Strike Force'?"

"Not a goddamn thing, but it sounds just like Renata Glover. Ask her."

Grabowski went in search of Diana Ringer's office. After several wrong turns, he found her tucked away down several unmarked hallways.

"Communications Department people are supposed to be invisible." She stored what was on her computer screen and waved him to a chair. "Senators want people to believe they write their own clever quips."

Two people wearing overcoats passed the door. Grabowski looked at his watch. One minute to five o'clock. "Don't let me get in your way of going home."

"No hurry. My cat probably isn't home yet, and even if he is, dinner can wait. Want to go somewhere for a drink?"

Grabowski looked at her in surprise. "Won't it hurt your job to be seen with a detective pumping you for inside information?"

Diana thrust her arms into a long green wool coat, wrapped a burgundy wool scarf around her neck, and crammed a matching beret onto her blond hair.

"Two types of people work for the state: lifers waiting to retire at age fifty-five and build decks onto their cabins in northern Wisconsin, or political hacks under age forty on the road to D.C. I'm category two. Another year and I'm gone."

At the door to the Capitol building, Grabowski turned up his collar against the biting evening cold. Diana was pulling on long leather gloves. "Meet me at the Italian restaurant on State Street where you went with Chief Mayerling. It's the only quiet place this time of day."

Grabowski arrived at the restaurant first, having parked in a no-parking zone. He slid into a cozy wooden booth, ordered an Andeker on tap, and sat looking at the kitschy Italian decorations and the nondescript oil landscapes of Wisconsin scenes. The booth was warm and comfortable, and he opened his notebook and started going over what he had learned.

First, he wasn't sure anyone was telling him the whole truth. Second, he had heard the word "rumor" more in the past two days than in his whole life.

"Who can I trust to tell me the truth around here?" Grabowski asked Diana after she had flung her coat over the back of the booth and ordered fried zucchini and a Cherryland Silver Rail beer.

Diana laughed. "Truth changes each minute in politics, so you'll only hear someone's particular truth at that time. Besides, staff watch their backs and smart ones won't go public with an opinion unless they know it's safe."

"Safe, meaning what?"

"We won't get fired for having it. Our job is to promote the opinions of the people we work for, not our own. Last year three people on staff went to a local printers' union meeting and sounded off about how union employees should get more active in Democratic politics. A year later, only one of the three still works here, even though the Democratic party is the party of labor."

"Isn't that unconstitutional?" Grabowski was amazed.

"Go to court and join the unemployed. Our only permitted public opinion is that of the senators we work for. Let anybody hear us get negative about our senators and we're toast."

"So how do I get the truth?"

Diana smiled. "Have you developed your secret sources?"

Grabowski considered the people he had interviewed. "You're it. Besides your honest face, you aren't a suspect, and whatever happens, you still will have a job."

Diana laughed. "Wrong, Detective. The basis of politics is loyalty, and I could be lying to save a senator whose patronage keeps my job."

"You're concealing information?"

"Relax. As much as I enjoy your presence and the diversion from my routine, I don't want your investigation to drag on. I'm tired of telling reporters I know nothing."

He tried a different approach. "Are rumors in politics ever true?"

"No smoke without fire. Rumor bubbles up out of the murky swamp of wheeling and dealing. A lot of what happens here I hear first through rumor but never understand until later, like secret agendas and shifting alliances."

"So how do you know if a rumor is true?"

"If a rumor survives more than two days, it's true. Or if a rumor is officially denied, it's true. Staff verify rumors as much as possible because passing on too many false rumors gets you dropped from the rumor network. I personally verify rumors through the security guards. People take their presence for granted and blab secrets in front of them."

"So who is going to get Senator Wisnewski's seat?" demanded Grabowski.

Diana smiled. "A real dark horse—a completely unknown woman from Milwaukee."

The beer and fried zucchini turned into veal Marsala and spinach salad, followed by deep-dish apple pie. It was eight o'clock by the time Grabowski and Diana Ringer climbed into his dented blue Plymouth and headed toward the bar off State Street where Senator Rubenstock had collapsed the night before. The smoky room was packed.

While Diana went to call the hospital for an update on Senator Rubenstock, Grabowski found an empty stool at the bar next to Senator Buford Chadwick, the Republican who had sat two seats away from Senator Wisnewski at the Senate Health Care Committee hearing. Chadwick was crouched over a martini and a bowl of nuts. He toasted Grabowski with his empty martini glass, then waved the glass at the bartender.

"To the police, always on duty to protect us."

Grabowski ordered a double Scotch and soda and looked around for familiar faces. Senators Wilk and McNulty were sitting in a booth. Clark was with another group.

Chadwick poked him with his elbow. "I'm taking a big chance drinking here," he said, slurring his words. "Old Beverly Rubenstock went facedown in her drink on this very stool only seventeen hours ago."

"Brave man." Grabowski noticed there were no women in the bar besides Diana.

Chadwick swayed on his stool. "Rubenstock was a lady

senator, and lady senators think they are Joan of Arc sent by God to reform politics. Then they see the compromising that gets laws passed and they get disillusioned. That's when they attack men. God help you if the pack of them is on your trail. You're a dead duck." Chadwick mopped his sweaty brow with a cocktail napkin.

"Women senators always work together?"

Senator Chadwick thought this over. "When they have to. It is not the nature of women to work together. Women are like cats. When one cat gets attacked by a dog, the other cats climb a tree. But when a dog gets into a fight, every dog in the neighborhood is on the spot to help him out." The senator's eyes grew misty.

"You have dogs?"

"Golden retrievers, and every one a beauty. Mouths like velvet; pick a downed duck right out of the water. The little woman is good with game."

Diana Ringer had returned and was listening from the barstool on the other side of Grabowski.

"Who do you think poisoned Senator Wisnewski?" Grabowski asked Chadwick.

"The female of the species is deadlier than the male. Women hold grudges for a lifetime. My sisters haven't spoken in fifteen years, and I can't even remember what set them off."

"Any particular woman senator?"

Chadwick swigged his drink and belched. He leaned close to Grabowski, his breath loaded with gin. "It had to be someone sitting near her so she could dump something in her coffee."

"How do you know something was in the coffee?"

"What else could have killed her—poison dart from across the room? The Senate Health Care Committee isn't 'Wild Kingdom,' even though it seems like it." The senator hiccuped.

Senator Clark, the other Republican on the committee, had taken the barstool next to Chadwick and was ordering a Virgin Mary. "Say," he interjected in his high, cheerful voice. "Did you test the coffee in Beverly Rubenstock's cup? I saw a movie where a woman put poison in her own cup, then swapped cups."

"Are you accusing Senator Rubenstock?" Diana's voice was loud enough to be heard over the din.

Senator Clark slid off his stool. "God no, but the detective asked, didn't he?" He retreated across the room.

Senator Chadwick ignored his departure. He narrowed his bloodshot eyes, thinking hard. "Those two biddies were thick as thieves, now I think of it, and cups could have been swapped. Put nothing past a woman, Detective. They're tricky and they tell each other everything. They put it in the computer pipeline. The phone is good enough for me. Of course, that's the other thing women do: sit on the phone day and night. Right on the senate floor they're on the horn to their aides, and as soon as they're home at night, they pick up the phone."

Chadwick tossed off his martini and signaled the bartender for another. Grabowski took a cautious sip of his Scotch. He grimaced. In this bar, a double meant twice the soda.

"A minute ago," Grabowski commented, "you said someone next to Irene might have dropped something strange into her coffee. Albert Clark was also next to her."

The senator held up a hand and burped. "You never heard me say anything about Albert or Beverly Rubenstock, even off the record. No, look for motivation and you'll have all the suspects you want, no matter the sex. Hell, I nearly choked Irene myself. She shot off her mouth to the press about a bill we were rewriting and I got burned. But that was too complicated for Irene to figure out. She wasn't a real politician like the rest of us; she was a factory worker. She should have stayed behind the sewing machine."

Chadwick started to climb down from his barstool. Grabowski put up a hand.

"One last question. Have you heard about a Feminist Political Strike Force?"

"No, and I hope I never do. The thought is terrifying. Talk to Renata Glover—the one who wears the purple

fringed cowgirl boots. She probably knows all about it."
Chadwick slapped Grabowski on the shoulder and walked a
wavy line to a group at a tiny table.

The bartender came over. "You a senator, sir?" he asked.

"I don't have the liver for it." Grabowski flashed his
badge.

The man smiled. "Senator Chadwick usually doesn't
drink this much. Most of the legislators dried out after they
passed the drunk-driving laws. Of course, they have immu-
nity in Madison—no parking tickets, speeding tickets,
drunk-driving tickets. Hard to believe these folks decide
what to teach schoolkids."

"You knew Senator Irene Wisnewski?"

"What barman in town doesn't? She could drink this
group under the table."

"Did she let out state secrets when she was drunk?"

"No more than most, but then I don't know the difference between state secrets and bullshit, if there is a difference. Plenty of folks bought her drinks."

"Anybody special?"

The bartender polished the counter, thinking. "Most
everybody except Senator Wilk. He stuck to her to keep a
lid on her mouth, I think."

Senator Clark came over to pay his tab.

"Still fishing for information, I see," he said, looking at
Grabowski's notepad.

Grabowski nodded. "Have you heard anything about a
Feminist Political Strike Force?"

"Is that part of the League of Women Voters?"

Diana laughed out loud.

"I'll check," said Grabowski, making a note. "Did you
know Senator Wisnewski well enough to guess why someone might have wanted to poison her?"

Clark dropped a fifty onto the bar. "Poison, huh? Rumor
was true, once again. I can tell you one thing. She had a big
mouth. Couldn't keep a secret if her life depended on it."

"Looks like it did," commented the bartender.

"Whose secret was she about to blab?" Grabowski asked.

Clark shrugged. "Democrats work against each other as much as they work with each other. Irene could have rubbed anybody in her party the wrong way." He tipped the bartender a five and left.

"How dare he say the poisoner was a Democrat!" Diana hissed at his back.

Senator Wilk had climbed onto the next barstool. He ordered a bourbon and branch water and glared at Clark's back. "Of course no Democrat would kill Irene. She was our leak to the press."

Grabowski didn't understand. "You told her, 'Go leak this information'?"

"Of course not—she would have flat-out refused. No, say we wanted a reaction to a new bill, or we wanted to spill the beans on something the Republicans were doing. We'd tell her something was strictly confidential, and half an hour later it was all over town. She blabbed to friends in Milwaukee and to her aide. The aide's son writes for a newspaper."

"Milwaukee paper?" Grabowski made a note.

"Some podunk afternoon paper, but reporters feed off each other. Tap into each other's computers, probably. Reporters are sharks—anything is meat, even themselves."

Diana took a big drink and leaned forward so she could see the senator. "Let me get this straight, Senator. You were using Irene Wisnewski as an information tool? Manipulating her natural verbosity to get your political dirty work done?"

"I wouldn't put it exactly that way, young woman."

"How exactly would you put it?"

"Just exactly as I did put it."

Grabowski leaned forward, cutting off the discussion. "Senator, what do you know about a Feminist Political Strike Force?"

Wilk's face turned bright red. "It's that damn aide to Senator Rubenstock shooting off her mouth again!"

"But what is this organization?"

"It's nothing! Female nonsense! The radical feminists in the senate, like Glover and Rubenstock's aide, want all women to vote alike on what they call 'women's issues.' There's a rumor that this group is forming a hit squad to force solidarity."

Diana had her temper under control. "I haven't heard that, Senator Wilk. It is simply a women's support group."

"For what? Women who work for the legislature get the same salaries as men. They have the same hours and the same working conditions. What do they need support for? PMS attacks?"

Wilk didn't wait for an answer. He snatched his fresh drink off the bar and stomped over to the table where Clark was sitting.

Diana ordered a gin and tonic and drank down half of it before she allowed herself to speak. "Women in the senate may get the same salary as men in the same job, but look at a salary chart and you'll see most women work in the lower-salary-range jobs where men won't work—secretaries, aides, cleaning people. I'm sure Wilk never picked up a toilet brush in his life."

The bartender leaned on the bar. "Can't type either. He was bragging about it the other night to Senator Rubenstock. He told her the reason women senators stay powerless is that they behave like secretaries and type their own letters."

"What did Rubenstock say?"

"She told him what an antiquated old fool he was, that he lived in the seventeenth century and that reality was about to catch up with him. She was really yelling by the time the woman with her calmed her down."

"The woman with her?"

"I've seen her in here before. She's a lobbyist. Once she told me she used to be a nurse."

Grabowski and Diana Ringer sat around until about midnight catching wisps of conversation and listening to the bartender gossip about the legislators milling around the room. When they had enough smoke and noise, Grabowski dropped Diana at her car and followed her until her taillights disappeared down a driveway in a neighborhood near the Capitol.

# CHAPTER

## 5

ST. CLAIR WAS having her usual ten-o'clock breakfast of two soft-boiled eggs, two pieces of toast with jelly, and a cup of black tea when the phone rang.

"Senator Renata Glover," the caller announced in a loud, firm voice. "We met at the Senate Hearing Room when Irene Wisnewski collapsed. Are you going to the funeral?"

The voice brought back a vague memory of red sweater and black miniskirt. St. Clair glanced at the morning newspaper spread out over the table. The front-page photo showed Senator Irene kneeling at prayer during Christmas Mass at St. Ignatius. The accompanying story included funeral information and listed the important people who would be there.

"I hadn't planned to."

"We need to talk," said Renata, "and the quickest way is at the funeral. You heard about Beverly, of course."

"I read about it in the paper. Talk about what?"

"Beverly collapsed night before last. Just like Irene, except Beverly is still alive and in the hospital. They tell me she's going to be all right. We're counting on your support. This is an emergency."

"Support what?" St. Clair asked.

"I'll tell you at the funeral."

St. Clair hung up, confused. On impulse, she called Grabowski's office, but the switchboard operator said he wasn't in. She was ready to call his home when the phone rang again. It was Karen Wolfson.

"You heard about Beverly Rubenstock?" she demanded. "I suppose that's why they want you to fill the slot."

"Fill the slot?"

"Be temporary senator for the remainder of session. You going to do it?"

St. Clair was astounded. "I hadn't even heard about it."

"Rumor travels at light speed. They'll tell you at the funeral, I assume. You're a natural. You're a doctor and you can talk the senate Republicans into passing Irene's health bill. It's the only women's-issue bill with hope this session. See you at the funeral. Want me to pick you up?"

"No." St. Clair hung up and looked at her watch. The newspaper had said the funeral was at eleven, with a reception afterwards at the senator's district headquarters on the South Side. It was ten-fifteen now. She made one last call, to Marquette University to a professor she used to work with. She wanted to describe the symptoms that had preceded the death of Irene Wisnewski and see if he had any ideas. He was teaching, so she left a message and got into the shower.

The funeral was at Jesu Parish, the cathedral-looking church called the Jesuit Pastoral Center, at Twelfth and West Michigan Streets just up from the Marquette University campus. Despite the sunny day, patches of snow clung in shaded spots. The sky was turning white, a sign of more snow. The two Gothic spires of Jesu stuck into the sky above the mildly pitched roofs of the surrounding buildings. St. Clair found a parking spot a block away.

In front of the church, people in heavy winter coats over dark clothing murmured among themselves. Karen Wolfson emerged from the crowd with an older man with strings of gray hair pasted across his balding head. The man grabbed St. Clair's hand.

"Senator Wilk," he announced. "Caucus chair and chairman of the Health Care Committee. You met me at the senate hearing."

"Of course." St. Clair shook the outstretched hand.

"We'll be talking to you later." He patted St. Clair's arm and escaped into the crowd.

Karen attached herself to St. Clair's arm and towed her into the foyer and up the crowded steps to the sanctuary. "See and be seen, that's success in politics," she murmured, smiling a careful sorrowful smile at everyone.

Once inside, St. Clair tried to detach Karen's fingers from her elbow. "No need to sit together. I'm sure you have people to meet."

Karen's grip tightened. "The coffin is downstairs in the chapel. After the ceremony, there's a short graveside service, then a reception at the district office. Most everybody will skip the cemetery scene and go straight to the reception. They've been setting up all morning. Food coming out your ears."

She spotted someone over St. Clair's shoulder and wrenched St. Clair around to be introduced.

St. Clair looked around for someone familiar who could help her escape the grip on her elbow. It had been so long since she was in a Catholic church that she wanted to just stand and get her bearings. Then someone's hand gripped her other elbow.

"Senator Renata Glover," the newcomer introduced herself. "Terrible. Good to see you, but terrible. Do they know what happened to Irene yet?"

"No, I don't."

"She smoked like a chimney," said a raspy-voiced, short, overweight woman reeking of cigarette smoke. "Probably had a stroke."

"I saw it and it was no stroke," snapped Senator Glover. She pulled St. Clair toward a pew near the back where a young woman was guarding two spots near the aisle by spreading her coat over them and leaning her body over the coat.

Karen Wolfson's grip on St. Clair's other arm tightened further. She tried to steer her down the aisle. Senator Glover hung on. The young woman gathered up the coats and moved over so St. Clair could sit. Karen Wolfson hesitated until it was clear that only two seats were saved, then she hurried toward the front.

"Was this planned?" St. Clair murmured, out of breath.

"Of course," said the young woman. "Nothing politicians do is accidental, except lose. I'm Kay Landau, aide for Senator Rubenstock and McNulty. You heard about Senator Rubenstock, didn't you?"

"Vaguely," said St. Clair.

"She's near death. There's an evil conspiracy to get rid of female legislators, and Senator Rubenstock was the second victim. I don't know how people can sit here calmly while she's lying in that hospital bed."

"She isn't near death," interrupted Renata Glover. "And we'll see her this afternoon after the funeral. Dr. St. Clair, I hope you'll overlook the fact that we're sitting at a funeral, but in politics, the unusual is the usual. The situation is this: We have just lost a major female force in the senate, and we must replace her with someone equally strong. We need a woman who can help pass some extremely vital health care legislation that will affect women and children across the state."

The priest had started the service with a prayer. Someone behind St. Clair made a shushing noise. Senator Glover scowled and lowered her voice to a hoarse whisper.

"We had a meeting of the Senate Democratic Caucus last night, and some of us decided that you will be an excellent candidate to be temporary senator until the session is over."

The priest had launched into a eulogy about Senator Wisnewski.

"Why me?" whispered St. Clair. "I know nothing about politics. I barely vote."

"You're a woman; you're an authority on the health care issue at stake; and you won't run for the seat when it opens up. We have our own candidate, but she needs time to get educated on the issues."

"And I don't?"

The priest was listing the Catholic charities Senator Wisnewski had supported. "And Senator Irene was trying to bring young people from our inner city into Marquette by providing state funds for scholarships. I hope this plan doesn't go to the dust heap just because this courageous woman has left."

Senator Glover raised her voice to be heard over the priest. "The only issue you'll be called to speak on, Dr. St. Clair, is the health care bill, and that, you'll have no trouble with. For the rest you'll be told how to vote."

"This is absurd. I couldn't possibly," said St. Clair.

"Why not?"

"I don't have time. I work for a living and I live in Milwaukee."

"Take a leave of absence for three months from your job. Listen, take some time to think this over. You can tell me by tomorrow or the next day. Here's the health care bill." She passed over a thick manila envelope.

St. Clair's jaw dropped. "Are you crazy?" she hissed.

Kay Landau leaned over. "Are you afraid to accept because of what happened to Beverly and Irene?"

The funeral service ended shortly after that. St. Clair followed Senator Glover and Kay through the crowd out to the sidewalk, where she ran into Father Vincent, vice chancellor of Marquette University.

"Dr. Maxene St. Clair! Such a pleasure! Not a nice moment to renew old acquaintances, but the Lord giveth, and the Lord taketh away."

"I suppose so." St. Clair couldn't think of anything else to say. Father Vincent usually reserved his friendliness for alumni who were big donors.

Father Vincent leaned down from his towering six feet and murmured in her ear, "A little bird told me that you are our new senator. Congratulations! They couldn't have picked a better woman to follow Senator Irene."

St. Clair's jaw dropped again. "You heard about this already?"

"I keep close touch with the senate; in fact, I spoke to Senator Irene the day before she died. She was getting us scholarship money. I know you'll make sure we get the grants. You used to be one of us; in fact, you still are. You're just on leave."

"I beg your pardon?"

"Senator Wilk was the lead, but Irene was delivering the women senators' votes by trading for something in her health care bill—all very political and mysterious. State money for private universities is touchy, even though the state allows elementary schoolchildren to use vouchers for private schools. Assemblyman Birnbaum, unfortunately, says that the use of vouchers breaks down the public school system, and that public money should go to public colleges. I explained that our scholarships pull students out of the ghetto, but I'm afraid our reputation as a rich Catholic university for rich Catholics has doomed us to poverty."

St. Clair smiled. "Or what passes for poverty here."

Father Vincent didn't share her humor. "Our endowments are inadequate. Now it's up to you."

"Excuse me?"

"As new senator, you can carry on Irene's support."

St. Clair's answer was cut off by Grabowski, who stumbled over her feet. Father Vincent took the chance to transfer his friendliness to Senator Wilk.

Grabowski's face was pale, his eyes red-tinged, and he had nicked himself shaving.

"You look hungover," St. Clair commented.

"Part of the investigation," answered a cheerful, tall, blond woman behind him. She was wearing a gray dress under a long, dark green coat. "I was worried when he got into the car to drive home, but he made it home in one piece."

The blond woman looked no worse the wear for the late night out, St. Clair thought, but Grabowski looked beat. "What did you find out?" she asked him.

"I found out politicians get a lot of work done in bars."

"Male politicians," interrupted Kay Landau. "Male chauvinist pigs who only make deals in the men's room or in bars after midnight."

The blond woman stuck out her hand to St. Clair. "I'm

Diana Ringer. I met you at the health care committee hearing when Senator Irene died. Actually I didn't meet you; I saw you in action. We were all impressed. I hear they're considering you for the temporary slot."

Maxene didn't know what to say, so she said nothing. Diana Ringer filled up the blank.

"Of course, we were all in shock when Irene died, but she did smoke like a chimney for fifty years. I saw a picture of her as a teenager; she had a cigarette in her hand. She must have had sheet-metal lungs to have survived as long as she did. You and Detective Grabowski know each other well?"

Kay interrupted before St. Clair had a chance to answer.

"How can we stand here making small talk when there's a killer out there loose? Senator Rubenstock is at death's door and one of us women is next."

Diana put her arm around her. "Take it easy, Kay. Beverly is going to be all right. Talk about sheet metal; Beverly invented the stuff. Isn't that right, Doctor?"

"Isn't what right?"

"That Beverly is strong as an ox. Detective Grabowski and I went to the bar last night where she collapsed, trying to figure out if she ate or drank something that caused the attack. And speaking of drinking, how about a leisurely glass before the reception, then get there in time for food before the cemetery crowd arrives? Who needs a ride?"

St. Clair and Grabowski watched them peel off to their cars. A few people lingered on the sidewalk to watch the hearse and the line of cars drive off to the cemetery.

"Going to the reception?" Grabowski asked.

"Can't think why I would."

"Because we could have a leisurely glass of wine at a nice restaurant, plus lunch, then arrive late."

St. Clair followed Grabowski's beat-up Plymouth south on Knickknick Street to a Slovenian restaurant famous for its stuffed zucchini. In the crowded dining room, the waiter found them a small table in a tiny corner with a candle that dripped red wax onto the white tablecloth.

St. Clair ordered cabbage-and-ham soup followed by stuffed zucchini with dumplings. She spread a thick layer of butter over the heavy brown bread.

Grabowski had picked up a newspaper in the bar. The front page had a large photo of Senator Irene shouting at other senators. It was flanked by other photos of her shouting at school board members, health department officials, hospital board members, and visiting congressmen. The caption read, "Woman of many words, mostly unprintable. Beloved by her constituents; feared by everyone else."

"Did somebody get tired of being shouted at?" St. Clair asked, scanning the captions.

"I've never seen so many possible suspects," sighed Grabowski. "Everyone has some good reason for throttling her."

"Her constituents, too?"

Grabowski tapped the photo on the front page. "These school board members lived or worked in her district, and so did the hospital board members. They didn't love her much."

"But no one ever ran against her."

"Which brings in another nest of suspects. Campaign politics is supposed to be nasty. The nicest thing I've heard said about her is she represented her district, which is usually meant as a slam."

"Any idea yet as to how she died?" Maxene asked.

"Nothing definite. Similar symptoms as Rubenstock, but could be entirely different cause. They may have ruled out strychnine, although the pathologist at the State Board of Health says strychnine is hard to trace since it doesn't take much to do the job. Got anything from your academic cronies?"

She shook her head. "Sorry. Have you talked to her neighbors? Maybe they saw something unusual."

"I went there this morning before the funeral. She lived in a little white stone bungalow surrounded by a white picket fence."

Grabowski sat remembering the scene. Roses, protected

for the winter with gunnysacks, lined a barbecue pit in the backyard. Miniature reindeer pulling Santa on a red sleigh sat in the front yard near five plastic choirboys holding hymnals, their scarlet lips in permanent song.

Inside, the house had smelled like furniture polish and bleach. Police fingerprint dust lay on the wooden cabinets in the living room, dining room, and study, and even was tracked on the deep green wall-to-wall carpeting.

Grabowski had gone methodically from room to room looking for the senator's missing briefcase or anything else that might give him a hint as to what happened. He found only a rigidly tidy house with clothing hung according to color in the bedroom closets, and shoes in shoe bags. The refrigerator had been well stocked with vegetables and fruit, plus tonic water and soda.

In the dark-paneled study was a heavy walnut desk, matching filing cabinets, and a bookcase filled with ency-clopedias and hardback best-sellers, each with a gift in-scription. Two walls were covered with photos of Irene posed with state and national dignitaries, and the liquor cabinet was packed with bottles still gift-wrapped.

The living room furniture was comfortably soft and well used. A half-finished afghan lay across a green sofa near the wide-screen TV, and a log fire was laid, ready to light. Grabowski sat down on the soft couch and listened to the heavy ticktock of the grandfather clock. It was a restful room but without spark: standard colors, standard furniture, standard northern Wisconsin landscapes on the walls. Several photos of an older man sat on the mantel, probably her husband, who had died a few years before.

Where was the briefcase? Not in her car, according to Mayerling. Grabowski spent an hour reading over every pa-per in her desk, including folders of information about transportation problems, crime, health care. In the bottom drawer he found another pink slip with MARK penciled on it. The date was two days before her death.

"I talked to the neighbor lady," Grabowski told St. Clair. "She said Senator Wisnewski's children live out of state;

they'll get here tomorrow. A green Camaro was there yesterday, Wisconsin plates. Some person tried the front door, walked around to the back. Could have been a man or woman. She didn't get the license number."

"Did the woman know Senator Wisnewski well?"

"They've lived there fifteen years. Senator Wisnewski was there before them. The neighbors had a few problems with her because of their dog. She told them dogs didn't crap in senators' yards."

Grabowski's beer came and he drank off the head. "I found two appointment cards with someone named Mark, but I can't find any Mark who is work-connected. Do women over fifty have affairs?"

Maxene laughed. "You think the sex drive stops after fifty? But why go for sex? Maybe it's her hairdresser."

"Maybe." Grabowski frowned.

"How are you going to figure out what happened? Or should I say, what's happening?"

"Hang around the senate, ask questions. Two lady senators poisoned in two days isn't the end. Something will surface."

"Something has," said St. Clair. "Senator Glover asked me to be temporary senator in Senator Wisnewski's place until the legislative session is over."

Grabowski choked on his beer. "You're joking."

"She made the request during the actual funeral, if you can believe that. She told me to take a leave of absence. What's even more ridiculous is that Father Vincent knew before I did. The funeral was no sooner over than he started pressuring me to give scholarship money for Marquette! Of all the nerve!"

"What are you going to do?"

"Turn her down, of course, Why me? I know nothing about politics; I barely vote. Senator Glover said that they chose me because, as a doctor, I would have the influence to push Senator Wisnewski's health care legislation through, but I haven't even read the whole bill. I'm just a body thrown into the line of fire."

Grabowski drank off his beer. "Isn't that what you're doing at St. Agnes? Holding the front lines? Why not say yes? They need you."

"What about my job? What about my apartment? It's too complicated."

Grabowski signaled for another beer. "It might be a good change, Max. You're becoming the kind of doctor you always disliked—boring. You were even planning to go to a medical convention in Palm Springs. Once, you told me that Palm Springs was full of people who are dead but don't know it."

St. Clair didn't answer, just sat looking at the red wax dripping on the white linen. Grabowski took her hand.

"Consider becoming a senator for a few months. If only to help me out. In that place I can't tell who is lying."

St. Clair smiled. "You want me to be a spy?"

"Just keep your eyes open. And don't worry. You'll be all right."

The funeral reception was at Senator Irene's district office on the South Side, in a tidy storefront wedged between a bookstore and a shoe repair shop. A wooden trash barrel bedecked with Christmas greenery sat near the curb bearing the sign "Keep Milwaukee Clean, Retain Senator Irene Wisnewski."

People were crowded around the doorway drinking out of steaming cups. Grabowski parked in front of a fire hydrant. By the time St. Clair had found a parking spot four blocks away, Grabowski had gone inside. She slid through the throng near the doorway and pushed inside the noisy room. Almost immediately, Diana Ringer appeared with a plastic cup of steaming cider.

"Have you known Detective Grabowski long?" she asked.

"A few years."

"But you see a lot of each other." This was from Kay Landau, who had come up behind Diana.

"It depends on our schedule."

"Mr. Efficiency," said Diana. "He understands the ins and outs of the senate already. Of course, he knows the criminal mind."

"He's a dream!" Kay exclaimed. "Sensitive, understanding. He really cares what happens to us. He'll get to the bottom of this. But it better be quick before more women senators get poisoned. I'm going to call the hospital and see how Beverly is doing." She left in the direction of the office, where Grabowski was visible at the doorway talking to a reporter wearing a *Milwaukee Journal* ID badge.

Diana scanned the crowd, then settled her attention back on Maxene. "Exactly how eligible is Detective Grabowski?"

"As eligible as he wants to be," St. Clair snapped.

A short woman wearing a fur hat, fur coat, and fur boots came up. "I'm Evelyn Brown, Assemblyman Birnbaum's aide. I heard you've been tapped to fill the temporary slot," she said to St. Clair.

The *Milwaukee Journal* reporter had followed her. "If Assemblyman Birnbaum died, he wouldn't get half this turnout. Is Birnbaum packing to move in here? Is he practicing saying, 'Senator Birnbaum'?"

The people around laughed.

The reporter turned on St. Clair. "I hear you've been tapped for the temporary senate seat. Is that because you're a doctor and you're going to push the Wisnewski Memorial Health Care Bill?"

"No comment," said St. Clair, edging away.

"You're a natural—no experience, no opinions." He laughed.

Senator Glover appeared and fastened her fingers into St. Clair's arm. "Come into the back," she said. "We're having a little conference."

Senator Wilk, Senator McNulty, and about six other senators were crowded into a small room. When St. Clair walked in, they stopped talking and began to clap. Senator Wilk took St. Clair's hand in both of his. "Congratulations, Doctor. Not only did you help us out medically, now you'll help us out politically."

"I only heard about this an hour ago," said St. Clair. "I must say, I'm hardly an appropriate candidate. I know nothing about politics. I'm not even clear how laws are passed."

Senator Wilk waved away the objection. "Details, details. It's your medical background we need. We have a dandy little health care bill that needs a sponsor who understands the medical system and can put together a package that will pass this year."

"You're still writing the bill?" asked St. Clair.

Senator Wilk cleared his throat. "The bill is final; we only need an articulate backer who will talk it up in committee hearings and on the floor."

"I have logistical problems," protested St. Clair. "I work, as you know, at St. Agnes Hospital, and I live in Milwaukee."

Senator Wilk made more waving motions. "Your hospital administrator will be happy to give you a leave of absence. And you can live in Madison for the session."

St. Clair looked around the room at the smiling faces. "Give me a day to think this over and check with my hospital administrator," she said. "At the moment, I'm expected at work."

Grabowski was nowhere to be found in the crowded outer room. St. Clair hurried to her car and got to St. Agnes barely by three o'clock. Joella, the ER clerk for the afternoon shift, and Shirley, the RN in charge of the ER for afternoons, were lounging at the nurses' station, picking through a gift box of chocolates. St. Clair picked up the gift tag. It was for her, from the Senate Democratic Caucus.

"Hope to have you with us," the tag read.

"What's this all about?" Shirley demanded.

"You won't believe. Just because I testified for their health care bill, some senators want me to take over Senator Wisnewski's seat until the session is over."

Joella took a careful bite of a chocolate-covered cherry. "No offense meant, honey, but they just want a female body who will vote as she's told while they fight over that senate seat. I've been reading the papers. There's a bunch of folks who want that spot."

"Senator Glover told me there's a woman who will get the seat as soon as she's properly educated about the issues," protested St. Clair.

"A woman and six others, including Assemblyman Birnbaum," said Joella.

"They think I can get their health care bill passed because, as a doctor, I carry some authority," said St. Clair.

"Have you read the bill?" asked Joella, hand on hip. "According to the papers, it's cat poo."

St. Clair held up a big manila envelope. "My homework for the night."

Shirley was frowning. "You want to walk into that mess? Senator Irene was poisoned and so was Senator Rubenstock. The newspaper said there's a rumor that a killer is out there poisoning lady senators."

"On the other hand," said Joella, "this is a chance to spend quality time with that cute detective of yours who's been assigned to the case, according to the newspaper."

"He's not mine, and there are women in the senate who have him in their sights." St. Clair yanked on a white coat.

"Why don't you marry the man and get it over with?" said Shirley. "We know he wants you."

"Maybe I don't want him," said St. Clair.

"Honey, don't let your feminist pride get in the way of your happiness," retorted Joella. "You can get married and still be independent."

"Says who?" St. Clair said, and marched off to see her first patient.

# CHAPTER

## 6

THE RECEPTION AT the late Senator Wisnewski's district headquarters was still going strong at three-thirty when Grabowski looked around the still-crowded reception for Maxene and learned from Diana that she had left. He drove to headquarters to check his mail. A pile had accumulated and a note from his captain said to see him. Grabowski poured himself a cup of coffee and tapped on the door.

"How's life in politics?" asked the captain.

"Everyone is a liar, but there's nothing to be done except keep your eyes open."

"Politicians lie. That's news?"

"I just never ran into it personally. They change their stories depending on who they're talking to and if they're being held accountable."

The captain yawned. "You got a plan?"

"I've talked to each of the senators on the Senate Health Care Committee and their aides, and I'll talk to a few people who testified that day for the health care bill. So far no leads."

"What about the vandalism reports we got from Assemblyman Birnbaum?"

"Birnbaum was too busy to see me in Madison, but he's going to his district office after the funeral reception today, so I'll go there, then over to Senator Wisnewski's house to open it up for the relatives."

The captain nodded. "I told Captain Mayerling that our technicians will take care of this end. They went to Senator

Wisnewski's house this morning and took away for analysis the contents of the refrigerator and the open containers in cupboards. The fingerprint report went into your box along with the key to the house. They didn't find much except the cleaning lady's prints and a few of Senator Wisnewski's. We had hers on file since she joined the 'Citizens Against Crime' group that works with our PR department."

Grabowski stood up to go, but the captain wasn't finished. "Newspapers say there's a conspiracy to knock off lady senators."

Grabowski frowned. "At first I thought that was crazy—the place runs on paranoid rumors—but now I'm beginning to wonder."

Assemblyman Birnbaum's office was in a storefront on West Greenfield Street. A dusty hardware store sat on one side and a small neighborhood grocery on the other. Both stores had steel mesh over the windows and doors. Birnbaum's didn't, and the window was broken. It had been crudely repaired with duct tape and a sheet of plastic. Inside, it was barely warmer than outside. A woman wearing fur boots and coat was sitting at a desk. A small space heater was going full blast and her gloved fingers were wrapped around a cup of steaming coffee.

"What do you want?" she demanded, opening a desk drawer and sliding her hand inside.

"Police." Grabowski held up his hands. He slowly opened his coat and pulled out his wallet. He let it drop open to show his badge.

The secretary closed the drawer. "That's right, I saw you at the wake. Assemblyman Birnbaum's car won't start and I don't know when he'll get here."

Grabowski held his cold hands over the space heater. "Are you this friendly with constituents, Ms., uh . . . ?"

"Evelyn Brown. This neighborhood gives me the creeps. I don't know why Birnbaum pretends he's like the people who elected him. He doesn't have to sit here afraid of being mugged. My sister wants me to quit."

Grabowski sat on an icy metal folding chair and took out his notebook. "The report from the district policeman said you've had a broken window, gum on the door handles, wet toilet paper stuck around outside. Anything more?"

"Dead rats on the doorsill, threatening notes in three languages taped to the door. Do you know what it's like to come to work not knowing what disgusting or frightening thing is waiting for you?"

"I have an idea."

Evelyn Brown was unmoved. "That's what cops get paid for. I'm paid to hear what intelligent people in Milwaukee want Mark Birnbaum to do for them in Madison. I'm not a U.N. observer in a combat zone."

"Any idea who's doing this?"

Evelyn Brown stood up and stamped her feet to get the circulation moving. "At first I thought it was Senator Wisnewski's henchmen, and I still think so. It stopped after she died."

Grabowski looked at her closely to see if she was joking.

"I'm not kidding," she said, reading his mind. "The woman was a maniac. She used to scream at us over the phone. She said Assemblyman Birnbaum's health care bill was ruining the chances of her health care bill. Of course, it was."

"You honestly think she had this place vandalized?"

"Whoever is doing it wants us out, and that's what Irene wanted. Frankly, I'm glad she's dead. Maybe the Democratic party will appoint someone pleasant and we can share the senate district office—safe neighborhood, restaurants with menus in English."

"You really think she was the vandal?" Grabowski persisted.

"Well, it isn't gangs. Birnbaum risked his life to talk to those hoods about politics and how they can make a difference by voting. What a joke. But they were friendly. One came in the other day looking for work."

The door banged open and a tall man wearing a heavy fur coat and hat with dangling earflaps stomped in and stuck out a cold hand. He pulled off his hat and a shock of white hair burst out.

"Mark A. Birnbaum. Saw you at the reception. You met Evelyn, I see. Any coffee, Evelyn?"

"Instant in the jar. Hot water in the kettle."

"Ah, yes. Detective, can I make you a cup of coffee?"

Grabowski nodded, wondering if he could pour it over the chair seat. His legs had gone nearly numb from the icy metal.

Birnbaum settled behind the second desk in the room and plowed through a pile of papers. "I have the letter somewhere I sent to the police department. I hope there's some way to stop this harassment, short of moving out." He shot a furtive glance at Evelyn, who was typing a letter.

"When was the last vandalism?"

The secretary answered. "The day Senator Wisnewski died. Somebody tossed a rock through the window as I was on the phone with her aide getting the news about Irene. Normally I'm not here during the legislative session—I commute to the Capitol—but I came to pick up mail. I'm lucky I wasn't hit by flying glass."

"We're all lucky." Birnbaum drummed his fingers on the desk. "Do you think this is related to Senator Wisnewski's death?"

"A pattern hasn't emerged yet. Maybe it had to do with her while she was alive."

Birnbaum glanced at Evelyn. "That rumor has been bandied about. We have no evidence, of course. Then again, strange things happen in politics."

"Do you have dates of the vandalism incidents?"

Birnbaum began shuffling through papers again, but Evelyn whipped a page out of a drawer and into Grabowski's hands.

"Dates," she announced. "Details. Most occurred while I was in Madison."

Grabowski glanced over the list. "Did the neighbors notice anything?"

"I don't speak Spanish and I don't have time to learn."

Birnbaum spoke up. "I don't speak Spanish either, or Cambodian or Laotian, which are the other languages in this neighborhood. Our translators think it's gangs."

Grabowski glanced at his notes. "What will happen with Senator Wisnewski's senate seat? I heard you want it."

The secretary gave a derisive snort. Birnbaum's face reddened.

"It's up for grabs, and you're right, I want the seat. I couldn't run for it while Irene was alive."

"Because she was doing such a good job?"

Birnbaum chose his words with care. "She was enormously popular, being a woman and Polish. It's a Polish district."

Evelyn Brown snickered.

"Will you get the position?" Grabowski persisted.

Birnbaum threw up his hands. "Those fools on the nominating committee want to name some woman doctor temporary senator. They think she can push through Wisnewski's health care bill. They also think she'll vote how she's told and not run for the seat in the general election, but let me tell you something, Detective, women do whatever they want. Women legislators smile sweet, but then they consult their fortune-teller or their hairdresser and vote as they damn well please."

Evelyn Brown snickered again. Birnbaum scowled at her.

"If the party moves you into Senator Wisnewski's seat, they will know how you'll vote." Grabowski repeated what he heard from Diana.

"Which they don't like." Birnbaum scowled and slumped in his chair.

"Could you win the general election?"

"Yes. If the state Democratic party backs me. I don't think they have another candidate, or they wouldn't want that woman doctor."

"Do you have any idea who poisoned Irene?"

"Poison? That's how she got it? Beverly Rubenstock, too?"

Evelyn was standing, stomping her feet and clapping her

gloved hands. "Is there really a conspiracy to murder women legislators?"

"We don't know," admitted Grabowski. "Heard any rumors?"

"I heard Renata Glover is next," said Evelyn.

Grabowski flipped to a new page in his notebook. "One last question, sir. Can you tell me exactly where you were the night before Senator Wisnewski died?"

Birnbaum swallowed. He started fumbling for his calendar. "Of course. I was at home. I made a lot of phone calls."

"To Senator Wisnewski?"

"I don't think so. Maybe. Why?"

"She had an appointment card with the name Mark written on it. For nine P.M."

"Well, it wasn't me. Maybe she meant Mark McNulty. They work together a lot."

Grabowski gave his home phone and work phone to Evelyn, who smiled for the first time. He left Birnbaum adding duct tape to the broken window while Evelyn phoned the glazier again. He went next door to the grocery, where he knew the owner from a previous robbery. The man was leaning on the counter reading the newspaper *El País*. His store was warm and smelled like coffee and fresh bread.

*"Buenos días,"* Grabowski said.

*"Muy buenos días a usted,"* said the man. "You catch those bastards who robbed me?"

"We have two suspects we can pick up any time you'll come look over a lineup."

"Not me, man. I got troubles enough not to stick my head in no hornet's nest."

"What do you know about this broken window next door?"

"Middle of the day, rock thrown out of a blue Chevy. Guy wearing a green parka and ski mask. Lucky thing that lady didn't get hurt. She got a mouth, that lady."

"Got any idea who's doing it?"

"I asked around on Russell Street, in the Mexican grocery, other places. Birnbaum's a gringo politician, no worse than the others. Not coming from this neighborhood, is what I heard. Maybe some other gringo don't like how Birnbaum votes." He laughed, gold teeth with black gaps.

"You see or hear something, call me." Grabowski wrote his home phone on the back of his card.

The owner stuck it between the cash register and the wall. "I heard Senator Irene died. She was some lady. She came down here once and started yelling about the holes in the street. Next day the city had trucks out."

Grabowski said good-bye and checked with the hardware store owner on the other side of Birnbaum's office, with no more success. He left his phone numbers and spun his wheels free from the frozen slush in the gutter.

It was nearly five and well past sunset. Grabowski had promised he would hand over Senator Wisnewski's house to her next of kin by five, so he turned toward the pleasant residential district farther west.

Four cars towing U-Haul trailers were parked in front of the late Senator Wisnewski's home, their engines running. In the back of one U-Haul sat the reindeer that had been in Senator Wisnewski's yard. The streetlights cast shadows over the trampled snow in Senator Wisnewski's yard and the plumes of exhaust from the cars. Neighbors were watching out the lighted windows of their houses.

Grabowski took his time parking. He knocked on the window of one of the cars. "Anybody here familiar with the contents of Senator Wisnewski's house?"

"I am." A woman got out of the passenger side and hurried around the car. The other car doors opened and three other women hurried toward them.

Grabowski spoke to the group. "I need people with me while I go through one last time. I want to know anything unusual that is present, or anything missing."

"All us sisters will come in together."

The man at the steering wheel laughed. "God forbid one of them gets something the others don't. I'm at the tavern at the corner." The other three car doors slammed and the four men got into one car and drove off while Grabowski followed the women through the icy dark to the house.

The house was cold and smelled of wood ashes. One of the sisters flicked on the lights and the furnace. The search didn't take long. The women spent equal time searching the house and watching each other. In half an hour, Grabowski turned over the house keys, ripped the police tape off the front door, and left them dividing up the goods.

It was six o'clock and he was beat. At home in his cold kitchen, he threw a frozen chicken dinner into the microwave and stepped into the shower. By the time he was out, the house was warmer. He ate dinner in front of the evening news and called Maxene. She was busy with a patient and Joella took the call.

"Sounds like you got some female fans there in the state capital," she chatted. "Politics could get interesting."

"I'm not interested," said Grabowski. He polished off his second beer and went to bed.

# CHAPTER

# 7

AT TEN THE next morning, Grabowski arrived at the Capitol in time to hear the pastor of the day pray over the senators assembled on the senate floor.

"Dear Heavenly Father," the minister intoned. "Help these industrious, dedicated men and women guide our great state through the rocky waters of today's politics."

"They pray for guidance, but never get it," someone behind Grabowski whispered. Diana from Communications was lurking behind the pillar. "You missed the excitement this morning. An aide got stuck in the elevator and started screaming she was going to be murdered next. By the time the maintenance crew got her out, three people had gone home with stomach cramps. If this panic keeps up, we'll have to call in the National Guard to cover the secretarial positions."

Grabowski smiled. "So how's my investigation going, according to rumor?"

"You haven't a clue, or you have too many, and you decided the show can go on as long as nothing comes to a vote."

"That wasn't my decision," Grabowski amended. "I said they could call a time-out as long as everyone was in the lineup when I wanted them. This morning I heard your lawyers decided that preconvicted felons can take part in discussions as long as no votes are taken that might have to be retaken later. They're assuming the investigation will be over fast."

Diana was looking out over the senate floor, half paying

attention to what was clearly old news. "What are you doing here on the senate floor today, picking over the chickens for carving?"

"Absorbing atmosphere. In two days I've heard so many rumors of deceit and corruption that I need a general impression of the place to put them into perspective."

"Deceit and corruption are harmless parts of the political process, at least in pristine Wisconsin," she informed him, scanning the senate floor. "The boys would be bored without wheeling and dealing."

"And the girls?"

"Female senators take their work more seriously, maybe because women haven't been in politics long enough to learn the fun side. Or maybe after raising children, they're through playing childish games."

"And how do you feel about playing childish games?"

"I get paid handsomely for the privilege, Detective, and though I could get fired any moment a senator decides he—or she—doesn't like my hair color, this job is more fun than any other I've had." She nodded at someone across the senate chamber.

Grabowski followed her gaze. Senator Wilk was lounging at his desk talking on his phone. Knots of senators were huddled, heads together, shoulders hunched, while a few dozed at their desks. The secretary of the senate was reading bill numbers into the microphone, ignoring Senator Clark, who was standing, tapping on his microphone for attention.

"I never heard Wisconsin politics described as pristine," Grabowski said.

"It's pristine because Wisconsin controls what corrupts other state politics, namely lobbyists." She hurried off to catch the attention of a balding man wearing a mismatched plaid suit.

Twice as many spectators stood on the sidelines as were senators on the senate floor. Most spectators chatted briefly with someone, then moved on, an eye on the senate floor action. Diana returned, scribbling in a notebook.

"I know what the senators are doing, but why is everyone else here?" Grabowski asked.

"Covering their asses. Jobs are lost if we don't leap to attention at a nod. The Research people who drafted the bills being debated today are here because they might have to write emergency amendments. The Communications people are here in case a senator says something significant that the press over there might miss. Here, watch us in action." She hurried off.

Senator Wilk was walking off the senate floor. Immediately five staff members swarmed around him, pencils scribbling on notebooks, sheaves of paper shuffling. Wilk said a brief word to two, then moved into a side office.

Diana returned slightly out of breath. "Staff in a feeding frenzy."

"Who's the man in the plaid suit?"

"Irene's biggest victim, Mark Lewis. Divorced twice, works twelve-hour days. He's an excellent writer and he used to head the research staff for the health care committee until Irene got mad at him and got him fired. Senator Rubenstock talked McNulty into hiring him on research staff for the Democratic Caucus. McNulty is senator in charge of staff."

"Irene actually got him fired?"

"After being terrible to him—demanding, overbearing, rude—even shouted at him on the senate floor. He rewrote her bills a dozen times. He moved to Caucus research staff, and the day before she died she was screaming at him again in front of everyone."

"Why?"

"She said he did bad research, wrote her a bad bill, same old stuff. Mark was beet red. People over forty shouldn't have to take that abuse."

As she spoke, the man in the plaid suit came up to speak to Diana. She made quick introductions, then hurried away. Mark Lewis began scribbling furiously in his notebook. Finally he came up for air.

"It sounds like people lose their jobs easily here," Grabowski commented.

"We live at the whim of prima donnas. And turnover is total when a senator gets unelected."

"You can't work for more than one senator in a row?"

"Senators don't want staff who are tainted by another senator's belief system."

"How did Irene do here?"

"Irene antagonized everybody—not just me. She won a few perks for her district, like money for more school guards, so her district kept reelecting her. But her only decent bills belonged to someone else. She just signed on. The trouble was, having her name on a bill was nearly the kiss of death because she had pissed off so many people. Of course, she insisted that no one would work with her because she was a woman."

Kay Landau had come to the sidelines and was listening to the conversation. "Irene was right. White men run this country. Women have to fight for every inch and we can lose everything through some clandestine agreement in the men's toilet."

She shoved a note into Grabowski's hand. "Senator Renata Glover wants to see you when the senate goes into lunch recess. How was your veal Marsala?"

"Quite good." Grabowski was startled.

"Try the ravioli stuffed with spinach and ricotta. How about tonight, say six o'clock? Come by my office." She hurried off.

Mark Lewis was scribbling in his notebook again. Grabowski interrupted him.

"I understand you had an appointment with Senator Wisnewski the night before she died," said Grabowski.

Mark looked up sharply. "I haven't spoken to that woman in months and I certainly wouldn't make an appointment to do so. She got me thrown off the health committee staff and she was trying to get me fired from Caucus staff. What a bitch."

"Why did she want you fired?"

"I made the mistake of telling her that if she'd let me write her bill my way, it might pass for once."

Senator Wilk was waving at Mark, who shuffled his papers nervously and hurried away.

At noon sharp the senate broke for lunch and Grabowski exited with the crowd of senators and staff. Senator Renata Glover got to her office before him and was sitting at her desk with her purple suede cowboy boots propped up on a pulled-out drawer. She held a sheaf of papers in her lap, but she was staring out the window. She waved Grabowski to a chair.

"Beverly is better," she said. "I talked to a nurse. Have you seen her yet?"

"This afternoon. A policewoman is sitting with her."

"I heard a rumor that there's a plot to kill women senators." Senator Glover yanked at her black leather miniskirt and stared at Grabowski through heavy red-framed glasses. Dark shadows were smudged under her eyes.

"You've been talking to Miss Landau, who is reacting in the extreme. I'm looking for a connection between the two women besides gender and political party. Were either of them worried about something or someone?"

Senator Glover looked out the window and shook her head. Her brass earrings jingled. "I can't think of a thing. I feel a nearly overwhelming sense of impending doom. Normally I'm not superstitious or moody, and I can't understand why I feel this way." She jangled her bracelets.

"Maybe you've been caught up in the sinister-plot mentality."

"Possibly." Senator Glover didn't concede the point.

Grabowski put his next question tentatively. "I heard from various people that women senators are different from men. Do you think this is the case?"

Renata Glover gave him a sharp look. "Are women senators being knocked off because we're different?"

"I'm just trying to get a handle on gender politics."

Senator Glover tossed the sheaf of papers onto the desk with an impatient sigh. "Both Beverly and Irene had become disgusted with politics, and Irene made no bones about wanting to retire. Why? Yesterday I spent an hour explaining my transportation bill to Senator Wilk, and he nearly patted me on the head and told me to run along like a good girl. Then in Caucus, he introduced an amendment that would decrease traffic jams in his district, but would cut the heart out of the long-range goals of the transportation bill. A retired dairyman with two brain cells to rub together gets more votes by riding a fire engine in a parade than a woman with a Ph.D. in political science and fifteen years lobbying for the Lung Association. That fool Clark never changed a diaper in his life and he's writing a child care bill. He knows no more about children in day care centers than what his hack writer tells him." She stopped, panting.

"I've met one of these hack writers. She seemed well versed in political subjects."

Senator Glover glared at him. "Depends on the hack writer. Some are political appointees who can't find the point of a pencil. It's a cushy job—watch the hour coffee breaks and two-hour lunches."

"Who's writing for you?"

"Diana Ringer, but I had to scream to get her. Otherwise I'd have a college graduate with more ego than brains."

"If you're so cynical about politics, why are you still here?" Grabowski asked.

"A lot of women think we can make political changes that help people. Finding out how difficult that is hits women hard because our expectations are so high. Men don't come with such hopes, or they're here for the power. Or they cope better with disappointment because they had it at work. Most women in elected office haven't held full-time jobs as long as men since many of us stayed home to raise children and do volunteer work. Also, a lot of women in politics were teachers—a powerless part-time job."

She paused to catch her breath. Grabowski cut in. "When did you talk to Senator Wisnewski about her burnout?"

"A few nights before she died. She and Beverly Rubenstock and I shared a flat here during session. After she died, I just closed the door to her room. I haven't the strength to pack up her things. And now Beverly is gone, too." Her mouth quivered.

Grabowski was astounded. "You shared an apartment with them? Why didn't I know this earlier?"

"I thought you did."

"No wonder you feel impending doom, Senator. I'm concerned about you myself. You can't stay in that apartment alone. Either I give you a female police guard or you move in with someone else."

Senator Glover blew her nose. "A few people have offered—courageous considering what's happened to my roommates. I'll move in with Kay, Senator Rubenstock's aide. She stays in a rooming house just off State Street during session, and it'll be better than looking at Irene and Beverly's empty beds."

"Give me the key to your apartment. I want to look around before you move."

He left Senator Glover staring out the window and called the hospital on her secretary's phone. Senator Rubenstock was awake, according to the ICU nurse, and he could visit briefly. He spoke with the police officer guarding the senator. She reported that all was quiet, no visitors allowed, although Kay Landau, Diana Ringer, and various senators had dropped by the waiting room and left flowers.

On the way to his closet office, he stopped by Diana's office. She was talking on the phone, typing on the computer, and keeping an eye on the television news. She hung up the phone and turned off her computer screen. "I heard Senator Glover is moving in with Kay Landau."

Grabowski handed over the pink scrap of paper that read, "From the desk of Mark" with the appointment time on it. "Can you find out who this person is without letting people know I'm looking?"

"Who already knows you're looking for him?"

"Senator Wisnewski's aide, Rhonda Schmidt."

"Then it's too late for secrecy. I'm surprised I haven't

heard already. First name and date, that's all you've got?"
She squinted at the paper.

Grabowski sat down on the visitor's chair. "I checked the
schedules of all the Marks on staff, and every one was
doing something verifiable at that time."

"Mark might be a lobbyist. This isn't Irene's writing, by
the way, or Rhonda's."

"You sure?"

"Senators drop notes off here and rarely sign their
names, so I've learned a few scrawls. And some clever for-
geries. A true political operative will sink to unbelievable
depths. Labor union lobbyists are the worst." Diana started
thumbing through the lobbyist book. "No Marks in here I
could imagine would want a meeting with Irene, but it
wouldn't hurt to follow up." She wrote down three names,
titles, and phone numbers and passed them across. "In the
meantime I'll make a few calls."

Snow had been falling all morning, and Grabowski's
tires made no sound on the yet-unplowed streets. He parked
in the doctors' parking lot at the hospital and went in
through the service entrance to save getting snow all over
his shoes.

Senator Rubenstock was in Intensive Care, lying on her
back with her eyes closed, propped up slightly in bed. The
respirator was gone, but green oxygen tubing was draped
around her head, the ends in her nose. Her fingers twitched
at the tubing, making the IV bag attached to her arm swing.
Grabowski leaned on the bed rail and spoke her name.

Her eyes opened, confused but definitely determined to
make order out of things. Her voice was hoarse. "You're
the Milwaukee detective."

"I'm here to find out what happened to you in the bar.
We're pretty sure you were poisoned; did the doctor tell
you?" Grabowski's experience with doctors was that patients were the last to know.

Senator Rubenstock shook her head. Her lips formed the
word "Poison?"

"We don't know which poison or how it got into you.

While we track that down, you'll have a guard sitting right here by your side."

Senator Rubenstock's wandering eyes settled on the solid policewoman in the chair by the door. Her fingers fluttered a tiny wave.

Grabowski smiled at the political behavior. "Can you remember exactly what happened in the bar just before you collapsed?"

Senator Rubenstock licked her dry lips. "Talking."

"To anyone in particular?"

"Lots of people." She coughed and a nurse appeared at the bedside holding a carafe of water with a straw stuck into it. The senator took a sip and waved the carafe away. "Put lemons in the water," she ordered in a weak, hoarse voice. "Real lemons, not concentrate."

Grabowski hid a smile at the nurse's expression. "What were you drinking?"

"Bloody Mary. Tasted normal."

"Is it possible that someone wants you out of the way?"

"Got to think," she said. "Got to talk to Kay."

Grabowski left Senator Rubenstock arguing weakly with the nurse about installing a phone next to her ICU bed and went out into the snowy parking lot. The snow had stopped falling and the sun had come out. It was his favorite kind of winter day: crisp cold with brilliant sun.

Chief Mayerling was skimming a pile of reports. He slid a parking permit across the desk to Grabowski. "Put that on your dashboard. I've already revoked three parking tickets on your car. Do you have to park by fire hydrants? This isn't Milwaukee. Cops here obey the same laws as everyone else."

Grabowski shoved the sticker into his shirt pocket and propped his feet on a box of teargas canisters. He flipped through his notebook. "Did you know that Senator Wisnewski shared an apartment with Senator Rubenstock and Senator Glover? Any chance you can send a lab person over there in an hour to take samples out of the refrigerator?" He scribbled the address on a bit of paper.

Mayerling shouted at his secretary to get the technical staff on the phone and pushed a folder across the table.

"Autopsy report," he said. "Poison still undefined. They've turned it over to the State Board of Health. Start harassing them—it's the only way to make them move. Ask for Ivan—baldheaded, works out with weights."

It was four-thirty by the time Grabowski drove through the slippery streets to the Capitol building. He left his car in the loading zone under the overhang with the police sticker on the dash. Upstairs in Senator Rubenstock's office, Kay was sitting behind a mound of papers with the phone parked on her shoulder.

"I'll come see you at seven," she promised the caller, smiling. She hung up.

Grabowski took a guess. "Senator Rubenstock got a phone installed by her bed and she wants something, maybe out of her apartment."

Kay blushed. "Renata shouted at me that I forgot to tell you about the apartment. I thought you knew. Maybe they were both poisoned by bad food from the refrigerator."

"Maybe," said Grabowski. "Come with me now. I want to look around before Senator Glover moves her things into your rooming house."

The senators' flat took up the second floor of a two-story bungalow on a quiet street near the Capitol building. The furnishings were sparse, and even the redbrick fireplace and built-in bookshelves with leaded glass doors failed to give it warmth. In the kitchen, the yellow gingham curtains with matching tablecloth and pot holders magneted to the refrigerator looked lonely. The two bedrooms each had twin beds with flouncy flowered bedspreads, and the bathroom cupboards were filled with cosmetics.

Kay felt the cold register and turned up the thermostat. "Irene grabbed the single room, even though she wasn't here much. She drove back to Milwaukee when the weather wasn't bad or when she didn't have a night meeting here. Beverly and Renata are here more since it's a long drive home for them and the weather gets worse further north. And both of them are on committees with night meetings."

She followed Grabowski into Senator Wisnewski's bedroom and sat down on the bed to watch Grabowski search the bureau. It held little: lingerie, a few sweaters, a bottle of aspirin, and a larger bottle of antacids. In the closet hung a heavy coat, boots, a red silk dress, and a bottle-green wool suit with blue blouse, all encased in plastic clothing bags. Two small suitcases sat on the closet floor.

"Do you see Senator Wisnewski's briefcase anywhere?" Grabowski asked.

Kay dragged herself off the bed and peered into the closet and under the bed. "I wish Renata would let me move in here instead of her moving in with me. I want to be here when Beverly gets out of the hospital."

Grabowski was surprised. "Won't she go home to recover?"

"Maybe for a weekend, but politicians are tough. They feed on stress, or maybe they feed their stress to staff."

Grabowski noticed the shadows under her eyes. He was about to suggest she make herself a cup of tea when the doorbell rang and the lab crew stomped up the stairs to take samples from the refrigerator.

There wasn't much: three cartons of yogurt, a quart of spoiled milk, a dozen eggs. There were also two bottles of wine, a six-pack of Miller, a quart bottle of brewer's yeast, a jar of lecithin. The lab tech sniffed it and make a face. In the freezer was a gallon of Absolut Swedish vodka, and instant meals: macaroni and cheese, veal Parmesan. In the cupboards were dry cereal, instant brownies, tea.

"They mostly ate out," said Kay, watching the lab tech pack food into evidence bags. "Fund-raisers, political strategy meetings. Chicken à la king."

When the lab techs finished, she wiped out the refrigerator with a paper towel.

Grabowski went into Senator Rubenstock's and Senator Glover's bedrooms and began looking through the two sets of bureaus and closets. Senator Rubenstock liked navy blue

and dark green, and Senator Glover liked red and pink.
There was enough in both closets to live comfortably for a
long time, mostly suits with skirts or wool slacks. Under
one bed was a suitcase filled with sweaters that opened out
flat as an additional drawer. Under the other was a box of
papers. He pushed it toward Kay.

She flipped through it. "Background information on various
bills. This is what she wanted me to bring."

Finished with the search, Grabowski walked through the
silent rooms. The flat had finally warmed up, but it still
seemed cold without the personal objects that made a
home—books, magazines, television, stereo. He didn't
blame Renata Glover for not wanting to stay there alone.

"Is this what the flat generally looked like?" he asked
Kay. "Didn't they give parties or invite people for dinner?"

Kay shrugged. "They weren't domestic. A cleaning service
came twice a week because they wouldn't even sweep
the kitchen. Beverly told me that after her four children left
home, she stopped providing any sort of service; she and
her husband graze out of the refrigerator. Renata never had
children; I don't think she knows how to cook."

"And Senator Irene?"

"Irene talked about her wonderful cooking, but she always
went to her daughter's for holidays. Do you think the
cookie-baking grandmother is gone forever?"

"Could be," said Grabowski. He himself ate out more
than he cooked, if you called heating a frozen dinner in the
microwave cooking. He turned off the heat and lights and
carried the box of documents out into the now dark and
snowy evening.

Kay cheered up over linguine with clam sauce washed
down by three beers and an after-dinner brandy.

"Senators have split personalities," she stated after the
second beer. "In Madison, they act sophisticated and politically
quick, and at home they act like regular folks. Voters
like to think they elect 'tame' politicians who vote as told
by the voters. Of course, it's the exact opposite. But if a

senator slips just once and shows the real ego under the 'I'm your public servant' facade, the public unelects them."

"Tell me about Senator McNulty," Grabowski asked.

"Mark McNulty is a sleight-of-hand artist in the positive sense: he works his legislation quietly around tricky corners before he goes public. Once I saw him get dumped on—by Irene, in one of her misguided moments. He had lined up the Democratic votes on a wastewater reclamation bill, but to pass, the bill needed Republican votes and he could only get the bare-minimum Republicans willing to vote for a gas tax raise to fund the system. On the senate floor, Irene broke her promise and voted against the bill. It got sent back to Environment and Natural Resources Committee, which she also sits on. It died."

"Why did she switch?"

Kay shrugged. "Irene could have caved in to pressure from industries in her district who have a lot of gas-fueled trucks and would be hit hard by the gas-tax raise. Or maybe she believed the Republican propaganda going around about high bacteria levels in gray water."

"How did McNulty react?"

"McNulty's face went white and he stomped off the floor. Before that, he never slammed a Democrat to the press, but after that, he never missed an opportunity to point out her voting vagaries. I think he decided her time in the senate was up."

"Is this motive for murder?"

Kay laughed. "If senators killed each other for double-dealing, lying, taking bribes, or sleeping with each other's wives, half the senate would be in the morgue."

# CHAPTER

## 8

THE NEXT MORNING at nine o'clock, Maxene St. Clair was curled up in front of a crackling fire wearing her at-home flannel-lined corduroy slacks, flannel shirt, and furry slippers. She had planned to sit there until it was time to go to St. Agnes, reading the newspapers and some professional journals and writing her mother. She had already called her ex-colleague at Marquette to discuss the poisoning question and was waiting for him to call back.

The other item on her agenda was to telephone Senator Glover and gracefully decline the honor of being temporary senator. The night before, St. Clair had sat down with the proposed health care bill during a lull in the ER and struggled through the pages of small print. The ideas were good—cost control by means of payment ceilings combined with opening preventive care clinics in high-risk areas—but she didn't like the overall bill. One clause said that each public clinic must have a full-time physician at all times, and another gave prescription-writing rights to physicians' assistants working with doctors. St. Clair opposed these as they didn't decrease costs. Both clauses were backed by the Republicans. One clause allowed for state-funded abortion on demand, but required that the procedure be done in a hospital after a counseling session and cosignature from a relative. The whole bill was a fight between doctors who wanted to control the medical system and other health professionals who wanted a piece of the action.

Still, for a brief period during her shift, she had entertained the idea of actually taking this limited opportunity to do something interesting and totally different from her daily, predictable routine.

Snow was drifting down and the sky was darkening. It looked like the predicted winter storm was on its way. The teakettle whistled at the same time the phone rang. It was Senator Rubenstock calling from her hospital bed in Madison.

"Terrible business," said Senator Rubenstock. "You know why I'm in the hospital, of course; you read the newspapers. I collapsed as suddenly as Irene, and they can't figure out what happened to either of us."

"The detective on the case told me something about it."

"Grabowski. I heard you know him. My aide, Kay, found out you did research in specialized drugs at Marquette University in Milwaukee. Well, I've been assaulted by a specialized drug, and I want to know what happened. I liked your take-charge attitude at the senate hearing. I want you to come here, read my chart, look me over, and find out what happened."

"You think I can figure out something the police and the State Board of Health can't?"

"The police have to follow certain procedures that private citizens don't."

St. Clair tried to think. Here was a request almost as absurd as becoming temporary senator. It was one thing to ask her medical colleagues for clues to help Grabowski. It was something else entirely to be directly involved. She changed the subject.

"Did you know that Senator Glover asked me to be stand-in senator for the remainder of session?"

"I did, and that's also why I'm asking you to look into this poisoning situation. I must keep this problem in the political family. Bad press can kill my upcoming campaign. Please, Dr. St. Clair. I need your help. I have nowhere else to turn and I am getting frightened."

St. Clair looked at her furry slippers and at the crackling fire. Oh, well, she thought, there will be other snowstorms and other warm fires. If I leave right away, I can make it back for work at three o'clock, even if it does snow heavily.

As she was changing into wool slacks and driving boots, Grabowski phoned. "Senator Rubenstock says you're coming to visit her."

"She thinks I can diagnose strange poisons."

"So do I. Let's have lunch after you're through. There's an Italian place on State Street that's good, except that I think it's bugged by senate communications."

"Grabowski, who's handling the case at the State Board of Health?"

"That short, bald Romeo with the bizarre sense of humor who helped us out last year with another poisoning."

"Ivan!"

"If I remember correctly, he tried to get you into bed."

"Relax. I like men with hair." But she smiled. She had known Ivan for fifteen years since they did a fellowship together at the University of Wisconsin in Madison. He talked a lot about his red satin sheets, but he was a good soul and a brilliant biochemist. She flipped through her address book to make sure Ivan's phone numbers were there and went outside to warm up the car.

The sky was getting darker. While the car was warming up, she ran a snow shovel down the new snow on the front sidewalk so the mail carrier would deliver the mail. Then she checked the trunk to make sure her gunnysack of sand, sack of wood ashes, wooden roofing shingles, and flares were there in case she got stuck in the snow. She put the snow shovel on top.

While she was there she could call up Ivan at the State Board of Health to find out what he knew about Senator Irene Wisnewski. Maybe there was a connection between the two senators.

Senator Renata Glover was sitting in a metal folding chair outside Senator Rubenstock's closed door, scowling and chewing her lip. St. Clair pulled up a chair.

"I want to talk about your request that I become temporary senator," she began.

Senator Glover wasn't listening. She started biting her red fingernails. "I must speak to Beverly privately after the nurse is through."

"You must be very upset."

Senator Glover exploded. "The situation is upsetting and unnerving and depressing. And I had to move to a hideous rooming house that's dark, reeks of meat loaf, and has red shag rugs. And I'm sharing a room with the aide for Beverly and Mark McNulty." Her voice trembled.

"It's hard to sleep when you're not used to sharing a room."

"I'm not a snob," said Glover, swallowing several times, "but certain knowledge should be known only to senators, and Kay is bound to put two and two together just from my phone calls and the documents I'm reading. Kay has a boyfriend and parents, and even though she generally keeps her mouth shut, if certain news gets out, it's me who suffers. Kay may lose her job, but aides quit eventually; nobody works long for senators. Even I know how impossible I am."

She stared at the floor. Her shoulders began to shake and her brass earrings jingled. St. Clair put her arm around her, but Senator Glover stiffened and sat up straight.

"It's PMS, type D. I'm low on magnesium." She gulped and inhaled deeply through her nose and exhaled through her mouth.

"It's stress," said St. Clair. "Could you go home for a few days?"

Senator Glover broke down completely. "I couldn't even pack properly," she sobbed. "That Grabowski person phoned my office and said a policewoman was coming in five minutes to help me move. I know he has my welfare in mind, but I had to pack with a policewoman watching! I can't go anywhere alone until after the investigation, whatever that means, and the only reason the policewoman isn't here this second is because she and the guard for Senator Rubenstock went for coffee. I shudder to think how much this is costing the taxpayers."

St. Clair handed her a packet of tissues from her purse. "I don't think the public will begrudge a few dollars for your personal safety."

Senator Glover mopped her eyes. "I'm safe, but I don't have a safe place to put my things!"

"Could someone take care of them for you?" St. Clair was thinking of jewelry.

Senator Glover blew her nose and looked at St. Clair. "You doctors keep your mouths shut, don't you? And you're going to be a senator."

At that moment, the door to Senator Rubenstock's room opened and a nurse breezed out. Senator Glover dodged in and St. Clair went to the nurses' station to read through the chart.

It took time. Senator Rubenstock's lab data was extensive and unusual, and each examining physician had written long passages in the chart. The nurses' notes were equally thorough, each profession forestalling malpractice claims. After St. Clair had read half, Senator Glover came out and tapped her on the shoulder. She pulled a large sealed manila envelope from her oversize leather bag.

"You'll look after this, won't you? I know you won't look inside." She marched off, policewoman in tow.

St. Clair looked at the brown envelope with surprise. It was thick, sealed with both glue and tape, and seemed to be papers. She stuck her head inside Senator Rubenstock's room and told her she was still reading the chart.

It was nearly noon before she finished. She found the senator sitting up in bed scowling at a tray of Jell-O, consommé, and soda crackers.

"I requested chilled mineral water with lemon wedges and they sent lemonade. The Jell-O is made with refined sugar, and the salt in the consommé will swell me up like a balloon. Is there no dietician in this hospital?"

St. Clair went back to the nurses' station and persuaded the nurse and dietician to send up pureed tuna salad with lemon wedges and whole wheat crackers. Senator Rubenstock cheered up with news of acceptable food. She pulled out a sheet of paper covered with purple ink.

"I made a few notes to see if I could remember more than I told the police. Basically, I was sitting at the bar listening to those drunken males make stupid deals with each other when I suddenly felt nauseous, began to sweat like a pig, couldn't breathe, and passed out."

"What were you drinking?"

"Vodka Bloody Mary. The police analyzed what was left in my glass and there was nothing but Bloody Mary mix, tomato juice, and a minuscule amount of vodka. That bartender is tight with liquor."

"Were you eating anything?"

"Olives. Same story."

"Smoking?"

"Certainly not."

"Anybody give you anything to eat—gum or mints?"

The senator shrugged. "Earlier that evening I went to a farewell party for a secretary and then to a fund-raiser, and both had appetizers. But I'm not allergic to anything and this never happened before."

"Your chart says that you have a cardiac arrhythmia for which you were taking quinidine."

"The quinidine is recent. I've never been ill in my life, then two weeks ago I went in for a routine insurance physical and my doctor found an irregular heartbeat. So he put me on quinidine."

"The diagnosis on your chart said quinidine overdose."

Senator Rubenstock smacked her hand on her tray. "Absolutely untrue. I took the pills exactly as prescribed. I even checked off on my calendar when I took them."

"I'm not saying the overdose was your fault. Quinidine is tricky. The dose has to be calculated according to a patient's reaction."

"Well, my bad reaction is being made to look like I overdosed," snapped Rubenstock. "My Republican opponent in the coming election is saying I'm incompetent, feeble-minded, and depressed. I want you to find out what happened and kill the rumors, which at this point are rampant."

"Mind if I look you over?" St. Clair pulled the curtains around the bed and went over every inch of the senator's well-nourished, well-exercised sixty-year-old body.

"Tell me," Maxene said, finally. "Can you think of any reason someone might want to poison you and Senator Wisnewski?"

Senator Rubenstock pulled a piece of paper from the drawer of her bedside table. "I've been making a list of people we may have offended or attacked politically. I worked with Irene on bills, state programs, community projects. We campaigned for each other, sponsored fund-raisers for each other, defended each other to the press. Jointly we angered, annoyed, and offended platoons of people, like good politicians do."

"Surely no one would poison merely for politics."

Rubenstock raised an eyebrow. "My dear woman, history is filled with political assassinations."

"But this is state politics!"

"Don't be naïve, dear."

St. Clair wondered where the border lay between naïveté and paranoia. "When are they letting you out of here?" she asked, changing the subject.

"Tomorrow. I'll go home for a few days, then move into the apartment, where the policewoman will sleep on the couch. What's your conclusion, dear?"

St. Clair shook her head. "Give me your number at home and at your office and I'll call you when I come up with something. Before I go," she added, "I want to talk about this idea to make me temporary senator."

"It's an honor," said Senator Rubenstock. "Not many people get the chance to serve their state in such a responsible position."

"I already have one responsible position."

"So do we all. That's the point of a citizen legislature. This is government *of* the people and *by* by the people."

Grabowski was leaning on the nurses' station counter

when St. Clair came out. He was picking over a box of chocolates and chatting with a blond nurse whose frizzed hair was bunched at the top of her head with a bright red ribbon.

Maxene felt a stab of jealousy, a feeling she experienced occasionally with Grabowski and which bothered her. She felt she was not a jealous person; she was an independent woman who could enjoy a relationship without the security of overt signs of fidelity. Why should women marry or even have permanent relationships? Modern life didn't demand communal living, and she could support herself. Still, jealousy attacked at unexpected moments.

Grabowski tore himself away from the blonde and joined her at the senator's door, slurping chocolate.

"Come back inside," he said. "I have a few things to ask the senator."

Senator Rubenstock smiled when she saw Grabowski. "I'm flattered that someone considers me dangerous enough to poison me. Women in politics have little power yet."

Grabowski pulled up chair. "You told me yesterday that you and Senator Wisnewski were working on bills that might anger someone enough to poison you."

Senator Rubenstock picked up her list and handed it over. "I jotted down a few names. Women legislators who vote a strong feminist ticket frighten males. I'm an eco-feminist, which is a threat to this state."

"Eco-feminist?"

"I believe that women are closer to the environment than men because we bear children, nurture them, and prepare food."

Grabowski wrote that down.

"Did Senator Wisnewski feel the same?"

"She was a feminist, but her idea of being close to nature was ordering a veggi-burger."

Grabowski was squinting at the list. "Senator, there must be fifty names here, all men."

Senator Rubenstock pulled another list from her drawer. "There are some other possibilities. Every bill written by a

Democrat has a Republican opponent. Organizations and private individuals also oppose bills."

"I have a hard time believing someone would poison someone just for politics."

"You sound like Dr. St. Clair. Clearly you haven't been around many politicians."

Grabowski rubbed his forehead and rose to go. "There are too many names on this list, Senator. Call up your political instincts. Somewhere you have a gut feeling about one person to fit the bill."

Grabowski waited until they had driven to the restaurant and were sitting over a glass of Chardonnay waiting for the spinach ravioli to cool before he moved his questioning to St. Clair.

"Any medical clues as to what happened to Senator Rubenstock?"

"She overdosed on her quinidine."

"What I drink with my gin?"

"That's quinine. Quinidine is an isomer of quinine. It's prescribed for people who have heartbeats that aren't rhythmic—short and fast together, or too fast. Senator Rubenstock's doctor said she had an arrhythmia of unknown etiology—meaning he couldn't figure out why. He thought it could have been the coffee she was drinking, or stress and exertion during extreme weather. Anyway, the senator responded to low concentrations of quinidine with marked lengthening of the Q-T interval."

"Speak English."

"On her electrocardiogram, the space between the Q wave and the T wave became longer than normal. She began to suffer the symptoms of quinidine poisoning: nausea, vomiting, and finally she had a sinoatrial block and collapsed. The bartender did exactly the right thing by doing CPR."

"Could be normal, except that it happened the day after another senator collapsed."

St. Clair frowned. "Plus her quinidine dose was quite

low. The cardiologist and her internist wrote in the chart that they were mystified how such a low dose could cause such a dramatic incident."

"Maybe she accidentally took her medicine twice."

"She doesn't seem absentminded. She checks things off on her calendar when she does them."

"Could she have been poisoned by something else?"

"She thinks so, and the hospital is still running tests."

Grabowski dug into his spinach ravioli as if he had not eaten in weeks. St. Clair spread out the bubbling pieces on her plate. The roof of her mouth was still recovering from a cheese burn incurred at another Italian restaurant.

"Grabowski, I think I'm bored with emergency medicine."

Grabowski forked in more ravioli. "Does this mean we can get married?"

St. Clair was shocked. "Is there a connection?"

"If you go back to research medicine, you'll have regular day hours, more or less. We would see each other like normal people."

St. Clair leaned across the table and kissed Grabowski, dragging her sleeve through the ravioli. "What a romantic thing to say, Grabowski."

"I can be as romantic as Ivan, the short, bald, Bulgarian biochemist." He wiped the sauce from her sleeve, then waved at the waiter and pointed at the empty basket of toasted garlic bread.

St. Clair reconsidered the thought of marriage, a subject Grabowski had brought up before. Her divorce was two years behind her, but the complications of another marriage worried her. It was easy living alone with a cat and a few plants. She liked her apartment, her neighborhood, her friends, her work. Marriage changed a person. Some British writer said that in every marriage one person dies. That was obvious after a divorce. Once belongings were split and separate establishments created, usually one half of the couple continued to live as before. The other half drifted as if lost.

Grabowski had returned to politics. "Have you ever met Assemblyman Birnbaum?"

"I never got into politics."

Grabowski put down his fork and leaned on the table. "If you're bored with medicine, maybe here's a chance to do something different. Think over being a temporary senator."

St. Clair narrowed her eyes. "You really are looking for a spy."

"Politicians aren't normal people and they're making our laws. They merit scrutiny."

Grabowski had left his car in a no-parking zone in front. He drove St. Clair the three icy blocks away to where her Ford Taurus Sho was mired in frozen slush. He sprinkled ashes in front of the back tires, wedged the wooden shingles under the tire, and watched her spin clear. She pulled out into the street and paused while he tossed the shingles into her trunk.

"Think it over," Grabowski said, leaning on the window ledge of her car.

"Being a senator?"

"Being married." He kissed her good-bye.

Maxene turned up the defroster full blast and watched the ice melt off the windshield. Occasionally she thought about moving to a softer climate, but Milwaukee held her despite the extreme weather and rising crime rate. Her life was comfortable and rewarding. And how could she leave Grabowski? To live somewhere else without him close by seemed unreasonable, or impractical. Not that she couldn't live without him; in fact, she did. She saw him only a few times a week, given their work schedules. For a while they were seeing each other more, but the prospect of a permanent relationship had made her nervous and she had retreated, pleading work.

As she drove back to St. Agnes, she decided to call Ivan at the State Board of Health, since there hadn't been enough time to visit. She also thought about Senator Irene's visit to the ER. Maxene had given the senator a white coat, but the senator stood out with her big, solid body and pierc-

ing eyes. Unaffected by the turmoil of the ER, she had
planted herself behind the nurses' station and talked to everyone. For an hour she had disappeared for coffee in the
cafeteria, then afterward had made the rounds of nurses'
stations in the hospital and chatted with staff. The next day
St. Clair caught hell from the hospital administrator, Sister
Rosalie, for not organizing the visit through the PR department, which was what Sister Rosalie called the part-time
woman who planned the doctor-appreciation dinners.

Shirley was sitting at the nurses' station reading the
newspaper stories about Senators Wisnewski and Rubenstock when St. Clair arrived. She tapped the paper with a
thick finger.

"I could have predicted this would happen to Senator
Irene the night she was here. She told a cardiac surgeon
that doctors should be healing people, not making a fast
buck, and she shouted out what he made on each bypass
surgery. He looked like he wanted to put a tourniquet
around her throat. If that's how she acts in the senate, I'm
surprised she lived as long as she did."

"Did she say how much Sister Rosalie pays ER doctors?" St. Clair felt the usual stab of guilt at the disparity
between her salary and Shirley's.

"Dr. Malek gets a third more than you, did you know?"

St. Clair's guilt vanished. "He has more experience."

Shirley snorted. "Sister Rosalie screws anybody who
puts up with it."

Maxene spent the next hour attending to minor burns,
shaken car accident survivors, and victims of stab wounds
while she thought about the temporary senator offer. It
would be an interesting change. Plus, she was sincerely
caught up in the problem of what happened to Senators
Rubenstock and Wisnewski. She had told Senator Rubenstock and Grabowski that she would help. If she accepted
the temporary spot, she would be closer to sources of information.

She thought over the scene at the hearing room. What
did she know? First, Senator Wisnewski's death had been

sudden and unexpected. Second, the chairman of the Senate Health Care Committee had been dead set against autopsy. And third, if it hadn't been for the ambulance medics telling Senator McNulty that this wasn't a usual heart attack, there would have been no inquiry.

St. Clair knew many ambulance paramedics, and the good ones had an instinct for reading people and situations. Ambulance medics sometimes helped St. Clair decide which patient needed care first. She had spoken to the Madison medics in the hearing room. She also should speak to the ambulance attendants who brought Senator Rubenstock from the bar to the hospital.

Shirley dragged a metal chair into the doorway of the supply room and took the weight off her thick legs. Her ankles bulged over the top of her white orthopedic nurse's shoes. She tossed over a telephone message.

"Senator Rubenstock called you from Madison. Wanted to know if you figured out what was wrong with her yet. Sounds like you might be getting involved in another police case. You be careful, woman. Last time you did that, you almost got yourself killed."

"Senator Rubenstock simply wanted me to help find out what happened to her."

"That's for the police, honey. What's the matter, you bored?"

"The senator was poisoned by an unknown chemical, and researching unknown drugs used to be up my alley."

It was an excuse and both of them knew it. St. Clair was surprised how easily Shirley had picked up that she was bored. Emergency room medicine was fulfilling professionally, but it lacked the intellectual puzzles of research medicine: collecting data, postulating hypotheses, following hunches. ER work also followed hunches—which patient required attention first; how extensive was the injury—but it wasn't the same.

Was it time to go back to research medicine? The dean of her department at Marquette had extended her year's leave of absence because he wanted her back whenever she was ready. It wouldn't hurt to drop by Marquette and make sure her options were still open. Maybe she did need a change from the hospital routine.

Shirley tossed the paper aside. "Does your good-looking detective know anything they're not reporting in the newspapers?"

"He says the State Board of Health has run through all the standard toxins and are moving onto imported ones. Senator Wisnewski had a convulsion followed by respiratory arrest, but Senator Rubenstock broke out in a sweat, couldn't breathe, and passed out. Maybe she got a smaller dose or she was a healthier person."

"Or it was a different poison. A poisoner who can get one fancy drug can get another. The senators didn't make somebody mad, did they, like trying to cut the amount of money doctors make?" She chuckled.

St. Clair studied her notes on her prescription pad. She sat down in the ripped red plastic armchair in the supply room behind the nurses' station and began making a list of who might have ideas about what happened to Senator Wisnewski. She wrote down the ambulance medics and the nurse-lobbyist, Karen Wolfson, who had sat next to her at the hearing and watched the whole event. Then she picked up the phone.

She first called the ambulance company in Milwaukee to find out how to know which ambulance company in Madison had answered which summons. In a few minutes they had transferred her to their Madison branch and looked through their records to find that two of their employees had answered both calls. The men were out, but would call her back.

The ER was still empty, so she dug Karen Wolfson's business card out of her wallet and called her number in Madison, charging it to her home phone.

Karen was eager to help but couldn't add much. "I was watching Senator Wisnewski while you testified, and she didn't appear ill at all—not even drowsy in that stuffy room. She was fidgeting, not dozing off."

"Did you notice any unusual reactions in the people around you?"

"Let me come to the hospital and talk to you tonight," Karen answered. "I also want to talk about Senator Wisnewski's bill. Now that she's dead, the bill may be dead, too, unless you back it when you get to be temporary senator."

Maxene answered with caution. "Before I decide to back it, the bill will have to be changed. Like Senator Wisnewski said in the hearing, the bill cut state welfare insurance for emergency rooms, and I don't agree. Besides, I haven't decided whether to be senator."

"Really? It sounds like you have."

Shirley had picked up the business card and was peering at it when St. Clair hung up. "Make All Relationships Kind? That's the name of her company?"

"She's a lobbyist for service professions like the State Nurses' Association. That's your union, Shirley."

"Unions, phooey. Nobody really represents me but me."

At six o'clock St. Clair went to the cafeteria and ordered the special, baked acorn squash and curried spaghetti. Sometimes her life seemed too contained by the walls of the hospital and her apartment. Work, rest, work, rest. It was comforting to have a schedule and people who needed her, but she had begun to wonder if there wasn't more to life. Part of the reason she had agreed to testify for Senator Wisnewski's bill was that it expanded her life. Passing laws seemed purposeful and defined, an orderly process carried out by intelligent minds. But Grabowski didn't seem to trust anyone in politics.

She was forking in yellowish spaghetti when Karen Wolfson plopped her tray across the orange tabletop and dug into a wedge of sugar-coated cherry pie dripping with vanilla ice cream. Karen drained a glass of orange soda and sighed.

"Senator Wisnewski's death really shook me," Karen confessed. "It's been years since I was a nurse, and my tough outer shell has thinned out. Last night I had nightmares and woke up drenched in sweat. Have they found out how she died?"

"The State Board of Health is working on it now." St. Clair took the prescription pad with her list on it and made a note to call Ivan.

"If I knew what line of thinking they're following, I might remember something I saw at the hearing," Karen said. "It could have been a natural death. She was over sixty, smoked like a chimney, drank like a fish, yelled at everyone. Probably had unbelievable blood pressure. What do you know about Senator Rubenstock?"

"Not a thing."

Karen pulled a sheaf of papers out of her briefcase and pushed them across the table. "Here are my suggested changes for Senator Wisnewski's health care bill. Her goal was to reduce costs in the health care industry, and I believe that can be done by using lower-paid personnel such as nurses and physical therapists to take the load off doctors. Nurse-anesthetists gave excellent anesthesia for decades until doctors forced them out. Nurse-midwives deliver babies. Nurses already run neighborhood clinics, especially in inner cities where doctors won't go."

St. Clair held up a hand. "You don't have to convince me. But I'm concerned that the bill cuts welfare money for emergency room care, among other things."

Karen waved away the concern. "So we keep working on it until you like it."

The switchboard paged St. Clair, and she left for the ER, trailed by Karen Wolfson. Karen plopped down in the ripped red chair and accepted a cup of coffee from Joella.

"I hear being a lobbyist is tough," Joella commented.

"Tougher than being a floor nurse, like I started out. I have to cope with senators who think my clients want too much. I have clients who think I don't push the senators hard enough. And then the press plays up lobbyists as evil self-interest groups who will lobby for anybody for money."

Joella popped a handful of popcorn into her mouth. "At least you know what people think of you."

"But it isn't true," Karen wailed. "All my clients are health care service groups, and everything they want helps the people they serve. If nurses can prescribe more, say for common things like strep throat that can be diagnosed with a throat culture, then people won't have to take time away from work or pay a lot to go see a doctor."

"They'd have to take time off from work to go see a nurse," Joella said.

"But nurses' clinics move more quickly, since nurses don't leave to make hospital rounds or do surgery."

"If a nurse wants to be a doctor, she should go to medical school," said Shirley, keeping an eye on the emergency room door.

Karen grew indignant. "It's hard enough being a woman in a man's world without having enough women senators left to help me. I was counting on women senators to get my amendments through, and now Irene is dead and Beverly is really sick. I don't know what to do. I can't even get appointments with the male senators. Even McNulty says we don't need any more changes to the health care bill. Most of my clients are women. Why should women be excluded from the medical dollar just because males control the purse strings? It's not fair."

Karen left shortly after. It was another hour before St. Clair could sit down in the red lounge chair and call Ivan at the State Board of Health. Ivan picked up the phone on the tenth ring.

"Maxene! My sweet! Where have you been hiding yourself? No, don't answer that; you'll tell me about your depressing city and I don't want to hear it. You're coming to see me; I can feel it. When?"

"This isn't social, Ivan. I want insider information about Senator Wisnewski, like her autopsy report and your conclusions."

"Come here and you can have all the information you want, Maxene darling. I knew already why you were calling. That Polish detective of yours who keeps calling me on the phone let it slip, casually, that you were working with him. It sounded like he was warning me off."

"Can't you tell me over the phone?"

Ivan's voice dropped to a whisper. "It's pages and pages, darling. Just put your long, beautiful legs under the steering wheel and head this direction. I'll give you what you want, we'll have lunch, then you can give me what I want."

"Forget sex, Ivan. I'm asking for a friendly favor."

His heavy sigh made Maxene smile. Joella began waving at her to hang up, so she promised to find a time to drive to Madison. Sister Rosalie was on the other line.

Sister Rosalie's sharp voice was unnaturally sweet. "I just now received a phone call from a Senator Wilk, chairman of something called the Senate Democratic Caucus. Are you familiar with this person?"

"Yes, Sister, I met him when I went to Madison to testify before the Senate Health Care Committee. When Senator Irene Wisnewski died."

"Yes, that's what he said. He asked me if I would give you a three-month leave of absence to be an interim senator in Irene Wisnewski's spot. Do you know anything about this?"

"Sister, I had no idea that Senator Wilk would call you," protested St. Clair. "He did ask me to serve as temporary senator, but I had decided to decline."

Sister Rosalie paid no attention. "Senator Wilk reminded me that Senator Irene was a good Catholic and a woman and that we need someone of equal stature in her spot. He also mentioned something about Senator Irene's health care bill that provides special state funds for Catholic hospitals, which you as temporary senator would be sponsoring."

"He did?"

"I've decided to grant you a leave of absence to serve in the Capitol. I have a warm spot in my heart for Senator Irene and I'm grateful that God gave me this chance to further her very admirable goals."

"Who will cover my position here?" St. Clair inquired.

Sister Rosalie's tone grew even sweeter. "My dear, you are not that difficult to replace. I've already spoken to the Medical Society."

St. Clair hung up slowly and stared at Joella and Shirley watching her from the doorway. "Sister Rosalie just granted me three months' leave to be interim senator in Senator Irene's spot."

"Don't you worry, honey," said Joella. "Whoever replaces you, we'll make his life hell, and when you're ready to come back, he'll be happy to leave."

St. Clair hunted through her purse for Senator Wilk's business card, where he had written his home phone.

"We're delighted you've made this very dedicated decision," said Wilk. "Come in tomorrow about noon; we'll do a quick swearing-in ceremony at one, and you'll be ready to start work."

"So quick? What if they can't find a replacement for me by tomorrow?"

"The senate has to get back to work, Dr. St. Clair. Each day costs the taxpayers money."

# CHAPTER
# 9

DIANA RINGER CALLED Grabowski at seven A.M. the next morning while he was shaving and thinking over the next step for the investigation. It was impossible to plan. Detectives who made lists of angles to follow spun their wheels and went nowhere. Grabowski ambled from point to point looking for something interesting.

His plan for the morning had been to go to the hospital at ten o'clock when Senator Rubenstock was discharged and see her safely into the state trooper car for her trip home. While shaving, he began to wonder if he was becoming a political groupie wanting the senator to notice his good work. No groupyism for him, he decided. The senator could get into the state trooper car by herself.

Diana Ringer's cheery voice changed his mind.

"We're planning a little hospital send-off. A few reporters, a chance for the senator to talk about the Irene Wisnewski Health Care Bill that Senator Rubenstock is sponsoring."

"Are you serious?"

Diana laughed. "You may want more security people."

"A double corridor of police dogs and state troopers escorting her to an armored motorcade?"

"That's a start. Incidentally, she's giving part of her get-well flowers to the children's ward and the rest to a nursing home in her hometown. Do you want to contact her hometown police?"

Grabowski groaned. "I have to, since I assume you've alerted the local paper, radio, and television."

"Her hometown has no local TV station, but the Milwaukee channels plan to follow her up there."

"Miss Ringer, please remember that Senator Rubenstock has already been attacked. Must you deliberately place her in more danger?"

"You don't understand politics, Grabowski. Senator Rubenstock is up for reelection, and this is the press opportunity of a lifetime."

"It may be her last."

Diana changed the subject. "Did you hear Dr. St. Clair has agreed to be interim senator? She's being sworn in today at one. Big press day for the senate."

Grabowski hung up and called Chief Mayerling, who groaned.

"The Rubenstock woman is behaving like a typical senator in an election year. I'll put more security on the hospital."

The county sheriff and city police of Rubenstock's hometown were equally displeased, especially when Grabowski refused to ride with Senator Rubenstock in the state patrol car and see her safely home. He hung up, feeling sympathy for professional bodyguards.

The roads were clear and wet and he made it to Madison by nine o'clock, enough time to stop by in person at the State Board of Health and see if Ivan the Lover had come up with anything yet.

Ivan was sitting at a long lab counter eating salami on Russian rye and reading a long, stapled report. Flasks of colored liquid bubbled on a Bunsen burner. Despite the winter, Ivan wore a deep tan and a pink-and-purple Aloha shirt. His bald head shone with oil.

"Ah, Grabowski," Ivan said. "You're still looking as young as you did last time we met, although I see there are a few gray hairs among the black. Don't worry, Maxene has a few of her own."

"How's the Wisnewski situation?" Grabowski demanded.

"No need to get hostile. There are chemicals for the gray

hair. Myself, I just shave it all off. Women find bald men sexy."

"Maxene says she likes men with hair. The Wisnewski situation, if you don't mind?"

"Still working on it, Detective. I've got a list here of everything I rejected. Got a clue to point me in the right direction? Any suspects who are doctors, pharmacists, chemists, biologists? If you think a senator did this, remember that senators are not all lawyers."

Grabowski made a note to get the professions from Diana and studied the list of drugs that Ivan had unearthed from a pile of papers. "How do you know which drugs to reject?"

"I start with the standard toxins from this part of the country, then move out. There are a lot of drugs that can cause the heart to stop suddenly, but most leave a trace. So far, we've found no trace. It could be some nerve poison from outside the country that we will never discover. Happens all the time: People go to Brazil, get sick, come back here, and we haven't a clue. The fact that Senator Rubenstock didn't die could mean two different chemicals. We could spend years testing. Find me a suspect who will crack under bright lights."

"We don't interrogate people under bright lights anymore."

"Another fantasy blown apart. Oh well, I have others."

"I'm sure you do."

Grabowski tucked the list into his pocket and stood looking around the lab trying to think of other questions. Maxene had said that fifteen years before, she had done a research fellowship in this lab with Ivan. It looked like the place hadn't been painted since, or aired out. The stench of chemicals was giving him a headache.

Diana Ringer was surrounded by a mass of people crowded outside Senator Rubenstock's hospital room when Grabowski got there at ten. Reporters were shooting pictures of nurses posed around a gurney piled high with flowers. Senator Rubenstock was just being wheeled out of her room in a wheelchair. Diana consulted her watch, pointed in the direction of the children's unit, and led out senator, flowers, and hospital staff. Grabowski trailed out of camera range.

It was noon before he watched the state trooper car finally head toward northern Wisconsin. Senator Rubenstock had decided at the last minute to pick up a few things from the office, which elicited a flurry of telephone calls from Diana Ringer to campus security. Finally, at twelve o'clock, the staff stood on the portico of the Capitol building and waved the senator off. Diana rolled up her event schedule into a megaphone and shouted into it.

"Everybody to Bernardo's Gourmet Italian Pizzeria for lunch!"

Grabowski decided to skip the lunch. Aside from being tired of Italian food, he wasn't convinced that lunching with political junkies who had just pulled off a PR coup would yield more information. He headed instead for police headquarters, hoping Mayerling might be free for lunch.

By the time he got back to the senate building, the Communications group had returned and were lounging at their desks watching television news. Diana Ringer was talking on the phone, feet on her desk, while she flipped through the television channels with a remote control. She waved Grabowski to a chair.

"All the television and radio stations, and every major newspaper in the state, were at the hospital," she crowed. "Senator Rubenstock won't have to campaign this year. She talked about her health bill, education bill, and safe streets bill. We're waiting to see what actually made the air."

"At the hospital, I heard a reporter ask her if there was a murder conspiracy against women senators," Grabowski said, "but I didn't catch her answer."

"She didn't answer, the sly vixen. She said the police have their theories and she's not going to be frightened by threats. She's a wonderful example to women of the state. I feel more courageous myself."

Grabowski pulled out his list of senators. "Can you tell me the professions of all the senators?"

"Whatever you need. Let's start with the Health Care Committee. Senator Wilk is a pharmacist, Senators McNulty and Glover are attorneys, Senator Rubenstock is a high school teacher, Senator Chadwick owns his own computer consulting company, and Senator Clark is an optometrist."

Grabowski put his feet up on a pulled-out drawer and began calling out the names of all the other senators, Democrat and Republican, and Diana rattled off the professions.

"What's the latest rumor about the poisonings?" Grabowski asked, when they were finished.

"Rumor says Irene had a natural heart attack and Beverly's illness is a fancy stall perpetrated by the Democrats to avoid having to vote on a tax package the Republicans are pushing that cuts out aid for education."

"What do you think?"

Diana sighed. "The only rumor I worry about is that Renata Glover is next. I know you practically have her under lock and key, but she gets restless and she's probably planning her escape. I hope you figure this out fast. Pressure is building—people are moody and have lost their sense of humor, and the coffee shop is going broke."

On the way back to his closet office, Grabowski stopped at Senator Wilk's office. The senator was out, but his secretary handed Grabowski some messages. Maxene St. Clair had called.

"Any news?" asked the secretary, tentative.

Grabowski shook his head.

He detoured through McNulty's office. The senator was lounging on his couch watching the news on a tiny desktop television. On the screen, Senator Rubenstock was climbing into a state trooper car and saying that female politicians hold the welfare of women and children foremost in their minds, and that women need to be brave and not be frightened by a male world. McNulty clicked off the sound and flung the remote control device onto the coffee table.

"I am sick of hearing about how women's motivations for going into politics are purer than men's. Rubenstock's holier-than-thou attitude is either naïveté or a massive ego. One single person—male or female—cannot make a difference in the politics of this country. Politics is a team game, and big egos can upstage the group agreements that make the real changes. Women politicians get a lot of press just for being female in a male world, and it goes to their heads. They start believing they personally can make changes. The same thing happens to 'people of color' or whatever the politically correct term is now. If a woman doesn't focus on the goal of making laws that benefit the people of Wisconsin, the press attention can make her forget why she came here."

"How did Senator Wisnewski fit into your theory?"

"Irene, for all her ego, had her head on straight. She lived her whole life in the same working-class neighborhood and she never forgot her values. I don't like that redneck mentality; in fact, I voted against her on parts of nearly every bill. But she went faithfully to her district meetings, she listened, and she voted what the people said. She also stood behind her votes. She wasn't tricky; I don't think she understood the ramifications of the legislation she voted on. But who does? Each year issues get more complicated. We're trying to cure cancer with clean air legislation; stop discrimination with equal opportunity laws; curb marital strife with no-fault divorce."

Grabowski steered him back on course. "I heard Irene was tired of being a senator."

"Nah, she loved it. We all have moments when our ideals are crushed by having our bill killed or when we're forced to vote for something we don't believe in just to pass something we do."

"According to Senator Glover, Senator Irene was ready to quit."

McNulty sighed. "Glover has double the IQ of the late Senator Wisnewski, but lacks her common sense. Glover also sees other people in terms of herself. Eighty percent of the time she's ready to quit and assumes we are, too."

"You didn't have an appointment to see Senator Wisnewski the night before she died, did you?"

"Not me, pal. I heard a rumor you're looking for Mark somebody, but it wasn't me."

Grabowski closed the door behind him and stood with his hand on the knob.

"Something I can help you with?" Kay Landau asked.

"How do you know when someone is telling the truth around here?"

Kay sighed. "McNulty does. But even he has a hard time keeping a clear head when information changes and people's priorities shift. Senator McNulty is a sensible person, but I like to think an occasional word from me reminds him of the real world outside politics."

# CHAPTER

# 10

ST. CLAIR CALLED Ivan when she woke up the next morning to say she could come to the lab around lunchtime. Then she stood staring into her closet trying to decide what would be appropriate for a woman senator being sworn in. As usual, she wished for a godmother who would do all her shopping and then tell her what to wear. Finally she settled on her one business suit, the same one she'd worn to the senate hearing.

At eleven o'clock she let the car idle while she scraped the ice off her back windshield. The lawn mower and gardening equipment stored in the garage made it impossible to pull the car in all the way, and a light snowfall during the night had frozen to the back window. Snow squeaked under her boots, sun sparkled on the icicles hanging from the garage eaves, and her breath left white plumes in the air. Everything looked simple, easy, clean. An icicle dropped and silently buried itself in a loose snowdrift against the garage wall, leaving only a tiny hole in the snow. Disappeared like the poison in Senator Wisnewski's blood, except that everything left a trace; even a white icicle in a white snowdrift could be found if one knew where to look.

She had slept late and awakened with an insecure feeling, as if she'd had a dream in which something important was missing. Maybe it wasn't a dream that had caused the insecurity, but rather the sense of incompleteness that she had felt just before she dropped off to sleep. Today she was to be sworn in as temporary senator, and all she could think about was Senator Rubenstock's chart.

Was she missing something very obvious in Senator Rubenstock's medical history? Mentally she reviewed Senator Rubenstock's chart. Physical assessment by doctors, nurses. Lab data. When she had worked in research medicine, she always felt as if her brain was working, even when she was not physically in the lab, and she had the same sensation now. She needed more information and something to make it jell.

Ivan was sitting on his lab stool eating an orange and dripping juice on the thick stack of paper he was reading. Peels were scattered around the stool. Foul-smelling gray liquid bubbled over a Bunsen burner. Ivan's bald head gleamed with oil. St. Clair could smell his aftershave, or maybe it was the oil.

Ivan jumped off his stool and threw his arms around her.

"Maxene! Or should I say, 'Senator St. Clair'? How have I survived without you? How have I got up morning after morning without seeing your beautiful face and that gorgeous red hair?"

"I'm sure you found someone compensatory." Maxene disentangled herself and climbed up on a tall stool next to the counter, a distance from the bubbling gray liquid.

"No, but you have. Your good-looking detective was in here this morning. He's developed a real attachment to you."

Ivan took two beakers from under the counter and filled them with the gray brew. "Herbal tea, my dear. Good for the nerves, the gums, the breath. Drink up. Here's the autopsy report for Senator Wisnewski."

Maxene looked at the debris floating in the beaker and picked up the autopsy report. "Anything special you want to tell me?"

"About Detective Grabowski, yes. Why him? Why not me?"

"About Senator Wisnewski."

"She had aortic stenosis, coronary artery disease, and

probably angina pectoris. She also had smoker's lungs and an enlarged liver. The hospital ran the usual blood work and came up with the usual three abused drugs: caffeine, nicotine, ethanol. People should not be allowed to desecrate their bodies. The body is a temple and should be treated with reverence."

Maxene ignored the usual diatribe and thumbed through the report. "These levels really are high."

"The caffeine is high because heavy nicotine users have increased hepatic enzyme induction and require more caffeine for a lift, plus they drink more coffee because their mouths are dry. The ethanol, well, look at the size of her liver. I may exhibit it in the fraternities to show what happens to hard drinkers."

Maxene absentmindedly took a sip of the hot gray liquid and coughed. She pushed it away and began to read the autopsy report more slowly. "What's this about a small square red patch on the back of her arm?"

"Nicotine patch. If she was trying to quit smoking, she wasn't having much success, according to the amount of residue in her throat and lungs. She added nicotine to her bloodstream through the patch." Ivan stirred sugar into his tea.

"Who prescribed it, her private physician?"

"Apparently. We still don't have her medical records because the old geezer wants a written request through proper channels. He should have retired years ago and probably doesn't even keep records."

"Did you talk to him on the phone?"

"His receptionist says he's busy."

"Who did the autopsy?"

"Medical examiner's office. They barely have time to breathe down there; you won't get much information out of them."

Maxene wrote down the name of the private physician and the official who did the autopsy. She read further. "What's this? 'Conclusion: strychnine poisoning'?"

Ivan sighed. "The medical examiner is grabbing at

straws and going by symptoms: tremor, convulsion, respiratory arrest. They didn't find strychnine in the blood, but it's
hard to trace strychnine; a tiny amount does the job."

"So what's your plan?"

"You mean why am I still working on something the
medical examiner has already decided is strychnine? Because the good senators at the Capitol don't want to hear
there's a poisoner sprinkling strychnine around the Capitol.
They want Senator Wisnewski to have died naturally."

"And I suppose Senator Rubenstock also had a normal
attack."

Ivan sighed. "I live in this town and I barely understand
the political mentality, so I can't expect you to. Politicians
write reality their way, and rewrite it if it doesn't turn out
as expected."

"So what are you going to do?"

"I'll give you an insider secret. I have more work than
I can do, and if I don't come up with another answer soon,
I'm saying it's nicotine poisoning. Her plasma nicotine was
high and would bear me out. It will also make the senators
happy."

"But nicotine poisoning isn't a natural death."

"Not for nonsmokers, but you'd be surprised at the nicotine self-poisonings that go on every day. Surely you've
seen it in the ER."

Maxene nodded. "Not so extreme. Is it actually possible
to get enough nicotine from smoking to kill you?"

"She smoked, she had nicotine patches, and she chewed
nicotine gum. She was also over sixty, had heart disease,
and also abused caffeine and alcohol. Plus, she took a lot of
cold and cough medications which don't fit with nicotine,
not to mention with alcohol and caffeine. The list of drugs
from her desk and her medicine cabinet at home goes on
for two pages."

He flipped to the last pages of the folder. St. Clair read
them over. "She had a lot of upper respiratory illnesses."

"Typical smoker. The pharmaceutical industry should

build a shrine to Sir Walter Raleigh for bringing us nicotine addiction."

"Can I photocopy this?" St. Clair unclipped the list from the folder.

"Let me. It's illegal, and this way you owe me."

While Ivan stood at the copier, St. Clair read the rest of the report. The medical examiner had even done brain tissue analysis and found nicotine receptors in amounts that showed a heavy smoker.

Ivan returned and pulled up a stool so close that their knees touched. "Lunch at my apartment? French onion soup? Toasted croutons? Bed?"

St. Clair moved her knees and looked at her watch. "Can't. I'm meeting Senator Wilk at noon, then I'm being sworn in as senator at one."

"One o'clock? Let me be the first to give you a congratulatory kiss."

Senator Chadwick was going into the coffee shop carrying a mug of coffee when St. Clair wandered down the hall looking for Senator Wilk's office. Chadwick shook her hand, spilling coffee.

"Welcome to the senate, Senator. We got a bulletin about your swearing-in ceremony. You'll be a welcome change from Warhorse Wisnewski. I bet you're looking for Wilk's office."

He walked with her to the elevator and punched the button.

"Was she that hard to work with?" The elevator came and they got in. In the tiny space, St. Clair could smell the gin on his breath. Chadwick moved close.

"The good Senator Wisnewski used to tell us over and over in health care committee how committed she was to the people of Wisconsin, but I think she was just committed to giving everyone a hard time."

A large bouquet of daisies and chrysanthemums sat on a long coffee table in Senator Wilk's office when Senator Chadwick presented St. Clair with a bow. Senator Wilk put

down the phone and hurried around the desk to wring St.
Clair's hand.

"We couldn't be more honored," he gushed. "We have a
nice little ceremony planned for one o'clock, and I've asked
Diana Ringer to fill you in on your press package, but
meanwhile, we need vital statistics—like where to send
your salary. Sit down with my secretary here and we'll get
that out of the way."

Before she knew what was happening, St. Clair found
herself holding a cup of excellent coffee and signing page
after page. She had just finished when Diana Ringer
breezed in.

"Senator!" She smiled. "I'll start calling you that now so
you can get used to it. You have quite an experience ahead
of you."

"I'm getting that idea."

"The senate convenes at one, and they're swearing you
in first thing. I happen to know that the Republicans are going to call an emergency caucus meeting as soon as we
convene, so Renata Glover and I have scheduled a women's
staff meeting to talk about sexual harassment. After that,
you're free to go to your office then and meet your staff."

St. Clair frowned. "Actually, I'm not free. They couldn't
find a replacement for my job today."

Diana appeared to be unfazed by any sort of news. "Oh,
well," she said. "Start tomorrow morning then. Now for
your press package."

St. Clair listened, feeling as if she had been skillfully removed from her life, which was being handled by someone
much better at organizing than she. Diana explained how
the Communications Department sent out press notices for
everything from parade appearances to comments on other
senators' bills. Then Diana read aloud two press releases—
one announcing St. Clair's swearing-in ceremony, and the
other quoting her saying how much she admired Senator
Wisnewski and hoped she could fill the role.

"I said that?" exclaimed St. Clair.

"It's appropriate," explained Diana. "Okay if I fax it

out?" She put another piece of paper in front of St. Clair and looked at her watch. "You are giving an acceptance speech after the swearing in. Two minutes, tops. Here's your speech. We're due on the senate floor in fifteen minutes."

Startled, St. Clair read about how grateful she was to have the opportunity to serve the great state of Wisconsin in this temporary emergency and how she hoped everyone would help her learn the ropes.

"Sounds fine," she said, feeling as if she had been pushed into a river and was being swept along by the current.

Diana slipped the speech into a gold folder embossed with the seal of the senate. "You'll find this at the podium. Senator Wilk will clue you in when to talk. Now, can I show you the ladies' room?"

"Have there been any more poisoning attempts?" St. Clair followed Diana down the deep-carpeted hallway.

"No, but stay away from the egg salad in the coffee shop. Seriously, is Detective Grabowski counting on you to keep him informed about insider secrets?"

"I beg your pardon?"

"Just a joke. As far as Senator Rubenstock, the latest rumor is that she poisoned herself to play up her feminist agenda. But I know who started that rumor—the Republican Communications director."

"Feminist agenda?"

"The health care package, money for women's studies, stiffer equal-opportunity sanctions."

"She got her stomach pumped for a PR stunt?"

Diana laughed.

Senators Wilk, McNulty, and Glover were waiting when Maxene and Diana returned. Senator Glover pinned a corsage to St. Clair's lapel. "Don't take this stuff too seriously," she advised. "The pomp and circumstance just makes us feel good until the shooting starts."

Wilk patted her arm. "Now, Renata, don't frighten the little lady." He steered St. Clair out the door.

Maxene St. Clair and William Wilk waited together just
outside the Senate Chamber while the secretary of the senate took roll. There was a moment of silence, then Wilk
took her arm. "Time to walk down the aisle. Like being
married."

As St. Clair entered the chamber, all the senators rose
and began to clap. But the only face she saw clearly was
Grabowski, smiling down from the visitors' gallery. And
sitting next to him was the tanned face and shining bald
head of Ivan.

St. Clair smiled up at them, and a few minutes later
formally promised to serve the people of Wisconsin and up-
hold the state constitution to the best of her ability. Diana's
speech was waiting for her at the podium, and in less than
ten minutes, Dr. St. Clair had become Senator St. Clair.

# CHAPTER

# 11

SENATOR ST. CLAIR'S work as Wisconsin state senator began immediately, but it wasn't what she expected. She had no sooner taken her seat at a desk that already held her nameplate than Senator Chadwick stood up and called for an afternoon recess. Senator Glover came over to St. Clair to explain.

"The Republicans haven't finished writing the amendments that will get their tax bill passed, so we agreed to take this afternoon off and convene Sunday at noon. In the meantime, Diana Ringer has asked if you and I could join her staff meeting. She's discussing sexual harassment in the senate. We've been having a few problems, as you can imagine there would be in a big men's club like the senate."

The meeting was held in a deep-carpeted conference room. Nearly twenty-five women sat around a long table or in chairs lining the wall. St. Clair recognized a few women she had met at the funeral and the wake: Kay Landau, Karen Wolfson, Rhonda Schmidt, Evelyn Brown. Diana knocked on the table to get everyone's attention.

"First, let me have the pleasure of introducing our new senator, Maxene St. Clair. As we all know, Senator St. Clair has come to the senate to back Senator Wisnewski's health care bill. She has jumped into emergencies before at the senate, and we are lucky to have her with us."

"Do you do surgical emasculations?" shouted out Kay, to general laughter.

Diana knocked on the table again. "I'm sure Maxene St. Clair is capable of performing whatever male surgery is needed in the senate. Now, to refresh all of our memories, we have been asked by the secretary of the senate to help draft policy regarding sexual harassment of employees. In other words, he wants us to give ideas about handling sexual harassment complaints from senate staff. Staff in the assembly are doing the same."

"Why should we waste our time on this?" demanded Rhonda Schmidt. "They aren't going to pay attention to harassment complaints. They never have and they never will."

Diana explained, in her firm, cheerful voice. "Times have changed, slightly. Since session started, several women have complained to their supervisors about unwanted attentions from male senators. The present attitude of the courts towards sexual harassment has become stricter, so the senate is complying with the new court attitude."

Kay banged on the table. "They are manipulating us again. They want to defuse our complaints, not help us. They want to figure out how to fire us for complaining without the senate getting sued. Watch. They'll hang us with our own words."

Evelyn Brown nodded. "This is tokenism. They're pretending to ask for our help only because the two harassment cases are ready to go to court and they want to look like they care what's happening to women."

Diana went on. "While this may be true, it's time we address the problem. Who knows? We may come up with some course of action so that women working in politics have recourse for sexual harassment besides the newspapers and the courts. Of course, the policy we propose will not preclude going to court. Any woman who wants to sue the pants off her harasser will have our full support."

A scattering of laughter and applause greeted Diana Ringer's last comment.

"Apparently," continued Diana, "part of the problem is that staff members feel there is no one they can turn to who can stop certain senators from sexually pressuring staff members."

"Can't women senators put in a warning word for them?" asked St. Clair.

Kay Landau answered. "How can a woman senator persuade a male senator to sign onto her legislation if at the same time she is warning him to stop harassing female staff? She wouldn't get a single signature, and he wouldn't stop the harassment either."

"Are you saying we have to ask male senators to fight our battles for us?" demanded Evelyn. "Like McNulty?"

"McNulty's no feminist," said Karen Wolfson. "But he's fair and he knows the old guard is on the way out and he might as well align himself with tough women."

"You're hard on him because he won't work with lobbyists," said Renata Glover.

Rhonda Schmidt added, "He also won't help stop sexual harassment for the same reasons that the women senators can't. If he annoys one of those sexist pigs, they won't sign onto his legislation and his bills will die."

Evelyn Brown stood up. "I've been around politics a long time, and the best you can hope for is a little ethics committee. When a hassled staffer complains, they'll make her write a report which will follow her the rest of her life. Then they'll meet with the senator in private so as not to embarrass the poor man. They'll slap him on the wrist, and then there will be a lot of jokes in the men's room."

"And the staff member will find herself without a job when session is over," added Kay.

"Which is why we asked you here, Dr. St. Clair," said Renata Glover briskly. "Women senators are caught in a bind. How can we stop the harassment of female staff while at the same time persuading the offending males to work with us to pass our legislation? How do you handle this in the medical world?"

St. Clair felt embarrassed. "Not wanting to be disloyal to my profession, I have to admit that sexism in the medical profession is rampant, and women are not united on how to deal with it. From what I've observed, most women cope by themselves."

"But isn't there hospital policy? As least group discussions?"

"Medicine is hierarchical, or at least strictly divided according to task," said St. Clair. "There isn't much group consensus about what to do."

"I was a nurse," said Karen Wolfson. "Doctors, including women doctors, treat nurses and other staff like handmaidens. If a nurse gets hassled by a doctor, there's no way she can ask another doctor for help."

"That's not universally true, but you're right in many cases," said St. Clair. "The problem is, what to do about it. I, too, have a bind. If I ask Doctor X, who is a private internist, to stop calling student nurses 'honey' or 'cutie' because it's demeaning to the student and to the nursing profession, the next time one of his patients comes to the ER and he doesn't feel the patient received proper treatment, he'll haul me in front of the hospital administrator and I could get fired. Private doctors bring business to a hospital. If they get pissed off, they go to another hospital."

Kay's voice was cold. "So you let some stinking doctor subjugate a student nurse because he's more powerful than both of you."

St. Clair didn't answer, but she nodded very slightly. What's to be done? she thought. A student shouldn't have to stand up for her rights as a human being without any support from other women.

"We're not here to talk about doctors, anyway," said Kay. "We're here to nail someone's hide to the barn door."

"Shall we avoid personalities?" said Diana.

"Avoiding confrontation is what got women into the situation we're in," argued Kay. "Face it. We're talking about that asshole Wilk, who makes my skin crawl every time I look at him."

"That old man? Sexual harassment?" St. Clair couldn't believe it.

Rhonda Schmidt nodded. "He's a paternalistic old coot who treats his secretary like a moron even though she saves his ass fifty times a day. But Chadwick is really why we're here. He's not in court yet on the two charges because he has a clever lawyer and the senate doesn't want trouble."

"Which brings us to the problem at hand," said Senator Glover. "The secretary of the senate has proposed that a committee be formed of two senators and two assemblymen who will impartially review any complaints and speak to the accused."

"And fire the complainer," said Kay.

"Can we offer anything else?" Senator Glover asked.

Diana answered. "How about nonsenators being on the committee—two staff members that a complainant can speak to privately, and who can advise the culprit that if he doesn't straighten out, he'll find himself in court?"

Evelyn shook her head. "Nothing remains secret in politics for more than a few hours. Too many mouths, too many computer linkups."

"I wish Beverly were here," blurted out Kay. "She'd have some excellent ideas. We know the reason she isn't: Wilk poisoned her to get her out of his way."

"You don't know that," said Diana, exasperated.

"You'd be surprised at what I know."

St. Clair stayed another half hour to hear Diana draft a page on the advantage of adding two staff members to the harassment review committee. She had a two-hour drive to Milwaukee with a ten-hour shift at St. Agnes at the end. Tomorrow she had a committee hearing at ten, which meant getting up at seven for the two-hour drive. Clearly she should move to a flat in Madison as soon as possible.

# CHAPTER

## 12

THE NEXT MORNING, Joseph Grabowski was watching his usual breakfast of two sweet rolls singe in the toaster oven while his sausages defrosted in the microwave when Diana Ringer called.

"Our senator is coming back this afternoon!" she announced with good cheer.

"Rubenstock? She just left the hospital yesterday!" Grabowski exploded. Smoke began curling out through the hinges of the toaster oven. He flipped the blackened sweet roll onto a plate.

"She said she feels fine and she shouldn't sit home twiddling her thumbs when she could be doing her job."

"Can't you argue with her?" Grabowski opened the microwave and stuck a fork into the sausages. Still frozen.

"She gets here at four o'clock. State troopers are bringing her."

"With campaign stops along the way."

"Don't get cynical, Detective. The senator can only serve the people if she is reelected. She's holding a press conference in the Senate Hearing Room when she gets here, in case you want to come, then she and Senator Glover and the policewoman will move back into the apartment."

"Will the press cover the move? They can carry suitcases."

"Again the cynic. See you later."

After a few hours at police headquarters catching up on paperwork, Grabowski drove to Assemblyman Birnbaum's office. The broken window had been repaired and the room was warmer, although Evelyn Brown still wore her fur boots. Grabowski avoided the metal folding chair and sat instead in Birnbaum's padded swivel chair. Evelyn was more friendly now that she was warm.

"I heard they know how Senator Wisnewski died," she said, making Grabowski a cup of instant.

"How?"

"Nicotine poisoning. Senator Wisnewski's aide told me. She herself has quit smoking. Again."

"Where did she get the information?"

"Rumor."

"Heard any rumors about the vandalism here?"

"It stopped after Irene Wisnewski died."

He went next door to the grocery to drink coffee in a mug that read "Hispanic Power Is Us." "You heard anything more about Birnbaum's broken window?" Grabowski asked.

"I might have something," reported the owner. "A couple boys live around the corner; they look like no-good hoods, but they just dress that way, you know? They told me they saw a man parked around the corner from Birnbaum's office. He was putting on a ski mask. The boys thought it was pretty funny, him wearing a ski mask. Then they heard somebody with a ski mask threw a rock through Birnbaum's window."

"Did they get a good look at him?"

"Boys like that, they drop out of school, but they aren't dumb."

"Where do they live?"

"I'll take you. It's early; they're probably still in bed."

The bungalow was a tiny, green frame building with icicles hanging from the split eaves and a garbage sack bursting with disposable diapers on the front stoop. Grabowski waited near the diapers while the shop owner stamped through the snow to the back. Soon after, the front door opened and a Mexican woman wearing a blue cotton dress and a heavy wool sweater motioned him inside, then went into the kitchen, where a baby was crying.

The store owner came out of a bedroom with two teen-age boys wearing jeans and leather jackets over T-shirts. They dropped onto the couch and looked sullenly at Grabowski.

Grabowski pulled a hard-backed wooden chair near the couch. "I hear you saw some man parked in a car near here put on a ski mask, then throw a rock from his car into the window of Assemblyman Birnbaum."

"We see everything, man. This is our territory."

"Would you be willing to come down to police head-quarters and help an artist draw a picture of the man? The artist could come here, but he'll get a better result if he's got his drawing table in front of him."

The boys looked at each other. "We ain't informers."

"I don't think this ski-mask person comes from your ter-ritory or your people."

"What if he did?"

"You can quit working with the police artist any time you want."

Grabowski led the way out to his car before they could change their minds. At headquarters, he sat with them and the artist long enough to see the picture begin, then left for Madison. Glare ice had caused a three-car pileup outside the city limits, but by three he was in Captain Mayerling's office.

"What's this about Senator Wisnewski dying of nicotine poisoning?" Grabowski demanded.

Mayerling drank a slug of Maalox out of the quart bottle and washed it down with coffee. "Don't know a thing about it. Right now I'm only worried about the se-curity of those two female senators in that flat. They'll have a police guard, but she can't go to their separate meetings."

Grabowski dropped by the coroner's office and found no more progress. He drove over to the Capitol building to catch Senator Rubenstock's press conference. It was packed with senators as well as television cameras and other press.

Grabowski spotted St. Clair standing next to Senator
McNulty and Kay Landau near the back. He pushed
through the crowd. Kay Landau was taking notes, all
smiles.

"How is it going, Senator?" whispered Grabowski.

St. Clair shook her head in amazement. "Yesterday I
heard about how women are harassed sexually in politics.
Today I sat in meetings without a clue of what's going on.
I have a list of how to vote in session. All the voting is decided before the senate convenes, and if something unexpected happens during floor session, they break for caucus
and line everybody's votes up again."

"Senator Wisnewski went along with that?"

McNulty answered, "Wisnewski didn't go along with
anything. I must say, Maxene has a political mind; understands nuances of what goes on in committee hearings that
Wisnewski never did. Of course, Irene slept during hearings."

"Do senators always show up for each other's press con-
ferences?"

"Solidarity. Wilk said make it look like the Democratic
senators are supporting each other for a change."

Senator Rubenstock began talking about how women of
the state must be brave. McNulty scowled.

"Press opportunity, that's all this is. She's only pushing
her legislation."

"You'd do the same, wouldn't you?" Kay asked.

Grabowski left the press conference early in order to
search the senators' apartment before they got there. He and
the policewoman toured the bedrooms, looking into every
closet and cupboard and under the beds. He prowled up and
down the back stairs that led to the empty, freezing attic
and to the pleasantly warm basement where the oil furnace
hummed. He banged on the back door of the downstairs
flat, startling two students at the kitchen table who were
eating spaghetti out of cans.

Search completed, Grabowski was waiting at the curb
when Senators Rubenstock and Glover drove up in Glov-

er's car, followed by St. Clair in her red Ford Taurus Sho. Diana Ringer pulled up behind them, bringing a ten-pound deli platter tied with a gift ribbon. They all marched up the steep steps, with Grabowski and the policewoman dragging four suitcases and two briefcases.

Renata Glover watched Grabowski look under the beds again. "I am not a paranoid person," she said, "but your behavior is making me nervous."

"Better safe than sorry," mumbled Grabowski, burning his hand on the radiator.

Diana had made coffee and laid out the cold supper. Senator Rubenstock began smearing Russian rye with garlic and mustard spread and added layers of prosciutto and goat cheese. Senator Glover stirred wheat germ into her low-fat cherry yogurt. Grabowski and St. Clair made themselves corned beef and pickle on rye doused with mustard and coleslaw. The policewoman followed suit.

"Senator Rubenstock," Grabowski started, "you have given me two very long lists of people who you say would poison both Senator Wisnewski and yourself. I have looked over the lists carefully and talked to many of the people. Here's what I have concluded: Political aggression is verbal. Nearly everyone grits their teeth when they talk about Irene Wisnewski, but they give no impression they would assault her. As for you, Senator Rubenstock, despite your claims that you angered enough people to provoke violence, you seem to be beloved by all, including your aide, whom you treat like a slave. There is something you aren't telling me."

A flicker of a glance passed between Senators Rubenstock and Glover. Grabowski said nothing, but he noticed the policewoman take a careful bite of her sandwich, meaning she noticed it, too. Every case had a turning point when facts showed themselves; reality poked through. More often than not, persons who were attacked had a good idea where the attack was coming from, even if only subconsciously. Humans operated more on instinct than they realized. He waited for the senators to come through with the truth.

Diana Ringer, however, sidetracked him. "I agree with you," she announced. "I heard these poisonings are entirely accidental. I heard a rumor that the State Board of Health says Senator Wisnewski died accidentally of nicotine poisoning from her own cigarettes."

She took a big bite of pastrami and mustard.

"Irene's death was an accident?" demanded Senator Glover.

"It isn't definite," Grabowski muttered.

"Ironic," said Senator Rubenstock. "Irene had finally quit smoking—even started stop-smoking classes."

"Couldn't have," corrected Grabowski. "The ashtrays in her office were full."

"Her aide smoked those. It drove Irene crazy."

Diana interrupted again. "This also means that Senator Rubenstock's quinidine dose was her doctor's mistake, not hers."

Grabowski shook his head. "Doesn't follow."

Rubenstock ignored him. "You think we can convince the press? Already my opponent in the senate race is saying I got depressed and I overdosed."

"Relax," said Diana. "Manipulating the press is my job."

Grabowski finished his sandwich and drained his coffee. The policewoman escorted him out.

"Keep your ears open," he said. "These poisonings were not accidental, and those two senators have something going that's related. Diana Ringer may also know what it is."

The moon was out and made sharp shadows of the trees against the snow and icy streets. Grabowski skidded to the State Board of Health where Ivan was still perched on his stool, reading his usual stack of reports.

"What's this about Senator Wisnewski dying of nicotine poisoning?" demanded Grabowski. "You were supposed to notify me before anyone else."

"Maxene told you?"

"Assemblyman Birnbaum's aide, Diana Ringer, director of Senate Communications; the news is all over town."

Ivan shrugged. "It's impossible to keep secrets in a political town."

"Is it true that Senator Wisnewski died from nicotine overdose?"

"She had a high plasma nicotine. She was a heavy smoker and she was under a lot of pressure, which made her smoke more."

"I was told she stopped smoking."

Ivan shook his head. "I doubt it, from her lungs, but she was trying, because she was wearing a nicotine patch to help her stop smoking. Unfortunately it also raised her plasma nicotine."

"Enough to kill her?"

"Apparently. Nicotine is absorbed rapidly by the body and filtered out through the kidneys. By the time the lab drew blood, some of the nicotine had been filtered out, so the blood levels were probably lower than when she went into convulsions. I don't know how much lower. She could have died by nicotine poisoning, yes."

"How long before you find out for sure?"

Ivan tapped the stack of reports. "I have other priorities, Detective. I don't have time to keep shooting in the dark. Find me a road to follow and I'll try again."

Grabowski stopped fuming by the time he reached his car. Ivan had a point, one that Grabowski used himself when he came up empty-handed at the end of a homicide trail. Plenty of homicides stayed unsolved due to lack of time or personnel. He was almost relieved. If nicotine poisoning was true, he could write off the case and go back to Milwaukee.

But what happened to Senator Rubenstock? Was it really quinidine overdose? He turned the car toward the hospital. He'd better get the facts from the hospital.

The same head nurse was working in coronary care. She was mildly informative.

"When I sent the chart down to medical records for final

filing, the diagnosis read 'quinidine overdose, causing prolonged Q-T interval and subsequent ventricular fibrillation.' "

"Why did she take so much?"

"Call the cardiologist or her private doctor."

Grabowski wrote down the phone numbers of both doctors with little hope of getting much from either. He went to a phone booth and called Maxene at her apartment in Madison.

"Listen," he said. "Is it really possible for someone to die of nicotine overdose by using nicotine patches to stop smoking?"

Maxene sounded sleepy. "I talked to some researchers at the Medical College about this. Nicotine is a powerful drug; it only takes fifty milligrams to kill you—that's the same as two cigarettes, if most of it weren't burned up before you inhaled it. In the ER I see heavy smokers with mild to severe cases of nicotine poisoning about once a month. Severe headache, vomiting, emotional jitters. Senator Wisnewski had heart problems which weakened her system and might have contributed to her death."

"How does a nicotine patch work?"

"There's a regimen: A patient gets a series of patches that release nicotine slowly into the blood, satisfying the body's addiction to the drug while gradually reducing the amount over a period of time."

"Would the amount ever be great enough to kill her?"

"I doubt it. But she kept smoking and chewing nicotine gum. And remember she had heart problems."

Grabowski scowled. "I don't believe it. Two accidental poisonings in two days is impossible. I don't think she died of nicotine overdose, and Senator Rubenstock didn't accidentally overdose on quinidine. Have Senator Rubenstock or Senator Glover said anything that would make you think they know what really happened?"

"I'm not much of a spy," confessed St. Clair. "After you left, I went to bed and read background material for various bills. Call me tomorrow. I'll be at the senate until one o'clock, then I'm back in Milwaukee. Sister Rosalie hasn't yet found anyone to cover my shift."

# CHAPTER

# 13

AFTER A RESTFUL night's sleep with quiet dreams of snow-filled fields, at eight o'clock Grabowski drove to police headquarters, where he found a note from his captain to see him.

"Senator poisoning case closed," announced his captain. "You're off the case. Accidental overdoses."

"What!" Grabowski couldn't believe his ears. "Two intelligent women with no history of drug confusion overdose two days apart and these are accidents?"

"You heard me. Chief Mayerling called this morning. I also had the misfortune to talk to some senator named Wilk. He says the legislature is going back to work."

"Mayerling is wrong. These are poisonings."

"Possible," agreed his captain, "but we're understaffed and overworked, and a cushy assignment like sitting around a warm Capitol building couldn't last long."

"Give me today to tie up a few loose ends."

The captain shrugged. "Take the morning. But check your box before you go; you've got catching up to do."

Grabowski pulled a stack of assignment folders from his box and dumped them on the desk, then called Chief Mayerling.

"That's right, case closed, and I couldn't be happier. Bring back the folders I gave you and we'll go out for a beer."

Grabowski then called Ivan at the State Board of Health, who was equally unhelpful.

"Give me a break, man. I'm overloaded, and the evi-

dence is conclusive. Nicotine addicts like the late senator
should have a nurse by their side if they use nicotine
patches and gum."

"What if I come up with evidence that points to something else?"

"Then call me."

The winter overcast had cleared, the sky was blue, and
the white-blanketed fields on either side of the freeway to
Madison sparkled as if it had snowed diamonds. The road
had been salted near the usual accident spot near the Belt-
line, so Grabowski made it to the Capitol building parking
lot in nearly summer travel time. The parking attendant
held up his hand.

"Case solved, I heard. Senator Wilk wants to see you."

A red Camaro was parked in Grabowski's allotted spot,
so he parked in a spot marked "Department of Agricul-
ture." On his way down the hall he ran into Diana Ringer
carrying a frosted doughnut and a cup of coffee.

"Senator Wilk wants you," she said. "When do I get the
key to my new changing room?"

"What makes you think I'm through with it?"

"It's all over the Capitol that the poisonings were accidental. Everyone is relieved, especially the manager of the
coffee shop."

"Two intelligent women without a single drug problem
in their lives overdose on prescription drugs in the same
week?"

"Listen, Grabowski, in politics this is best forgotten. Senator Rubenstock's opponent in her senate race is saying she
was depressed and deliberately overdosed. American voters
will put up with lying, cheating, stealing, and spousal deceit
in their elected officials, but they will not tolerate mental
illness. Drug overdose is mental illness."

"Forget the political nonsense, Diana. We need to find
out what's going on. These are human beings we're talking
about."

"Wrong again, Detective. People who risk their bank accounts, reputations, and family relationships to run for po-

litical office are not ordinary humans. Some are superhuman, some are barely human, but none are normal. Now, where's the key?"

"You'll get it at noon."

Senator Wilk's secretary called within seconds of Grabowski's unlocking his closet office to say that Wilk wanted him, on the double.

"Have you been dialing every five minutes?" Grabowski took his time going upstairs. As he passed the late Senator Wisnewski's office, he saw the nameplate had been replaced with "Senator St. Clair." Rhonda was on the phone, smiling, happy she still had a job. Grabowski paused to peer into the inner office. The new senator was sitting at her desk, reading a stack of papers.

"I have five minutes before my next meeting; can you believe it?" she exclaimed.

"I've got something even more unbelievable. I'm off the case. The poisonings were accidental."

"I heard. Rhonda told me."

"This can't be true, and you and I know it. Two intelligent women made the same blunder? Okay, they're politicians, but they aren't dumb."

"You think I'll be poisoned next?" St. Clair asked.

Grabowski sat down in the visitor's chair. "You sound worried. What happened to your old sense of invincibility?"

"I don't know, Grabowski. Maybe I'm out of my own territory and I don't feel secure. Maybe trying to manage two full-time jobs for a few days and commute in bad weather is wearing me out."

"I think you've got so settled in a comfortable pattern of life that you've lost your sense of adventure. It sounds like you've even lost your curiosity."

"It's not a fatal illness."

"For you, it's not a good sign. Maxene, I want to tell you the truth about why I pushed you to accept this senator foolishness. You were getting fearful of change,

Max. You were turning into a hermit, with your work and your cat."

"And now this radical change is going to get me poisoned."

Grabowski stood up. "No, Renata Glover is next. Do me a favor. Call your friend Ivan and find out if he's telling the truth about this accidental nicotine poisoning. He may be buckling under pressure. Find out who's putting on the pressure."

St. Clair drew a deep breath. "Okay, Grabowski, I get your message. You want me to find my courage, wherever I put it, and start trying to fit the facts together here."

"Thanks, Max. Call Ivan. Hell, go out for a drink with him. Maybe he'll pull you out of this Milwaukee stupor you've fallen into."

St. Clair smiled. "Ivan can't be pressured. He's too unconventional."

"Ivan is civil service, and the heads of civil service divisions are appointed by the legislature—even if not directly. Ivan or someone above him can lose his job if he doesn't occasionally yield to pressure."

Senator Wilk was on the phone when Grabowski walked in. "He's here," he said into the mouthpiece, then hung up and pasted a smile onto his chubby face. He came around his desk to shake Grabowski's hand with both his sweaty ones.

"Congratulations." He smiled. "Case solved. Back to business as usual."

Grabowski removed his hand. "You're convinced that two poisonings in two days are completely accidental."

"If the State Board of Health is happy, so am I. We've been waiting for you to come up with something for quite some time, and I'm pleased that at least someone else has."

"You know it's up to Chief Mayerling and me to decide whether the case is closed."

"I spoke to him and he's happy to close it. Now, if you'll hand over your office key; a personable young woman plans to turn it into a women's aerobic center, something we sorely need."

On his way down the hall, Kay beckoned Grabowski inside, closed the door, and turned the key. She waved him into Senator McNulty's inner office and closed the door behind them.

"Our electronic mail this morning said your investigation is officially over and we shouldn't answer any more questions," she said in a shaky voice. "I smell a cover-up. Irene and Beverly were too smart to overdose on their own medicine. I don't want anything more happening to my senator."

Grabowski handed her his handkerchief. "I'll do what I can. The latest rumor is that Renata Glover is next, and as nutty as she is, I like her. Have you heard anything new?"

Kay dried her eyes. "Diana told me you were looking for someone called Mark. I came up with something. Mark could be an acronym for a lobbyist's organization, 'Make All Relationships Kind.' MARK."

"You're joking."

"It sounds dopey, but it's a social service lobby headed by Karen Wolfson. She handles the State Nurses' Association, the State Social Workers' Association, the Physical Therapists, and several of the subpharmaceutical lobbies. The acronym isn't in the lobbyists' book because they're listed by lobbyist's name, not by company name. I was going through my book of business cards and I happened to see hers."

She handed Grabowski a pink business card.

"Did she work with Senator Wisnewski?"

"Ask her aide, Rhonda. I would think so. Irene's big bill this year was health care, and Karen's card says she lobbies for health care agencies."

"Do you know Karen Wolfson personally?"

Kay frowned. "She came here once to make an appointment, but Senator Rubenstock was busy and I don't know if Karen Wolfson ever caught up with her. Lobbyists don't

come here much. Neither Senator Rubenstock nor Senator
McNulty are easily influenced, and they especially distrust
special interest groups who have money to spend persuading senators how to vote. We have excellent staff and the
senators make up their own minds."

"You make your senators sound like real statesmen."

"They are. I hope you don't still think Senator McNulty
is the Mark you're looking for."

He handed her his card. "Call me if you hear any rumors."

Next, Grabowski dropped by Senator Glover's office.
Her handshake was icy and there were shadows under her
eyes.

"Why are you here?" she demanded. "This morning at
caucus Senator Wilk said Irene died of nicotine poisoning, self-induced. We all told her that she shouldn't be
chewing nicotine gum plus putting on the nicotine
patches. And Senator Rubenstock told us herself she took
too much quinidine. I told the policewoman who is
guarding us that she is no longer needed. She called Chief
Mayerling, then left."

"You're convinced that these two events were coinciden-
tal."

"Totally. Everybody has calmed down and is getting
back to work. Even the food in the coffee shop has im-
proved."

"Tell me about this Feminist Political Strike Force I've
heard about."

Senator Glover frowned. "Where did you hear about
that?"

"Senator Rubenstock's aide claimed that Senators
Wisnewski and Rubenstock were poisoned because they
were part of a Feminist Political Strike Force that could
prevent male senators from ramming through a nonfeminist
agenda."

"Ah." Senator Glover stopped frowning. "It is true that
quite often female senators vote in similar ways, especially
on issues affecting women and children. Women senators

are still a minority, despite our majority in the population, but we are one of various minorities in the senate, and as such, women shift alliances from time to time."

Grabowski's mind began wandering, a sign he was being handed bullshit.

"Senator Glover," he interrupted. "I don't believe in co-incidences or accidents. While not every event in life can be predicted or prevented, every event has a cause and a consequence. This appears especially true in politics."

"Detective Grabowski, even if I adopt your deterministic philosophy, the poisonings of my two colleagues remain noncriminal. Both were a natural consequence of drug misuse."

"You're hiding something," said Grabowski.

"Of course. Politics is deals, most of which remain hidden until they can withstand scrutiny."

"Any particular deal might have caused these two poisonings?"

"Possibly, but I'm not at liberty to reveal it."

"Are you such a fool?" Grabowski exploded. "Are you so caught in the half-truths of politics that you've lost your common sense?"

Senator Glover stood up. "We have been told by experts that Senator Wisnewski and Senator Rubenstock are victims of accidents. You have no proof of poisoning. Go see Senator Wilk. He told us to delete your office phone number from our computers."

Grabowski went back to his office and glowered at the cement walls. He knew there was more to these "accidental" overdoses. Slowly he began pulling his papers together, reading over every scrap of scribbled notes. He came to the pink paper with the appointment with Mark. Mark McNulty, Mark Lewis, Mark Birnbaum. Grabowski dialed the next Mark, from the number on the pink business card. Karen Wolfson was in.

"Of course I know you," she said, all enthusiasm. "I was at the Senate Hearing Room when Senator Wisnewski died, then I met you at the funeral. I was there with a good friend of yours, Maxene St. Clair. I've been helping her figure out what happened to Senator Wisnewski and Senator Rubenstock."

"You have?"

"Since I was in the hearing room, I was helping Maxene remember what happened."

"Is there a chance we can meet today?" asked Grabowski. "I'd like to talk to you further about this. Do you have an office?"

Karen laughed, a musical trill. "I'm a lobbyist. I spend my life in other people's offices. How about the legislature coffee shop in half an hour?"

Grabowski continued reading through his papers. He still had not traced the person who had prowled around Senator Wisnewski's house trying the doors. He called the woman who lived across the street. No, the only people she had seen recently were relatives emptying the house of valuables. Yes, the person could have been a man or woman.

He went over his notes again. Should he take Maxene's suggestion and try the hairdresser? He called Diana. Senator Wisnewski's hairdresser was a woman, Betty something.

"A lover?"

"I honestly don't think so," she said. "She dressed well but not for male attention. She just liked clothes and she had money for them."

"From where? From her salary? Her pension? Did she still work part-time? From lecturing?"

"Don't know, but she had money. We used to compare the cost of her outfits with Senator Glover's. Renata has expensive taste, but Irene bought designer stuff. Her clothing consultant used to drag in boxes full of designer dresses. She made the senator try them on in Beverly Rubenstock's office to keep cigarette smoke away from the clothes the senator didn't buy."

"The consultant's name?"

Diana named an expensive Milwaukee dress shop. "But aren't you off the job?"

"Not until noon."

Grabowski called Rhonda.

"You still here?" she asked. "I heard the case was solved."

"I heard that too. Did you ever trace the Mark that Senator Wisnewski was supposed to meet the day she died?"

"No. I've been looking for a job. It's tough to find a secretarial job with good medical insurance."

When he got to the restaurant, Karen had already arrived and was working on a coffee and a sweet roll. She was wearing a purple turtleneck, a blue wool skirt, and black boots.

"Detective!" She waved from her booth.

Grabowski picked up a coffee at the counter and brought Karen a refill. Karen leaned across the table, hands clasped.

"I'm so thrilled you're including me in your investigation! How's the case going?"

"The case is closed. The State Board of Health investigator says Senator Wisnewski OD'd on nicotine by continuing smoking while she was wearing nicotine patches."

Karen stared at him. "And Senator Rubenstock?"

"Took too much of her quinidine." Grabowski watched Karen digest this. Her reaction was mixed amazement and disbelief.

"Accidents?"

"You surprised?"

"Well, yes. Everyone was saying they got sick so close together that it couldn't be accidental."

Grabowski leaned over the table. "I still think the poisonings were deliberate. However, I'm not convinced that the poisoner wanted the poisonings to be fatal. Someone just wanted them out of the way temporarily for some reason. So somehow the person caused them to overdose on their own medicine."

"What makes you think that?"

"Just from watching the kind of manipulating that goes on around here. Politicians aren't killers, like Senator Wilk said, but they aren't above manipulating events and people to achieve what they want."

Karen Wolfson nodded. "Absolutely true. Do you have any particular person in mind?"

Grabowski pulled out the two pink slips of paper with the name MARK printed on them and the appointment time.

"One of these was found in Senator Wisnewski's desk, with an appointment for the evening before she died, and one I found in her desk at home. Did you keep your appointment?"

Karen's face paled. "What are you saying? The meetings were about Senator Wisnewski's health care bill. My clients are very concerned about that bill. The physical therapists want more diagnosis capability, the nurses want more prescription-writing authority. I was trying to convince both senators Wisnewski and Rubenstock to broaden those clauses."

"With any success?"

"Yes, in fact. Both senators were open to giving opportunity to qualified people."

"Did you get definite promises from them?"

"Senator Wisnewski was all for my ideas. Senator Rubenstock had some changes." Karen stared into her coffee.

"As a lobbyist, do you always get what you want?"

"It's not what I want, it's what my clients want, and the answer is no. Everything's a compromise, but try to explain that to an animal rightist who thinks everyone should be a vegetarian and hasn't two nickels to pay my fee."

"Are lobbyists expensive?"

"Depends on the lobbyist and the lobbyist's record for persuading legislators. In Wisconsin our hands are pretty much tied, as far as expense accounts. Lobbyists aren't allowed to give gifts, although some get around that by donating to a campaign fund under another name—making sure the senator knows, of course. In an election year, everything helps."

"Did you do that?"

"I stay within the limits of the law, Detective."

She finished her roll and polished off the coffee. "But with the case closed, all this speculation is moot."

"I wouldn't be surprised if I'm back before the month is out. I don't think our poisoner is through."

Back at his closet office, Grabowski looked through his notes again. After a few minutes, he locked up and went in search of Assemblyman Birnbaum's office.

Nearly every square inch of Birnbaum's office was covered with something about him: news photo, clipping, citizen award. Blue matchbooks with his name in gold were lined up in a ceramic dish.

Evelyn looked happier than she had in the South Side Milwaukee storefront. She was wearing a miniskirt and silk blouse and was chatting on the phone. She waved Grabowski cheerfully to a chair and hung up.

"Case closed, I just heard," she said. "Now you can concentrate on who is chucking rocks through our window in Milwaukee."

"I thought that stopped when Senator Wisnewski died."

"Really, I was joking when I accused Irene, but we'll never know, will we?"

"Not unless my witnesses come up with a face."

"Witnesses?" Evelyn frowned.

"Two neighborhood boys saw someone parked around the corner put on a ski mask. They spent some time with the police artist. I haven't seen the drawing yet."

The phone rang and Evelyn brusquely told the caller to call back in two months. "I must take ten calls a day from people wanting to know if Birnbaum is going to get the senate seat," she said.

"And will he?"

"It's possible. There was a lot of opposition to the appointment of that woman stand-in. Of course, much of that was generated by Mark Birnbaum."

"So Assemblyman Birnbaum had good reason to get Irene Wisnewski out of the picture."

"You think he poisoned her? Not a chance. First, Mark Birnbaum couldn't organize his way out of a paper bag. Second, he couldn't keep his mouth shut afterward, and third, he doesn't have the guts in the first place. Besides, I heard she OD'd on her own nicotine gum."

"You don't seem to have much respect for your employer."

"I'm simply being honest. He didn't poison her."

"How do you know?"

Evelyn Brown smiled. "I've worked for a lot of legislators and I can read them like a book. I feel no particular loyalty to Assemblyman Birnbaum, but I want to be fair."

"Just a job."

"That's right, Detective. Political junkies who get caught up in hero worship fall like a ton of bricks when their hero loses an election or fires them for a silly mistake. Some staff here believe that whatever a legislator wants, they should provide, even if it means going outside legal boundaries. For example, Communications people can't help a legislator campaign, but everything Diana Ringer writes for Senator Glover is in one way or another a push for reelection."

"Do legislators try to get staff to cross the border?" Grabowski asked.

"Sure. I'm always reminding Birnbaum of my limits. Assemblyman Birnbaum doesn't push, but that's because his district is safe. It's straight Labor-Democrat and he grew up there; half the voters are fishing buddies or old girlfriends and would vote for him even if he switched parties. With the rest of the senators and assemblymen, staff has to keep their perspective. Lose your perspective and you're dead."

"Is that what happened to Senator Irene? Some staff member lost perspective?"

Evelyn narrowed her eyes. "You think she was murdered, but you're a cop. Oncologists think every pain is cancer."

Grabowski went back to his closet. It was nearly noon.

He packed up his papers and took his key to Senator Wilk's office. Wilk was in caucus and wouldn't be out for an hour, according to his secretary. That meant all the Democratic senators were in caucus and unavailable, including St. Clair, who would leave for Milwaukee at one o'clock. Grabowski went in search of Diana.

Diana was sitting at her desk, typing furiously on her computer, listening to the radio news, and watching a video about the school system. She switched off her computer screen, turned down the volume on radio and TV, and offered Grabowski a mint.

"I heard my aerobics center key is at Wilk's office. Want lunch before you go back to the big city?" She reached for her coat.

Tucked into a cozy booth at the Italian restaurant, Diana ordered Pumpkin Lager beer and linguine al pesto.

"I hear you're convinced there will be another attack," Diana said.

"In nearly every case, at a certain point I get a wild hunch that has nothing to do with the evidence or the witnesses. I've come to believe in instinct."

Diana took this seriously. "Some behaviorists believe that humans absorb more about our surroundings than we realize—from nuances of language, people's expressions, smells. So what we think is a wild hunch is really sound logic based on facts we don't even know we have. Trained observers, like you, probably have these hunches more than the rest of us because you absorb more information."

Grabowski nodded. "Since I've been hanging around the senate, I've also come to believe in the value of rumor. Maybe rumors start because people unconsciously witness things, then pass them on. Kay told me once, information here is currency; you trade it."

"So what's the rumor about who will be attacked? Renata Glover?"

Grabowski nodded. "I've heard it from several people. I believe it, and I also believe that she will not be the last. I was also told that people in politics verify rumors, and I think this rumor persists because someone knows something."

"And that's why Renata Glover won't be last?" Diana's normal casual attitude had deserted her. She was staring intently at Grabowski, her face close enough so Grabowski could smell her faint perfume.

"It's only a matter of time. The way things are happening around here, that means hours or days."

# CHAPTER

## 14

AT FIVE O'CLOCK that afternoon, Maxene St. Clair was wearing her white lab coat and sitting in the ripped red plastic armchair in the supply room behind the nurses' station. Her feet were propped on the third shelf and she was reading the health care bill when Karen Wolfson called.

"I had coffee with Detective Grabowski today. He says he's off the case. Or I should say, the case is closed."

"That's what he told me, too."

"Nice speech today on the senate floor. Diana Ringer wrote it, right? I made an appointment to see you on Monday. Your secretary said you'd be in at eight o'clock. I want to hear your ideas on my proposed changes to the health care bill."

"My secretary?" St. Clair looked up in surprise at Joella, who was standing in the doorway buffing her nails.

"Rhonda Schmidt."

Joella pointed at her phone with her buffer, and switched over the second call to St. Clair. It was Senator Glover.

"Sorry to bother you," said the senator in a brisk voice. "I need those papers I left with you. Can you bring them to Madison tomorrow?"

Maxene was taken aback. "I hadn't planned to come to Madison until Sunday, for the special session. I can send them in the mail."

"No, no, I need them now. Call the state patrol and tell them to pick up the envelope from wherever you have it and bring it to Madison tonight."

"The state patrol?"

But the senator had already hung up. St. Clair looked at Joella. "I'm supposed to call the state patrol and tell them to pick up a package I've been holding that Senator Glover needs."

"You hang around with politicians, you get treated like a servant. When my cousin became alderman, he demanded so much service, we nearly ran him out of the family."

Maxene pulled the phone book out of the drawer and started hunting for emergency numbers. The state patrol dispatcher answered on the first ring.

"Send a package to Madison tonight?" he demanded. "I thought Senator Wisnewski was dead."

"Senator Glover requested it."

"We're not a courier service. I'll call the senator."

St. Clair hung up, relieved that state services were not completely subject to the will of capricious senators. Then she remembered that Grabowski had asked her today to talk to Ivan and find out if he was being pressured to come up with his diagnosis of accidental death. She punched in his lab number and waited for the usual ten rings. She felt a momentary stab of guilt at using the hospital phone to make personal long-distance calls. Next time, she'd bill it to her home phone, then see if the people of Wisconsin would reimburse her.

When Ivan answered, she could hear bubbling in the background.

"Ivan," St. Clair began, "we go back a long ways."

"That's right, my love, and we could go forward a long ways if you would give up on that detective."

"Ivan, we're not going to go forward even one day until I feel I can trust you."

"What are you talking about, my sweet?" But his voice had lost its banter.

"I'm talking about when I ask you for the truth and you give me garbage. Your conclusion that Senator Wisnewski died of accidental nicotine overdose is shaky. Are you getting pressured to say this?"

Ivan sighed. "Maxene, why strain our perfectly good relationship by asking absurd questions that could endanger my career?"

"Your career is toast if Detective Grabowski finds out you're giving false information. Who's pressuring you, Ivan? Who wants accidental death on the death certificate?"

Ivan's voice sounded strained. "Maxene, she died of nicotine poisoning. This is the truth and no one is pressuring me to say it."

"Then what's this about 'endangering your career'?"

"A joke."

St. Clair scowled as the phone went dead in her ear. She called Grabowski's home, but he wasn't there, so she called his switchboard and left a message.

Joella was standing in the doorway, arms crossed. "Is this what politicians do, spend all their time on the phone?"

Shirley peered over her shoulder. "What's in the so valuable package that Senator Glover wants?"

"Don't know. It's in my car," said St. Clair. "I decided to give it to Grabowski, so I've been carrying it with me."

"You've got something so all-fired important in your car?"

"Nobody but you and I know it's there."

"And anybody who decides to steal your car."

St. Clair had to admit she was right. Even though the parking lot was fenced and a security guard watched from the building, cars were broken into all the time. "I'll go get it when I have a minute."

While they were talking, Senator Glover called back. "I'll come pick up the package myself," she said. "I'm coming to Milwaukee for a fund-raiser speech that Irene was scheduled to give. Can you bring the package to the hospital?"

It wasn't until four hours later that St. Clair finally found a minute to go out to her car and get the envelope. She was putting on her coat when Joella picked up the phone and waved frantically at her.

"Ambulance coming in five minutes from a restaurant in the Blatz brewery. Another woman senator was poisoned.

Senator Glover. She ate something at dinner and fell off her chair. Somebody called the Poison Control Center at Milwaukee Children's Hospital. They said it sounded like strychnine."

"What are the ambulance medics doing?"

"They gave her a face mask respirator during the last set of convulsions and put her in the ambulance."

"Get the Poison Control Center on the phone, and find me a copy of Goodman and Gilman, and *Rang Pharmacology*."

St. Clair talked to the Poison Control Center from the supply room, where it was quiet but she could see the outer emergency room door. She listened carefully, taking a few notes on the back of a prescription pad. As the outer door opened, she came out, issuing orders.

"Get an IV with D5W ready, plus three syringes of ten milligrams diazepam," she told Shirley, then turned towards the ER door. Senator Glover was being wheeled in on a stretcher.

Senator Glover's face was pale and damp with sweat. She was gasping and staring wildly around the room. She let go of her grip on the blanket and grabbed St. Clair's arm.

"They got me," she gasped. "I don't know how, but I'm going to die."

"No, you aren't," said St. Clair firmly. "I know it's scary when your muscles tighten up, but I'm going to give you something to make that stop."

Senator Glover was panting. "In the ambulance the spasms got so bad, I couldn't breathe. I'll suffocate."

"We've got a respirator ready. You're going to be all right." She scrubbed the upper arm muscle with alcohol and injected ten milligrams of diazepam, then took the IV needle from Shirley and inserted it quickly into an arm vein.

Shirley hung the plastic bottle from a metal standard and scribbled quickly on the chart as St. Clair stepped back a few paces to speak with the ambulance medic.

"How many episodes of convulsions?" she asked, glancing over their chart.

"Two."

"Severe?"

"I don't know about the first one, I only got the story from the people at the dinner. It sounded severe, but who knows—they were pretty upset. The second started in the ambulance. Twitching of the extremities, then stiffness of the face and legs, then arched back and extended arm and leg muscles. That was five minutes ago. We gave her oxygen."

St. Clair turned to Shirley, who had laid out syringes for drawing blood and was taping the IV in place. "Get a respirator ready in case she has another episode, since severe convulsions can lead to respiratory arrest. Get a gastric lavage set ready. We'll put her in the corner with curtains drawn."

St. Clair and Joella wheeled the stretcher over to an examining table in the corner.

"Turn off the overhead light on this side of the room," she said to Joella, "then call ICU, tell them that in fifteen minutes we're sending up a possible strychnine patient. We need a separate room with absolute quiet. She should have no stimulation whatsoever—that means no intercom noises, no beeping respirator, no radio. Move a staff person in to sit with her for at least four hours. Somebody quiet."

She patted Renata Glover on the shoulder. "Hang on. The injection I gave you should be working by now. Shirley will draw some blood, then we'll wait a few minutes to make sure you're okay, then we'll take you up to a quiet ICU room and a nurse who will sit with you."

Renata grabbed her hand. "They're trying to kill the women legislators," she gasped. "They can't beat us, so they're killing us."

"Who's they?"

"Where is Beverly? She said she was coming in the ambulance with me, but the medics wouldn't let her."

"Take it easy," said St. Clair. "The ambulance goes faster

than cars. I'll tell the receptionist to call the place where you were and find out where she is."

"I wish we had a quieter place," St. Clair murmured to Shirley, who was laying out the blood sample tubes, respirator equipment, and gastric lavage set on a tray table. "According to the literature, one way to reduce the likelihood of convulsions is to keep the patient from being stimulated at all. We'll wait ten minutes to see if the diazepam will relax her muscles enough to prevent another episode of convulsions. If she goes into convulsions, we have to worry about respiratory arrest. If there are no convulsions in ten minutes, we'll do gastric lavage, then send her upstairs."

St. Clair hurried over to Joella. "Tell the lab to send somebody for this blood work. Then call the restaurant where Senator Rubenstock is. Then call Grabowski. And turn the intercom and the phones to low. Thank heavens it's quiet at the moment."

Joella held up a hand. "I already called the lab and Grabowski," she said. "And I don't need to call Senator Rubenstock. She's here." Joella pointed a long, red-painted fingernail at the entrance. The electric doors hissed open and Senator Rubenstock marched in. She was wearing a long muskrat coat, fur boots, and a fur hat pulled tight over her black hair.

"Where is she?" demanded Senator Rubenstock. "Those idiots in the ambulance wouldn't let me go with her, and it took ten minutes for people to decide who would drive me here. What kind of city is this, where people are afraid to drive to an inner-city hospital at night? And why in God's name did they bring her here, anyway? Aren't there any non-ghetto hospitals?"

St. Clair took Rubenstock's arm and moved her toward the gurney where Shirley was holding Renata's hand.

"This is a good hospital and we were closest to your restaurant. Renata will be all right. We'll keep her here a few minutes, then we'll pump out her stomach and send her upstairs. The best therapy for her now is to stay calm while we get the results of the blood work and see if the muscle relaxants are stopping the convulsions. Help her keep quiet. And don't tell her about the stomach pump."

Her advice slowed Rubenstock's charge and she moved quietly behind the curtain. St. Clair turned around to find herself face-to-face with Karen Wolfson, blond hair frizzed around her hat.

"I can't believe it," whispered Karen. "Another woman senator. There aren't any other women Democrat senators left."

"Except for you," Joella said to St. Clair.

# CHAPTER

## 15

AT ELEVEN O'CLOCK that evening Grabowski was standing in front of his microwave thawing one of the casseroles that the cleaning woman had cooked and put in his freezer. After lunch with Diana he had turned in his folder of information and rumors to Chief Mayerling, then spent his afternoon at police headquarters in Milwaukee catching up on the unending reports.

The indistinguishable frozen mass began to turn into macaroni and cheese with peas and chopped red peppers. He was on the verge of exchanging it for another unlabeled frozen mass when the phone rang. It was Joella at St. Agnes.

"Senator Renata Glover was just brought into St. Agnes. This is unofficial, but she probably was poisoned. Dr. St. Clair is treating her for strychnine ingestion."

Grabowski sat down on the hard wooden chair. "I knew it. I just didn't expect it this soon. How's she doing?"

"She's alive. There's another senator with her. You want to talk to her?"

Grabowski listened to Muzak briefly before Senator Rubenstock's precise tones came on the phone.

"Renata has had an attack," she said. "Actually, I don't know if I should say 'attack.' We were joking around about me poisoning myself with my own quinidine and she popped in one of her vitamin pills and a few minutes later went into convulsions. The ambulance got there in ten minutes flat."

"Vitamins?"

"From her own little pillbox that was in her own purse."

"Do you have the pillbox?"

"In my purse, under my arm. Renata has bottles of vitamins in our apartment in Madison and in her desk at her office. God knows what she's got at home. Do you think they're all poisoned?"

"We'll find out. Who is there with you?"

"A hospital security guard who says the police chief in Madison is sending that policewoman here. I told him I don't want her. Wait, I have to go; the doctor is coming out."

Grabowski pushed down on the receiver button, but before he could call Chief Mayerling, his phone rang again. It was the chief.

"They're at it again, knocking off the women. This time strychnine. That Rubenstock woman thinks it was in her vitamins and she's got the container on her. You get it. I've sent someone over to the apartment for the rest of her supply."

The phone rang almost as soon as he put it down. It was Senator Rubenstock again.

"I'm calling from the Intensive Care Unit nurses' station. They're moving Renata up here. She's had her stomach pumped out, an experience I also had recently and which I never want to repeat. Chief Mayerling wants to send that policewoman to guard me, but I told him I want you."

"I'll be at the hospital in half an hour." Grabowski hung up and watched the mass in the microwave begin to bubble. He dialed St. Agnes' ER again. Maxene was free, having transferred Senator Glover out.

"What do you know about strychnine poisoning?" he asked.

"It's hard to diagnose because it takes such a small amount to do the job. Mostly it's treated by the symptoms, not by diagnosis through lab tests."

"What are the symptoms?"

"Mainly those arising from stimulus, or rather reduction of the normal inhibition, of the central nervous system. Senator Glover had a classic case: tremors and slight twitching that occurred within fifteen minutes of ingestion, then stiffness of the face and legs. She may have had convulsions at the dinner; she certainly had them in the ambulance, with arched back and extended arms and legs. The problem I'm worried about now is that she may stop breathing because of the convulsions. We have a respirator waiting."

"How much strychnine did she get?"

"Well, fatalities have occurred with doses of ten milligrams or less, so I suppose she got less than that, although I don't know if she ingested less or we pumped it out in time. The muscle relaxant I gave her stopped the convulsions long enough to pump out her stomach, and most of the food was still undigested."

"Senator Rubenstock says the strychnine was in the vitamins."

"That's possible. She took the vitamins on a full stomach, and most were in tablet form, so they had not yet dissolved."

"So there could have been a lot of poison in the vitamins but it just hadn't got into her system yet, or there could have been just a little and she digested it all?"

"Both are possible. Why?"

"I'm trying to decide if someone was trying to kill her or just put her out of commission for a while."

"I've sent her stomach contents to the lab, and I'll let you know when I hear something. She'll be weak for a couple of days, but she'll probably go home tomorrow."

Grabowski groaned. "Can't she stay in for a while? I have enough trouble trying to protect them."

St. Clair smiled. "These women senators are tough. Senator Rubenstock sat here calmly like she was waiting for her moment at the microphone. But listen, Grabowski, Senator Glover gave me a manila package to hold for her while she was living in that rooming house. She was worried about security, so she handed it to me at the hospital when I went to see Senator Rubenstock. I've got it here with me; well, it's in my car."

"What's in it?"

"I don't know."

"Three women have been poisoned and you're holding some sort of secret information?"

"Sorry. Really. I've been meaning to give it to you, but I kept forgetting. I'll go out to the car now and get it."

"Take the security guard with you."

Grabowski hung up. Leaving his macaroni to bubble, he climbed into the shower. Refreshed and slightly more alert, he spread the macaroni out on a plate and ate about half, then stuck the plate into the refrigerator, threw some clean shirts, slacks, and underwear into an attaché case he used as a suitcase, and left for St. Agnes. He detoured through the emergency room. It was empty of patients, so St. Clair came with him upstairs to the Intensive Care Unit.

Senator Rubenstock was seated next to a security guard on a straight chair outside the Intensive Care nurses' station, her feet flat on the ground, her purse held tightly between her crossed arms. She rose when she saw Grabowski and held out a small jeweled pillbox.

"Senator Glover is still in serious condition, and I won't give up the box of pills to anyone but you."

Grabowski extracted a plastic evidence bag from his jacket pocket and deposited the pillbox inside. Then he took an evidence card from his wallet and wrote the date, the name of the object, and "Received from Senator Rubenstock" on it. He tore the adhesive paper off the back and attached it to the outside of the plastic sack.

Senator Rubenstock watched the procedure closely. Her tense posture relaxed. "I apologize for saying you were wrong about these poisonings being accidents," she began. Then her voice broke and she started to cry.

Grabowski handed her a clean handkerchief, mentally thanking his cleaning lady for ironing them and putting them in his jacket pockets, then took her elbow and guided her back to the straight chair. Senator Rubenstock blew her nose and took a deep breath.

"We were sitting next to each other at the head table of

a Nurses' Association dinner that Karen Wolfson had arranged for Irene to speak at. Karen had just finished giving her speech, and someone passed down a package of gum. Renata made a stupid joke about how she hoped it wasn't the same kind of gum Beverly was chewing before the senate hearing. Then she remembered she hadn't taken her vitamins all day. So she poured most of what was in that little pillbox into her hand and chugged it down with her coffee. And a few minutes later she went into convulsions." Senator Rubenstock shuddered.

"Did she eat anything after the vitamins?"

"Coffee. Same pot mine was poured out of. It was even after the dessert."

"What did you eat for dinner?"

"Chicken à la king. Ice cream and cake. We drank wine from the same bottle. The only thing we ate different was the vitamins. I don't take vitamins. I believe a person can get all the required nutrients by eating a balanced diet and avoiding refined sugar."

"Senator Rubenstock," said Grabowski. "It's time to start telling the truth. What did you three women have going on that is making you the target of these attacks?"

Senator Rubenstock shook her head slowly. "Routine back-room, under-the-table politics. One of our bills gave money for women's studies programs at state universities and private colleges. We wanted to cut funds from their university sports programs to fund women's studies programs. You can imagine the uproar."

"I can't picture any Wisconsin politician voting money away from college sports."

Rubenstock waved her hand vaguely. "It was all politics—we'd support their bills if they would support ours."

"What was happening with the scholarships to Marquette?" asked St. Clair. "Wasn't that tied to the health care bill, somehow?"

"Everything is tied together by trading off votes. Irene and Wilk were buying the Catholic vote by giving state money for Catholic universities. Renata and I wanted state-funded family planning services through the health care bill. It was a straight swap."

Grabowski shook his head. "Nobody would poison three women senators to kill a women's studies bill. There are plenty of other ways to trench a bill. You three have something going that is frightening someone, or several people."

Rubenstock shook her head. "When you find out what it is, let me know. In the meantime, I'm sitting right here until I know Renata is all right."

Grabowski beckoned to the security guard and rose to go. "I'll be back after I send these pills to the state crime lab. If you get hungry, you can try the cafeteria. But take a security guard with you as a food taster. I don't want you back in the hospital, too."

Grabowski spent some minutes on the phone, then waited outside the front entrance for the police officers in the patrol car who would take the pills to the State Crime Lab on the South Side. Then he took the elevator down to the ER, where he found Maxene sitting in the supply room behind the nurses' station, feet propped on the third shelf, reading a medical text. He dragged up a metal folding chair.

"Senator Rubenstock says she's going to sit by Senator Glover's bed until she's better. How long could that be?"

"Couple of hours. She's much better."

"Rubenstock still wants me to be her personal guard at her apartment in Madison, without telling me why some person is after her. I'm convinced she knows. Come up with any more information about strychnine or anything else on this case? I had a little chat with Chief Mayerling. The case is open again. He says the hell with what Wilk wants."

St. Clair flipped through a couple of pages of her medical text. "What I know about strychnine, I already told you. Convulsions may recur repeatedly and be followed by periods of relaxation. Few patients survive more than five episodes of convulsions, death usually occurring due to respiratory arrest. She still may have secondary effects from the severe spasms, like kidney problems, but I doubt it. I gave her two doses of muscle relaxants that stopped the convulsions until we could get the poison out. Now she just has to stay in a quiet place until all the toxin is out of her system."

"So where do people get strychnine?" Grabowski accepted a cup of coffee from Shirley, who pulled up a chair.

St. Clair squinted at the small print. "In this country, it's tough. In some countries, like Mexico, it may be in pharmacies, but in the U.S. it's only used in some types of rat poison, if even that. There are a few medications with strychnine salt in them, but they're all sold in Europe, as far as I can tell."

"Was Senator Glover taking any of these medications?"

"Senator Glover wasn't taking anything except vitamins, according to what she told Shirley. You could ask her again; maybe she'll remember something."

Grabowski looked at his watch. "Nearly midnight. I'll check with your lab to see if they have any results yet, then I have a date to spend the night with a senator, in a city two cold hours drive away. Then tomorrow I get to drive back here and pick up another senator and take her I don't know where, probably home to northern Wisconsin. Let's hope we don't have another of our freak snowstorms."

# CHAPTER

# 16

AFTER HE LEFT, St. Clair put the two medical books on the floor and stretched. "Call the lab and tell them to give Grabowski whatever information he needs," she told Joella. "I'm going out to the car to get that package. I want that thing off my hands before I go home tonight."

"Wait ten minutes until the guard gets back from coffee break," Joella advised.

St. Clair shrugged into her coat. "It will only take a minute. I put it in the trunk."

Shirley frowned. "I'm coming with you. Gotta look after people with more brains than sense."

The phone rang, however, someone who had been to the ER and needed advice from Shirley about refixing the bandage. St. Clair hurried out alone into the dark cold.

The parking area was fenced with a seven-foot hurricane fence and an electric entrance gate that opened with a private card or cash. The gate was closed now, and the lot cold and deserted. St. Clair's car remained by itself in the far corner to the right of the entrance.

The evening snowfall had covered the frozen slush with a deceptive white blanket. St. Clair tripped several times over hidden ridges and nearly fell. She was watching the slippery footing so closely that she didn't notice that someone else was also at her car.

He was crouched on the far side of the car, a bundled-up figure in dark clothing, with a dark wool cap over his head and heavy wool scarf around his mouth. As she pulled out her keys, he stood up.

"Just hand over the keys, lady," he said in a heavy, rough voice. "Then you don't get hurt and the car doesn't get hurt."

Sudden anger overwhelmed St. Clair. She was fed up with having to worry about burglary, robbery, and violence to her person during what seemed like every waking minute.

"Don't give me this shit!" she shouted, the rage overwhelming the fear. "I just bought this car. In fact, I just bought it from Rolondo's brother-in-law, who probably stole it; I don't care. The point is that when Rolondo hears you stole my car right out of the hospital parking lot, he's going to be plenty pissed, and you know what Rolondo does when he's pissed."

The thief hesitated. "What do you mean, Rolondo?"

"Rolondo, the biggest pimp in Milwaukee, who has plenty of unpleasant people working for him, and who doesn't like having his friends' cars ripped off, and I happen to be one of his friends."

St. Clair was running out of breath, and the surge of adrenaline that was the source of her courage was ebbing. She clenched her keys tightly and backed up. The thief moved forward. St. Clair turned and ran. "Help!" she screamed, slipping and nearly falling. She felt as if the attacker was right on her heels.

The electric doors of the ER hissed open and the guard ran out, pistol in hand. "Stop! Freeze!" he shouted, pointing the gun in St. Clair's direction.

Oh, hell, St. Clair thought, now I'm going to be shot by the guard. She ducked as low as she could and kept running for the lighted doorway. When she got behind him, she turned. There was no one in the parking lot.

Shirley and Joella were hovering just inside the doorway.

"Someone was stealing my car," panted St. Clair.

Shirley got a tight grip on St. Clair's arm. She pulled her away from the glass doors. "You sure he wasn't after the senator's package? God knows how many people at that dinner Senator Glover told that she was coming here to pick it up."

The muscles in St. Clair's legs were quivering. She sank into a chair. "You're right. You could be right. I have to go back out there and get it."

The guard was back and was hovering anxiously over her. "You going out there? You crazy?"

"If Shirley is right, the thief will be back."

This time St. Clair followed the guard with his drawn gun and flashlight. The parking lot was empty, but so was her trunk. The lid had been popped open and the envelope that had been sitting on the sack of sand was gone. She searched under the sack of ashes, under the snow shovel, under the wooden shingles, the guard flashing his light everywhere. Inside was empty, too. Back inside the hospital, she accepted a cup of hot tea from Joella.

"It's stolen," she said. "Either that or I planned to put it in the car and then forgot. Maybe it's at home."

"What was in it?"

"I didn't look. We'll have to ask Senator Glover." St. Clair suddenly stood up. It wasn't so long ago that someone had got past the police guard and poisoned a witness who was recovering in the ICU.

"Call Grabowski at the lab," she said. "Tell him to meet me up in ICU."

Senator Glover's guard was still sitting outside the senator's room, reading a magazine.

"Where's Senator Rubenstock?" St. Clair demanded.

"Inside, with Senator Glover. She goes in for a few minutes every half hour. That's the allowed time."

St. Clair hurried in. Senator Rubenstock was leaning over the bed rails giving Senator Glover a sip of water. Senator Glover gave St. Clair a weak smile.

"You were right," she quavered. "I'm going to live."

"Of course you are."

"The package," whispered Senator Glover. "Is it safe?"

St. Clair hesitated, not sure whether to tell the truth. Lies never worked out for her, maybe because she was a bad liar. She was saved from having to answer by Grabowski, who hurried in with the police guard. St. Clair took his arm and guided him outside.

"I just went out to my car to get the package that Senator Glover gave me to hold, and it's not there. Maybe it's at home."

Grabowski grimaced. "I wish I had even a clue as to what was going on. I'll put another guard on Senator Glover tonight, then you and Senator Rubenstock and I will all proceed to your apartment and find this document. Whether it's there or not, the good Senator Rubenstock is going to tell us what's in it. Let's hope they're not up against someone who's tougher than they are."

Senator Rubenstock strode out, shoulders back, lips firm. "What a mess!" she exclaimed, in a loud, brisk voice. "Although I must say this means we're getting somewhere. Before, we only had idiotic rumors that Irene and I somehow overdosed on our prescription medications. Now everyone will see we were right; we couldn't possibly have overdosed by accident. We were poisoned."

St. Clair tried to cope with this opinion change. "You mean you were deliberately poisoned? It wasn't an accident?" she repeated.

"I said it all the way along. Now we go full force and find the criminal."

"With no brakes on the investigation." It was Grabowski, lips tight.

Senator Rubenstock took no notice of the comment. "Renata will have a full-time guard and so will I, which I want to talk to you about, Detective Grabowski. That policewoman gets on my nerves. I want you. I'll feel much safer and you can ask me anything you want, whenever you want."

Grabowski was looking glum, St. Clair noticed. She looked at her watch. "I have a suggestion. Why don't we go to my apartment, look through the papers that Renata left me to take care of, then you can spend the night there. It's quite late to be driving back to Madison. If Senator

Glover is released in the morning, you can drive back together."

Senator Rubenstock thought this over for about thirty seconds. "Is there room for Detective Grabowski?"

"On the living room couch."

Grabowski waited until Senator Rubenstock had gone back into Senator Glover's room to give her the news, then he took St. Clair's elbow.

"Do I have to stay on the couch all night?" he murmured.

"Depends on how fast Senator Rubenstock goes to sleep."

"You care what she thinks about your personal life?"

St. Clair hesitated. On one hand, she didn't care at all. She was over forty, reasonably liberated, in charge of her own life. On the other hand, Senator Rubenstock was not an intimate friend, and St. Clair felt like keeping her private life private.

"We don't have to push our relationship in her face," she equivocated.

"Coward," Grabowski said, but remained cheerful.

St. Clair felt more cheerful herself. It had been a while since Grabowski had stayed over, and she missed his warm, furry legs. Senator Rubenstock could have the hot water bottle.

The problem was how to explain when a search of her apartment didn't turn up the brown manila envelope. She was sure it had been stolen out of her car.

It was nearly one A.M. by the time St. Clair had opened up the Hide-A-Bed in the guest room that doubled as her study and extra closet. Senator Rubenstock took one look at the big enamel bathtub with the brass claw feet and announced she was taking a hot bath. She borrowed a flannel nightgown and bathrobe from St. Clair, asked for a cup of tea, and took it with her into the bathroom. St. Clair could hear her humming as the water splashed into the tub.

St. Clair closed the connecting door between the bedrooms and the kitchen and sat with Grabowski at the kitchen table, St. Clair over a cup of instant hot chocolate, Grabowski with a beer.

Grabowski drained half his beer. "I notice you're not hunting for the famous manila envelope."

"It's not here. I put it in the trunk to give to you."

"It really was stolen this evening?"

"I bet Rubenstock knows what's inside. If she doesn't, Glover does. Also, I talked to Ivan. He claims Senator Wisnewski really did die of nicotine poisoning and that he's not being pressured to say it." St. Clair frowned.

"Do you believe him?"

"I think he's telling the truth, but not the whole truth."

"You know anybody who tells the whole truth? Now, give me that sleeping bag and I'll hang out on the living room couch until I hear the senator snoring."

# CHAPTER

## 17

THE NEXT MORNING, the fragrance of brewed coffee raised St. Clair out of bed and into the kitchen. It was ten-thirty, the previous night having taken a toll on her normal energy. Grabowski had returned to his sleeping bag on the couch in the early hours of the morning. She peeked into the living room. Grabowski was sleeping on his back, smiling.

Senator Rubenstock was in the kitchen, fully dressed, eating scrambled eggs with toast and reading a thick document.

"I hope you don't mind me making myself at home," she said.

"Not at all." St. Clair poured herself a cup of coffee. She found some sweet rolls in the freezer and put them in the toaster oven, then sat down across the table.

"What was in the envelope that Senator Glover gave me to hold?" she demanded without preamble.

Senator Rubenstock went back to reading. "Legislation we were working on."

"Why didn't she leave it in her office, or yours, instead of giving it to me?"

"Anyone can get a key to our offices."

"Please understand my concern." St. Clair was trying to be patient. "Senator Glover gave the envelope to me the day after you were poisoned. Shortly after, she herself was poisoned. Am I sitting on a bomb?"

Senator Rubenstock pushed her papers away and shook her head. "I appreciate your concern, but don't worry."

St. Clair got up and flipped the hot sweet rolls onto a plate and placed it on the table. "The envelope was stolen out of my car last night after Senator Glover was brought into the emergency room. Somebody tried to get rid of it and Senator Glover in the same night."

"The envelope was stolen? It's not here in the apartment?" Senator Rubenstock's eyes widened.

The ringing phone interrupted Maxene's answer. It was Kay Landau, fairly shrieking.

"Is Beverly with you? Is she safe? Why didn't anyone call me? I just heard on the radio that Renata had been poisoned and was at St. Agnes. I had to threaten to cut off all state aid to hospitals before the nurse at St. Agnes would let me talk to Senator Glover."

Maxene passed the phone to Senator Rubenstock and let her do the calming down while she tossed butter into the skillet and beat up two eggs to scramble. Senator Rubenstock was rattling off instructions about letters to write and memos to send. Maxene had finished making the scrambled eggs before she hung up.

St. Clair dumped the eggs onto a plate. "What was in the envelope?"

Senator Rubenstock rearranged the papers in front of her. Her fingers trembled. "Somebody stole it?"

"Broke into my car."

"How did they know it was there?"

Maxene thought this over. "I mentioned it to Shirley about four hours before I went out to my car to get it. I don't believe anyone else heard, or if they did, they wouldn't have known what I was talking about. Could Senator Glover have told someone at the dinner that she was coming to St. Agnes to pick it up?"

The answer came from Grabowski, who was standing in the doorway. He handed the phone receiver to St. Clair. "Let's ask Senator Glover," he said, pointing at the phone. "Maxene, mind getting us through the ICU nurse barrier?"

The ICU nurse took some time coming to the phone, and when she did her voice was sharp and strained. "Senator

Glover left about fifteen minutes ago, right after her phone call. Got dressed and discharged herself."

St. Clair was astounded. "Did she say where she was going?"

"No one saw her go except for another patient who says she simply walked out of her room and took the stairs. I was busy in the treatment room. Her police guard had gone to the bathroom."

Maxene put her hand over the receiver. "Senator Glover has checked out," she relayed.

Grabowski snatched the phone out of her hand and shouted at the ICU nurse. "Let me talk to the police guard! Well, then, get me hospital security."

After another few minutes, he hung up the phone and splashed coffee into a cup.

"Hospital security has no idea of where the senator or the police guard have gone. They're writing an incident report."

"Maybe she's coming here," Rubenstock offered. Her voice was calm, but her face was pale.

"The envelope. What's in it?" Grabowski was grim.

This time Rubenstock didn't argue. "The Irene Wisnewski Memorial Health Care Bill. Renata and I were working on it in the apartment. When she had to move to the rooming house, Renata decided that the papers were safer with you. Mistake."

Maxene stared at her. "Somebody broke into my car to steal a health care bill? Why was the bill so secret?"

"We made some radical proposals: birth control and abortion on demand, a hundred percent covered for welfare patients. We didn't want that made public until the bill actually made it to committee, when we could defend our stand in public. Even McNulty wouldn't back us on that."

St. Clair was trying to remember what Karen Wolfson had said about the health care bill. "Were you proposing that nurses could prescribe certain medicines, and physical therapists diagnose certain muscular ailments?"

Rubenstock frowned. "Physical therapists make diagnoses? I don't think so. Incidentally, remember we have a special Sunday session. Some Republican amendments on the health care bill will be discussed when we break for caucus."

The phone rang and Grabowski snatched it up. "Where the hell were you?" he shouted. "Couldn't you have checked that the fool senator was getting dressed before you decided to go to the bathroom?"

He listened for a moment, then slammed down the phone. "Disappeared into thin air," he said. "The guards at the main hospital entrance and emergency room don't remember any women getting into taxis, and so far no taxi has reported picking up a fare at St. Agnes. Where the hell did she go?"

"Renata is a strong-minded woman," said Rubenstock.

Grabowski turned to St. Clair. "Is she in any condition to be taking city buses in freezing weather?"

"She's probably weak, but the strychnine should be out of her system. I wonder what she said to Kay. Kay called her at the hospital to find out that Senator Rubenstock is staying here."

"Why didn't you say so?" Grabowski flipped through his notebook and found Kay's number at the senate. "What did you and Senator Glover talk about?" he demanded, without explaining the situation. When he hung up the phone, he poured himself more coffee.

"Renata told her she knows who's doing the poisoning. When Kay told her where Senator Rubenstock is, Senator Glover said something like, 'Good; she'll be fine while I clean up some details.' Kay asked if she wanted some help, and Senator Glover said, 'Not yet.' "

"Clean up some details?" St. Clair said to Senator Rubenstock. "What did she mean?"

The senator shook her head. "I don't know, but Renata is a resourceful person."

"I heard," said Grabowski. He narrowed his eyes. "Was there anything in that envelope about the Feminist Political Strike Force?"

Senator Rubenstock sighed and sat back in her chair. "I suppose I have to tell you. Irene, Renata, and I were forming a support group for women in the legislature. We had written an introductory letter that we were going to put on the E-mail of all women. We didn't want anyone to know what we were doing."

"Why not? You're senators. Can't you do what you want?" Grabowski hurried to the living room and returned with his notebook, shuffling through the pages. "Did part of your introductory letter have anything to do with preventing male senators from 'ramming through a nonfeminist agenda,' like Kay said?"

"Kay doesn't understand the situation. We were simply forming a support group. To answer your question, Detective Grabowski, female senators cannot do anything they want any more than women in general can do anything they want. Many males in society are frightened by the prospect of women helping each other to gain equal status. If the legislature in general found out about this feminist group before we had a chance to gain popular support, they would find some way to outlaw it."

Grabowski sat sipping his coffee and watching Senator Rubenstock after she had finished speaking. Finally he picked up his coffee mug and stomped into the living room, where St. Clair could hear him talking to someone at police headquarters. From there he went into the bathroom and slammed the door. The shower ran.

Senator Rubenstock shuffled through the stack of papers in front of her and began to read again.

St. Clair put her sweet roll back into the toaster oven to reheat it, then sat looking out the window. She watched the snowflakes multiply. The basement furnace clicked on and the faint rumble from below was followed by a hot blast of air from the vent under the table. She shuffled off her slippers and propped her bare feet on the warm metal grid.

Senator Rubenstock turned the page of the tightly typed document she was reading. Without taking her eyes off the document, she picked up her coffee mug and took a sip.

When she put her mug down, St. Clair picked it up and replaced it with hers. After a minute, the senator picked up the substituted mug and took a sip. She kept on reading, not noticing she had sipped milky coffee instead of black. St. Clair switched the cups back and thoughtfully finished her sweet roll.

She was contemplating heating up another one, slathered with melted butter, when the phone rang. It was Ivan.

"I read in this morning's paper that another senator was poisoned and Grabowski has reopened the investigation," said Ivan, without preamble. "I'm calling to confess. You were right: I was pressured to close the case. I didn't have trouble saying yes, because the nicotine level in Senator Wisnewski's blood was very high."

St. Clair held the phone tight to her ear. Ivan had a loud voice and she wanted to think about this before she passed on the news to Senator Rubenstock.

"I understand your dilemma," she said.

"You asked me who the person was," he went on. "I'll tell you on one condition: that Grabowski stays out of my lab. Last time he came in I became insanely jealous about you and him, and I made lab errors."

St. Clair smiled. "It's a deal."

"You'll be surprised to find out who it was," he went on, "because it doesn't make any sense at all. The person who called and told me to close the case or lose my job was Senator Rubenstock."

St. Clair stared wildly at Senator Rubenstock, who was peacefully turning a page of the thick document. The senator looked up.

"Problem?" she asked.

"Not at all, Senator Rubenstock," Maxene said. "It's the lab."

Ivan's voice exploded in her ear. "Rubenstock is sitting there with you? She could be the poisoner! Senator Wisnewski could have died from strychnine like the medical examiner said initially; strychnine sometimes doesn't leave a trace. From what I read in the papers, Rubenstock was sitting right next to Senator Glover and could have dropped the strychnine right into her Chardonnay."

"But what about the intervening event?" St. Clair was trying to remain ambiguous.

"You mean Rubenstock's poisoning by quinidine? She did it herself. Watch it. She could have dosed your breakfast coffee already."

St. Clair looked at her half-empty coffee mug and at her watch. Had the requisite time passed before the convulsions would start?

"I'll get back to you," she said, and hung up.

At that moment Grabowski came in the kitchen, hair still wet from the shower. "Was that for me?" he demanded.

"No." St. Clair tried to figure out how to get Grabowski in private. Should she write him a note? Or ask him to check the furnace or a frozen pipe?

Grabowski was already on the phone to police headquarters. "Any news on Senator Glover? Remember, she's resourceful. She could have flagged down someone—probably a woman—and talked her into driving all over the state."

He slammed down the phone. "They're checking car rental agencies, bus terminals, taxi companies. Nobody in her hometown has heard from her. The only thing to do now is to take Senator Rubenstock back to Madison and wait."

St. Clair stood up. "Grabowski, my furnace isn't working right. Could you take a quick look?"

"It seems fine to me; I'll look at it when I get back."

"When are you coming back?"

Grabowski looked at Senator Rubenstock, who was putting on her fur boots. "It depends on when Senator Rubenstock will agree to having the policewoman move in as guard."

After they left, St. Clair called police headquarters and left a message to have Grabowski call her as soon as he was in private. Then she called Karen Wolfson.

Karen picked up the phone on the first ring. "Make All

Relationships Kind, Karen Wolfson speaking," she said with a smile in her voice.

"Maxene St. Clair here. Did you hear Renata Glover is out of the hospital?"

A gasp burst into St. Clair's ear. "That's wonderful!"

"Not really. She left without saying where she was going."

"You mean she wasn't supposed to leave? Have you checked her house up north? How about her apartment or her office at the senate? Maybe she went to a friend's house, or even a hotel. It would be just like Renata Glover to find a quiet hotel with good room service and spend the next two days sleeping off her terrible experience."

"Karen," St. Clair said, "have you heard of a Feminist Political Strike Force?"

Karen waited a moment to answer. "Senator Wisnewski told me once when she was half-plowed that she was checking the voting records on feminist issues of the male Democratic senators. She was using any bad votes to force the men to support her bills this session."

"What would she do with the bad votes on feminist issues?"

"Blast the news to the press. This is the year of the woman, at least some people think so, and Irene could make them look very bad—insider information, you know."

"I don't get it. Why is this such a crime—checking voting records?"

"Normally this is campaign activity carried on against opponents. Senate staff shouldn't be doing the voting-record research, and Irene made them."

"Did she ever try using this information?"

"I don't know anything more about it."

"Did Beverly Rubenstock and Renata Glover know about this?"

"I don't know."

St. Clair hung up totally confused. Was Irene Wisnewski poisoned by someone she was accusing of antifeminism? Was Renata hiding because she was in with Irene Wisnewski? Maybe she was in a hotel, as Karen Wolfson said. She called Grabowski's switchboard again and left a message for him to check all the hotels in the Madison/Milwaukee areas.

Then she hunted for her senator orientation packet. Diana had penciled in her home phone number. Diana was her usual effervescent self.

"Dr. St. Clair—woman-on-the-spot for senatorial poisonings. We heard Senator Glover is doing fine, thanks to you. Did Senator Rubenstock bring her to St. Agnes because you were in charge? Part of their feminist agenda?" She laughed.

"Diana, Senator Glover has disappeared. Checked out of St. Agnes half an hour ago without saying where she was going."

"You're joking. What happened?"

"She told Kay that she knows who has been doing the poisoning."

"And she's off to track down the culprit like an intrepid lady senator. What an idiot. The woman hasn't a grain of common sense. What can I do?"

"Find her," said St. Clair. "I think Renata Glover is up against more than she can handle, despite her reputed resourcefulness."

"Do you know who the person is?"

"No. Tell me something. Grabowski asked Senator Rubenstock about the Feminist Political Strike Force and she said it was a women's support group. What is this organization?"

"I've heard of it by rumor only and I thought it was a joke. I heard Senator Wisnewski was compiling the voting records of male senators on feminist issues like child care, abortion, equal opportunity. She was going to use them as pressure to support her health care bill. Voting-record research is actually campaign activity—strictly forbidden for state employees. There is a mildly legitimate reason why a senator should know other senators' voting records—to know which senators are likely to oppose or support similar new legislation. But the press always points out that senate staff has enough work. They shouldn't be compiling data that probably will be used in a senator's next campaign."

"Who was doing the voting-record research for Irene?"

"I don't know."

"Were Beverly and Renata in on this?"

"Possibly. I don't know."

"Can you think of a particular senator who might be especially damaged by this?"

"The senate is full of male chauvinist pigs. If you ask my honest opinion, none would be hurt much by having antifeminist charges leveled at them. In some districts, it might even help them win the next election."

"Keep thinking," said St. Clair. "In the meantime, Renata Glover may try to contact you. You seem to be a central source of information. If she does, please tell her to call me. After three o'clock today, I'm at St. Agnes Hospital ER."

St. Clair hung up frowning. Diana Ringer, source of all knowledge and information about everyone and everything in the senate, suddenly knew nothing about Irene Wisnewski's Feminist Strike Force—a strike force that was using senate staff. St. Clair called Grabowski's answering service again and left another message: "What do you really know about Diana Ringer?"

# CHAPTER

# 18

GRABOWSKI GOT THE message on his car phone from his switchboard to call Maxene St. Clair before he had even reached the outskirts of Milwaukee. The message was to call as soon as he was alone. The second message, relayed the dispatcher, was telling him to check all hotels, and the third was asking him what he knew about Diana Ringer. Grabowski asked that Chief Mayerling be notified that Senator Rubenstock was on her way to her apartment. Grabowski frowned as he put down the phone.

"Problem?" asked Rubenstock.

"Don't know yet. What do you know about Diana Ringer?"

"Why? Did something happen to her?"

"Not at all."

Senator Rubenstock didn't answer for a few minutes. "She's an extremely smart woman who understands politics enough to know that she's better off working for a politician than being one."

"Can you trust her?"

"She will always take the correct political action. At least until she sees that the benefit to her is negative. Then she will opt out immediately."

After that Senator Rubenstock seemed caught up in her own thoughts. She stared forward, not watching the scenery, her gloved hands firmly holding her leather briefcase in her lap. After about an hour she broke the silence.

"I've been thinking. It's unrealistic for me to demand that an upper-level homicide detective be my personal guard. The policewoman will be satisfactory. We senators get carried away with our own importance. I plan to go to my office at the Capitol building today, where there are already security guards."

"What made you change your mind?"

"A good night's sleep put life back into perspective."

Grabowski made a quick search of the apartment while Senator Rubenstock waited in the car. Then he escorted her upstairs and called Chief Mayerling, who said he would send a policewoman over to the Capitol building. He called Maxene, but the line was busy.

Senator Rubenstock had changed into a pair of dark green wool slacks and a sweater and was packing her briefcase with another set of papers. He carried the stuffed briefcase downstairs and put it and the senator in his car.

The Capitol building was warm and quiet. Even though it was Saturday, several people were working at their desks, including Kay. She jumped to her feet and clasped her hands when they walked in.

"I just called Senator St. Clair and she said you were coming to Madison, so I rushed over here knowing you'd come here. Are you all right? Where's Senator Glover? I heard a rumor that she disappeared! Senator St. Clair said she doesn't know anything."

Rubenstock ignored the excited babble and went into her office. "Coffee?" she called, and closed the door.

Kay ran for the coffeepot down the hall.

Grabowski sat down at Kay's desk and called St. Clair again.

"Two things that will throw you for a loop," said St. Clair. "Ivan called this morning while you were in the shower. He was, indeed, pressured to close the case, and the person putting on the pressure was Senator Rubenstock. Grabowski, does this mean Beverly Rubenstock poisoned Irene?"

Grabowski looked up to see Senator Rubenstock standing in the doorway.

"Where's Kay?" she demanded.

"Went for coffee."

He waited until the senator was back at her desk. "What else?"

"Ivan says Senator Wisnewski could have died of strychnine and that Rubenstock could have put strychnine in Renata Glover's coffee at dinner. He also asked that you don't go see him because it makes him jealous."

St. Clair went on to explain what Karen Wolfson and Diana Ringer had said about the Feminist Political Strike Force. And what Diana Ringer had not said.

"Also, I heard from the hospital lab. There was a trace of strychnine in the stomach contents, but they didn't find any in the vitamins that had not yet been digested."

Grabowski put the phone down slowly and sat thinking until Kay came back with four cups of coffee and the policewoman who would guard Senator Rubenstock. He watched her give one to the senator, and pass the others to the policewoman and himself. Then he took his coffee, went into the senator's office, and closed the door.

"Senator," he said, "I've just received some interesting information that puts you in a difficult position. I understand you told Ivan at the State Board of Health to close the Wisnewski poisoning case."

"I did what?"

"Told Ivan to file a nicotine-poisoning report and close the case."

"I did no such thing. That's criminal activity. Obstructing justice."

Grabowski frowned. "Ivan himself says you contacted him."

"He's mistaken. Ask him if he spoke to me personally. He didn't."

Grabowski started again. "I also found out about the Feminist Political Strike Force. It's you, isn't it? Collecting damaging information on nonfeminist senators. What were you planning to do with the information? Blackmail them?"

Senator Rubenstock punched the button summoning Kay and folded her hands on the desk. She motioned Kay to a

seat and waited until the policewoman had locked the outer
door and come in, closing the inner door behind her.

"I'll give this to you straight, Detective Grabowski," said
Rubenstock. "Since Kay is involved, she should hear. Certain male Democratic senators have made it their goal to
eliminate or, at minimum, defuse the effect of female Democratic senators. To stop ourselves from being denied our
role in the senate, Irene, Renata, and I were gathering data
on these Democratic senators. We were going to use the information as barter to give us our rights. Kay was doing
much of the research."

"Such as?"

"Compiling voting records of male Democrats on feminist issues like child care, abortion rights, work equity. We
were also tracking campaign promises versus actual voting
records on other issues."

Grabowski stopped scribbling. "That's it? Voting records? That's hardly murder material. Voting records are
public information."

"But for a legislator, compiling voting records can be
construed as campaign work, and Kay and a certain Communications officer were doing this on state time. They
were risking their jobs."

"But these voting records were on people from your own
party. How could that be campaign work?"

Rubenstock sighed. "You're right. Our problem is that
our shaky female authority here would collapse completely
if reporters found out that female Democrats were being
rendered ineffective by males from our own party. Irene,
Renata, and I wanted to get the goods on the offending senators, then tell them we would feed it to their Republican
opponents in the next election if they didn't allow us our
rightful role."

Grabowski started writing again. "What exactly were
they doing to render you ineffective, as you say?"

Rubenstock sipped her coffee. "In the last five years,
since Wilk became caucus chair, no bill introduced by a
woman senator has ever lived more than a few days. Prac-

tically no male senator will sign onto a woman senator's legislation, except for McNulty. If a female senator's bill actually made it to a committee hearing, it died a quick death."

"Why would they do this?"

"Fear, Detective. Politics has always been a men's game. It's poker, with different stakes. Men know that if women get one toe inside the political arena, men's power is gone. No more calling secretaries 'honey.' No more sexual attacks on everyone wearing a skirt."

Senator Rubenstock's eyes glittered and face flushed. Kay nodded vigorously.

"You tell him, Senator."

Grabowski shook his head. "I don't believe that any male would seriously worry about a bad voting record on a feminist issue in this state. Especially given the antifeminist behavior you have been describing."

Senator Rubenstock sighed. "Detective, you are politically naïve. Any voting record on any issue can defeat an incumbent in an election if the voting record is used correctly. A good campaign writer can put out negative campaign mail that makes a senator's vote to improve the food in nursing homes look like he's trying to starve out the Head Start kindergarten program."

Grabowski carefully changed the direction of the conversation. "Let's go back to your being undermined by male senators. What about Senator Wisnewski's health care bill? Why wasn't that killed?"

"Irene Wisnewski was cochair of the Health Care Committee and kept it alive. She got to be cochair by default. She was vice chair two years ago—a token job invented by Wilk to prove to the press that he was profeminist. So when Wilk had bowel surgery, she took over as chair. When he came back from the hospital and wanted the position of chair back, she made such a stink in the press that the caucus voted to create a cochair position."

Kay added, "Also a token job. If she were male, she would have kept the lead position until the end of session.

Irene kept her own health care bill alive by tabling it when it looked like it would get voted down in committee. Then she let other senators make amendments by trading their amendments for their support. Her final bill wasn't her original bill, but it wasn't bad."

Rubenstock nodded. "Then Irene was poisoned. And we lost the envelope with all our information."

"Okay," said Grabowski. "You were compiling male Democrats' bad voting records on feminist issues to force these men to vote profeminist. Did Senator Wisnewski use this information to get votes for her health care bill?"

Kay Landau and Beverly Rubenstock looked at each other. Beverly shook her head. "If she did, she didn't tell me."

Grabowski let a minute go by. "You understand. If she did, this could be her poisoner."

Grabowski had entered Senator Rubenstock's office convinced that she was a poisoner and a blackmailer. Now she seemed like a reasonable woman coping to the best of her ability in a harsh world.

"Who do you think stole the envelope?" he asked.

"That's obvious. Senator Wilk. As caucus chair, he had the most to lose if women got in control."

Grabowski left, after a private word with the policewoman in the hall to stick like glue to Rubenstock and keep as much of an eye on Kay Landau as possible. He detoured by Wilk's office, but it was locked. In the security guard's room, he called Information for Wilk's phone in Madison. It wasn't listed and the telephone operator refused to believe he was a cop. Wilk's district phone in Okonomowash was listed, but the recorded message gave only the senate office number.

Then he called Diana Ringer.

"You've been misleading me," he said. "You told me that you only knew rumors about the Feminist Political Strike Force and that it was a women's support group. Then you told Maxene that you heard by rumor that some senators were collecting voting-record information. Now I've learned from Senator Rubenstock that Kay was doing the research—along with a Communications person. You wrote for Senators Glover and Wisnewski. That person had to be you."

Diana sighed. "Got me. Highly illegal; that's why I didn't tell you."

"What else didn't you tell me?"

"Nothing! I used the Legislative Computer Data System to pull up records and I was always flicking off my screen when people came through. Even though I have every right to pull up records, Senator Rubenstock didn't want anyone to know what I was doing. Printing out the records on my lunch hour and after work was giving me ulcers."

Grabowski didn't know whether to believe her. "Were you just researching senators?"

"And Democratic assemblymen from the same districts as Irene, Beverly, or Renata since they could carry the senators' legislation through the assembly. We didn't find anything. The members are younger and more liberal, and there are more women."

Grabowski hung up feeling deceived. Diana should have told him what she was doing, even though technically it could ruin her career. Her activity was related to the poisonings.

His bad mood lingered through the drive to Milwaukee. The detective room at police headquarters was quiet, only a few officers writing reports. Grabowski's box held a large sealed envelope from the police artist. He ripped it open and stared with disbelief at the detailed drawing compiled by the two neighborhood boys with the artist.

It was Assemblyman Mark Birnbaum.

The Milwaukee phone book didn't list Birnbaum's home phone, but this time when Grabowski called Information, the operator could tell he was calling from police headquarters and she came up with the phone and address. A woman answered on the third ring. Birnbaum was outside shoveling snow.

"Tell him Detective Grabowski is on the way over,"

Grabowski snapped, surprising himself at the anger in his voice.

Birnbaum lived on North Frederick on the well-to-do North Side, in a graceful brick home with a rounded blue wood door and matching window trim. A Christmas wreath still hung on the lamppost. A green Camaro like the one described by Senator Wisnewski's neighbor sat by the curb. Birnbaum was watching out the window. He opened the door as Grabowski marched up the curved walk.

"Sounds like you've got an emergency on your hands." Birnbaum's smile was weak.

Grabowski yanked off his leather jacket and threw it over the back of the couch. Then he threw the police artist's envelope at Birnbaum. Birnbaum pulled out the paper slowly and closed his eyes. He sank into a chair.

"Evelyn said you found witnesses. I should have known. People were everywhere."

"Did you do all the vandalizing?"

Birnbaum nodded. "I borrowed a friend's car. Pretty stupid, huh? Sometimes I can't believe it myself."

Birnbaum's wife sat down on the arm of his chair and put her arm around her husband. Birnbaum leaned his head against her.

Grabowski felt his anger dissipate. "Why did you do it?"

"Irene. She was driving me crazy. She was burying every bill of mine before it even passed out of committee in the assembly. My colleagues told me that she had called every assembly member and said anything with my name on it would never pass the senate. She was destroying me politically. She hated me because I vote so far left."

"So you vandalized your own office and blamed it on her."

"To destroy her credibility. But no matter how much I tried to start a rumor in the legislature about her being the vandal, the rumor always died."

"Did your aide know you were responsible?"

"I think Evelyn started suspecting me the day I threw a

rock through the window. I didn't know she was there. Rotten luck." Birnbaum's shoulders slumped.

Grabowski smiled, remembering what Evelyn had said about Birnbaum being unable to organize himself out of a paper bag. "Was that all it was—political mudslinging? Nothing connected to the Feminist Political Strike Force?"

Birnbaum's eyes flickered. "Did you ask me about that before? I don't know what it is."

Grabowski waited and Birnbaum began to fidget. For some reason, the topic was making Birnbaum nervous.

"You do know what it is, don't you?" said Grabowski.

"I may have heard something; some women legislators want more rights for women."

"It was Senator Wisnewski, Senator Rubenstock, and Senator Glover. They were compiling antifeminist voting records on certain legislators who refused to cooperate with them. You run as a profeminist, proenvironmentalist Democrat, isn't that right?"

Birnbaum nodded.

"If it became known that in your past you had worked against women's rights, you'd lose your next campaign."

Birnbaum frowned. "Are you saying that I vandalized my own office because of evidence from Irene that I was antifeminist?"

"That's right."

Birnbaum's eyes flickered around the room. He licked his lips. "You're right."

"Where's the evidence?" Grabowski demanded. Something was wrong here. Senator Birnbaum's wife was sitting like a statue, her eyes frozen onto the coffee table.

"I destroyed it. No, I never saw it. Irene told me over the phone what she had."

"Did you steal the envelope with the evidence out of Maxene St. Clair's car? Is that what you mean when you said you destroyed it?"

"I didn't steal anything."

"What was the evidence?"

Birnbaum mopped his forehead with the doily that was

on the coffee table. "My voting record of five years ago on not voting for providing welfare money for abortion on demand."

Grabowski picked up the artist's drawing and stuffed it back into the envelope. "Despite what you and other politicians say about how voting records can kill a campaign, I don't believe you. Voters are not so stupid. Nor do they have such short memories. Five years ago a negative vote on an abortion issue wouldn't hurt you—not in Milwaukee, not anywhere in Wisconsin."

Grabowski stomped out of the house. Birnbaum was lying. But about what?

# CHAPTER

## 19

SENATOR RENATA GLOVER had not come to St. Clair's flat by two-thirty when St. Clair was ready to leave for St. Agnes. St. Clair hadn't expected her. Renata was off pursuing her own agenda. Or was she caught in someone else's agenda? Was she being manipulated without knowing it? For that matter, was St. Clair?

Manipulating was a big part of politics. Politicians manipulated words and events in order to manipulate people's thinking—their perception, as Diana called it. Senator Wilk wanted St. Clair to be interim senator because, as a doctor, she had power to influence people's thinking. A few speeches from her and the health care bill would probably pass, even though she herself had not written it. Renata Glover and Beverly Rubenstock had said they wanted her because she was a woman. Presumably, by mere presence, she would keep women's issues in the public mind.

The weatherwoman had predicted another storm, so St. Clair called a cab to take her to St. Agnes. In bad weather, taking a taxi was easier than digging her car out of a snowdrift in a parking lot at midnight.

At six o'clock she was sitting in the supply room behind the nurses' station having a cup of coffee and reading the *Drug Interaction Physician's Desk Reference* when an ambulance pulled up with a shooting victim. The damage was light, a graze, and while Shirley was prepping the wound, St. Clair got the details from the ambulance attendants. They were the same pair who had brought in Senator Glover.

"I read in the newspaper that the strychnine victim we brought in is okay," said one. "I never saw anything like those convulsions."

"Did she say anything to you about how she got the poison?" asked St. Clair.

"No," said the other, frowning. "The only weird thing was, as we were putting her in the ambulance, two of her friends wanted to ride in the ambulance. Sometimes we let close friends do that, but the sick woman grabbed my hand with those long red fingernails of hers and started saying, 'No! No!' So I told the ladies to take their own car. One of them got so mad, I thought she was going to hit me!"

St. Clair smiled. "Senator Rubenstock can be quite forceful."

"Even so, she should have been nicer," said the attendant. "She was shouting she used to be a nurse."

After the suturing and the patient had been sent up to the ward, Shirley pulled another chair into the supply room.

"I read in the newspaper you gave a nice acceptance speech when you were sworn in. Did it take long to write?"

"I don't write anything," answered St. Clair. "Communications and Research do that. And if I slip and say something wrong, my press person sends out a press release explaining why I didn't mean what I said."

Shirley wrinkled her nose. "I hope lying isn't contagious."

"I'm beginning to think it is."

The phone cut into the discussion. It was Senator Chadwick.

"Sorry to bother you at work, Senator St. Clair, but we've got a special Sunday emergency session tomorrow at two, and I was hoping we could have a chat before then, maybe lunch?"

"I guess so," said St. Clair. "I was planning to get to Madison about noon."

"Shall we say the Italian restaurant on State Street? The lasagna isn't bad."

Joella was signaling that St. Clair had a call on another

line, so she promised to meet Chadwick at noon and took the next call. It was Senator Clark.

"I was chatting with Chadwick and we agreed that it might be nice to talk over the health care bill with you a little before the next health care committee meeting, which is Monday morning. Any chance we could have lunch tomorrow before session?"

St. Clair decided honesty was the best policy. "I'm already having lunch with Senator Chadwick."

"Ah. Where, may I ask?"

"The Italian restaurant on State Street. I'm having lasagna."

"Sorry?"

"A joke. Will you be joining us?"

"I just might."

Wilk was the next caller. Joella passed over the phone as St. Clair was standing at the counter, signing charts. Wilk cleared his voice.

"I hear you're having lunch with Chadwick and Clark. A warning. They're Republicans. They want you to change the health care bill. They oppose the state-funded abortion clause and the clause about nurses prescribing antibiotics. They're also against physical therapists making diagnoses. Of course, we're against that, too."

"I'm not," said St. Clair. "As written, physical therapists get limited privileges. Besides, they are professionals—they wouldn't overstep their knowledge bounds."

Wilk went on as if he hadn't heard. "In committee on Monday we'll delete the physical therapist clause and send the bill to Rules Committee as amended."

St. Clair slammed down the phone after Wilk's good-bye. "They don't want a senator; they want a rubber stamp," she fumed.

"Told you," said Joella. "You think they're going to let some newcomer mess up their plans? Of course, if you were a man, they wouldn't be telling you what to do."

St. Clair scowled. "I'm beginning to believe you."

At seven o'clock, Joella transferred a call to the cafeteria, where St. Clair was eating curried split pea soup and wondering how to remove the curry from the hospital kitchen. It was Senator Glover.

"Where are you?" demanded St. Clair.

"Never mind," snapped Glover. "I'm safe and that's what counts."

"Who are you afraid of?"

"I'll tell you when I'm sure. Right now I need information. I spent the afternoon in a medical school library reading about nicotine poisoning. I learned that you can't die of nicotine poisoning from overdose in cigarettes, that the vomiting would make you stop smoking or you would take off the nicotine patch, or stop chewing gum."

"Yes. I've been reading up on it here, too."

Glover went on. "What if you couldn't stop taking in nicotine? What if it got inside you? Could it be pumped out, like strychnine?"

"Depends on how much you ingested. The treatment involves making a person vomit or pumping out their stomach, plus giving drugs to slow or speed up your heart, depending on what stage the poisoning has reached," explained St. Clair. "But nicotine enters the bloodstream fast; that's part of its addicting quality. In liquid form, two drops will kill you. There's nausea, vomiting, diarrhea, headache, dizziness, high blood pressure. Then convulsions and coma. With a big dose, death takes only a few minutes."

"I know. I saw Senator Wisnewski. Where could someone get the stuff?"

"Probably through a medical supply house that sells to research labs. Or a good chemist could distill it from cigarettes."

"Or scrape it off a nicotine patch?"

"I'll call the drug company. They have twenty-four-hour hot lines."

St. Clair had no sooner gone back to her now tepid curried pea soup when Shirley transferred another call to the cafeteria. It was Grabowski.

"Weird stuff is going on," he said. "I found out who was vandalizing Mark Birnbaum's office."

"Wait, don't tell me," interrupted St. Clair. "One rumor said Irene Wisnewski was behind it, but Diana said Irene wasn't so stupid. The other rumor I heard was Birnbaum vandalized his own office and blamed it on her."

"Right. Remember the Feminist Political Strike Force? Irene Wisnewski found something antifeminist on Birnbaum, and he was trying to get her off his back by making her look like she was vandalizing his office. Unbelievable. As if real people care a gnat's whisker what politicians do or say."

"Grabowski, I just got a call from Senator Glover. She wouldn't tell me where she was, but she's safe. She's calling back in half an hour."

"Maybe I'll come by. I want to talk to her."

St. Clair returned her tray with the uneaten curried pea soup and hurried back to the ER. A patient with a bandaged hand was filling out insurance forms with Joella's help. St. Clair grabbed up the *Physician's Desk Reference* from under the counter. She found the twenty-four-hour hot line number for the drug company that made nicotine patches and picked up the phone in the supply room.

Shirley stood in the doorway with her arms crossed. "You going to spend all night on the phone? Maybe I should find another doctor."

"Sorry," apologized St. Clair, punching in the number. "This really is an emergency. Senator Glover is calling back in half an hour."

"Will you have time to see patients before your next call?"

Grabowski had not yet arrived by the time Senator Glover called back.

"Got the information?" she asked.

"You were right," said St. Clair. "and I see what you're driving at. This pretty much narrows down the list of possible people who could have poisoned Senator Wisnewski. Let me explain this to Grabowski. In the meantime, I have a question. Is the Feminist Political Strike Force compiling voting records on antifeminist votes?"

Glover laughed. "Hell, no. We were after personal dirt. Every man has a story somewhere he wants to hide. Stuff went on in those wild parties during session that you wouldn't believe. Drugs, sex, prostitutes. We have pictures. Doctor, that folder could blow the career of half a dozen people."

"It was stolen out of my car."

"Stolen!" exclaimed Glover. "Shit! Who did it, I wonder? Wait, I have an idea. Call you back, maybe. If I don't, I'll see you at the senate at two o'clock tomorrow."

"Wait!" said St. Clair, but the phone was already dead.

She quickly looked up Diana Ringer's home phone. The answering machine was on, but as soon as St. Clair started to leave a message, Diana picked up the phone.

"Senator Glover called me, too," reported Diana. "She's in a hotel and she wants me to pick her up tomorrow for session. She's calling me at noon to say where to pick her up."

She left a call on Grabowski's answering machine that she had come by taxi and if he was still awake at midnight, it would be wonderful to see him. Then the ER got busy and she didn't have time to think. At midnight Grabowski appeared, tired and grouchy.

"I've been lied to by people I didn't believe would sink to those depths," he said, as they hesitated in the covered drive-up to St. Agnes to turn up their collars and get used to the shock of cold air in their lungs. "I hate it. Promise me you'll never lie to me."

The snow was falling heavily, turning the parking lot, sidewalks, and streets into a silent, white mystery. Their footsteps made no sound in the feathery whiteness. The windshield wipers couldn't move fast enough to remove the thick flakes. The streets were virtually empty, only an occasional car with headlights muffled by falling snow passing silently in the deepening white blanket.

"Who else besides Mark Birnbaum?" St. Clair asked, her eyes glued to the white street ahead.

Grabowski peered through the small area of the windshield freed of snow by the windshield wipers.

"Diana Ringer. She told me she knew only rumor about the Feminist Political Strike Force and she was actually doing the research."

"Beverly Rubenstock was lying to you, too. The research for the Feminist Political Strike Force wasn't voting records. It was actually blackmail dirt. And she and Renata Glover knew all about it."

Grabowski swore under his breath. "This means Diana Ringer was lying even more than I thought. I'm starting to think that whoever is poisoning these women has plenty of good reason."

He pulled into St. Clair's driveway and parked behind the white mound that was the back of St. Clair's car. The light over the side door had a cone of snow on it that fell off onto St. Clair's hair as she opened the door. Grabowski brushed it off and kissed the snow on her nose and lip.

"Hot toddy?" she asked. "Curl up in front of a crackling fire? Or straight to bed?"

"Bed," Grabowski said. "And I don't want to hear a single word about senators or feminists until well after breakfast tomorrow."

# CHAPTER

## 20

SENATOR CLARK AND Senator Chadwick were already seated in a booth at the Italian restaurant and were drinking highballs when St. Clair tucked her hat into her coat sleeve and hung up her snowy coat at noon the next day. She waved at Karen Wolfson and Kay Landau, who were having lunch near the back.

"Sorry I'm late," she said to Chadwick and Clark. "The roads were hideous."

"You need a drink." Chadwick waved at the waiter.

St. Clair ordered a Vodka Stinger and a plate of fried zucchini for appetizer. "What's up?" she asked.

"It's the health care bill, as I mentioned." Clark smiled. "We have some excellent amendments that will help it pass the floor vote. Without these amendments, we happen to know the bill will die in the senate."

"Are the amendments related to the abortion rights clause?"

Chadwick answered. "That's right, honey. The clause should be deleted, along with the clauses about nurses writing prescriptions and physical therapists making diagnoses."

"Your AMA lobbyist doesn't like those parts?"

Chadwick shrugged. "The Republicans don't. That's all you need to know."

St. Clair ate a crispy zucchini. "Have you heard of the Feminist Political Strike Force?"

Chadwick yawned. "Rumors. What about them?"

St. Clair accepted her drink from the waiter. "They're a

198

research group that promotes feminist issues, like the abortion rights clause in the health care bill."

Chadwick dabbed at his lips. "Abortion rights is something we'll have no trouble killing on the senate floor. You were thinking this feminist group could somehow get it passed?"

Senator Clark had downed his drink and was waving at the waiter for another. "We want the nurse-prescribing section out, too. And the physical therapist section."

St. Clair took a long drink of Vodka Stinger. "I think they're good ideas. So does the Feminist Political Strike Force."

"Think it over, Dr. St. Clair," said Chadwick. "You're only here for a few months and you have no political future to worry about, but try to see the situation our way. You can rewrite the clause now or we can defeat the health care bill. That would be a waste of everyone's time as well as the taxpayers' money."

Clark cleared his throat. "I heard Senator Glover was poisoned by strychnine."

"That's right. I was covering the ER when she came in."

"I suppose whoever poisoned her still has strychnine left. What a horrible death."

The lasagna was excellent. After a cup of coffee and an after-dinner mint, St. Clair followed Senator Clark's Buick back to the senate parking lot. Senator Glover and Diana Ringer were getting out of Diana's car by the door to the inside. Diana handed her keys to the garage attendant. St. Clair pulled up behind them and handed the attendant her keys. They waited while the attendant put the cars away and came back with their keys.

"Normally I park my own car," said Glover in a low voice, "but I'm taking no chances. There's a maniac out there."

"Do you know who it is?" Diana asked.

Karen Wolfson hurried up and put her arm around Senator Glover. "We're so relieved you're all right. I was worried sick. What a horrible experience!"

"You can't imagine," said Glover.

It was nearly two o'clock and St. Clair had only a minute to drop by her office to hang up her coat and pick up messages. Rhonda handed her a sheaf of papers and held out a dish of leftover Christmas candy. St. Clair popped a toffee into her mouth and hurried back to the Senate Chamber just in time to stand for the flag salute and the prayer of the day.

The Vodka Stinger seemed to be making her dizzy. Or maybe it came from working late the night before, driving two hours on snowy roads, eating a heavy lunch, and now standing in a hot room. She sat down gratefully and opened her sheaf of papers.

The room began to tilt. St. Clair hung on to her desk and fought back the nausea. Her heart seemed to be beating a hundred times too fast. Sweat dripped down her forehead. She fumbled for the phone on her desk. Rhonda answered immediately.

"Call Senator Glover's desk and ask her to come over. I'm going to throw up," whispered St. Clair. She put down the phone carefully and took hold of the desk again. In a minute, Senator Glover was bending over her.

"I'm going to throw up," whispered St. Clair. "Get me to a bathroom."

She felt Senator Glover grip her arm and pull her up. She walked as straight as she could through the tilting room, out the Senate Chamber door, through the crowd of lobbyists, and around the corner to the marble-tiled ladies' room, where she threw up.

Senator Glover handed her a damp towel to wipe her sweaty face.

"You were next," Glover said, grim. "We've got to stop this person. Look how easily you were caught."

St. Clair looked in the mirror. Her face was yellowish green and mottled red. Her eyes were bloodshot. But the room had stopped tilting. She drew a deep breath. "Let's go back to the senate. I can cope with just sitting. But if I wave my hand, come over. I may have to throw up again."

Back at her desk, the light on the phone was on, meaning Rhonda was trying to reach her.

"What happened?" Rhonda said.

"I felt sick suddenly and had to get to a bathroom. I'm all right now. Listen, did anyone come into the office this morning?"

"Sure. Lots of people."

St. Clair could hear her chewing. "Stop eating!" she exclaimed suddenly, then lowered her voice. "What are you eating?"

"Potato chips. I know it's not on my diet."

St. Clair cut her off. "Put that candy that you gave me into a sack and staple it shut. Then get Grabowski on the phone. Can you transfer him here?"

"Sure," said Rhonda. "Anything else?"

"Tell me what the hell they're talking about here."

Grabowski's voice came over the line in ten minutes. "What happened?" he snapped. "The radio said you were led off the senate floor, sick."

St. Clair explained. "I've been sitting here putting these pieces together," she said. "Things you told me; things Renata Glover and Diana Ringer told me."

"Anything I don't know?"

"I can't tell you everything now—I'm supposed to be voting on something. But tomorrow morning the Senate Health Care Committee meets. That's where this whole thing started, and I think that's where we can make it end." Then she explained the other things she wanted Grabowski to do.

"I'm coming to Madison now," said Grabowski. "Wait in your office until I get there. Don't eat anything and don't plan anything for dinner. I'm bringing the food."

# CHAPTER

## 21

THE SENATE HEALTH Care Committee convened early Monday morning. A few spectators had arrived, but senate security held them in the hall.

In the senate room were only those people specifically invited: the health care committee, which included Senators Maxene St. Clair, Renata Glover, Beverly Rubenstock, Mark McNulty, William Wilk, Buford Chadwick, and Albert Clark. Assemblyman Mark Birnbaum was there, along with aides Evelyn Brown, Rhonda Schmidt, and Kay Landau. Diana Ringer and Karen Wolfson were sitting together in the front row. A policeman and a senate security guard stood at each door, and Grabowski leaned against the wall.

St. Clair sat down in the witness chair.

"I've only been a senator for five days," she began, "but I've learned a lot about politics. I've learned never to rely on one source of information, and I've learned that when you put power, money, and political egos together, something is bound to explode."

At this moment, the policewoman came in and held up a manila envelope. St. Clair acknowledged it with a nod and went on.

"The poisonings that went on here—including my own—were a result of a lot of under-the-table goings-on that everybody knew a little about, but nobody knew totally. They happened because too many people were putting on too much pressure and the weakest link snapped.

"I'm here because of the health care bill. It's an important bill that could make or break the political career of many senators. However, it had become too complicated. It required a major tax hike and had big problems because it gave medical privileges to nonmedical personnel. It also gave state money for private Catholic hospitals who traditionally have refused to perform tubal ligations or abortions. Everything in that bill was bought dearly by trading off votes for other unrelated bills. Senator Irene Wisnewski was center of all the trade-offs. The health care bill was so important that three women were poisoned because the trading wasn't working.

"I was told that I was drafted as temporary senator to get it passed simply because I was a doctor. This wasn't true. I was simply a credible body to fill a hole while the underground work continued.

"I was also told that I'm here because I'm a woman and could raise the status of women in politics. From what I see, average salaries of women employees are lower, there are no adequate women's facilities, and bills introduced by women senators always failed."

"Because they're stupid bills," snapped Wilk.

McNulty shook his head. "Wilk, join the twentieth century. There are worse things than gender equality."

"Those dames don't want equality—they want power!" exploded Wilk. "That's why they formed that stupid Feminist Political Strike Force. Irene Wisnewski was the ringleader. She went too far and that's why she was killed."

"We were compiling voting records," said Senator Rubenstock, calmly. "Granted, that's not completely sanctioned for a senator's staff, but it's not illegal."

"Senator Rubenstock is telling half the truth," said St. Clair. "The Feminist Political Strike Force was also compiling blackmail information."

Diana Ringer stood up. "I heard about it, but I drew the line."

Kay Landau's face was flushed. "I helped, but nothing criminal. I only passed on to Senator Wisnewski rumors about where the parties were and who would be there. I never used any of the information."

"Somebody did." Grabowski looked at Assemblyman Birnbaum.

Birnbaum jumped to his feet. "That bitch Wisnewski! I didn't kill her, even though I told her I would. Okay, there were prostitutes at that party, but that's no reason to ruin a political career. Feminists are not responsible for all women. Those prostitutes were there because they wanted to be."

He sat down and put his face in his hands.

St. Clair went on. "Other people had received calls from Senator Wisnewski. Senator Wilk did, and so did Senator Clark and Senator Chadwick. The Health Care Committee. From their reactions when I asked them about it, they all knew what the Feminist Strike Force was, even though they claimed they didn't."

Senator Chadwick flung his pen down on the table. "Irene Wisnewski wanted her health care bill passed as she drafted it, and she was willing to blast my picture all over my district to get my vote. I told her what she could do with the pictures, which was the same thing I told her to do with her health care bill. I'd have to explain away those pictures in my hometown, but it wouldn't ruin me. No Democrat has won in my district in ten years. I had nothing to worry about, and I told her that."

"Same here," said Clark. "The newspapers in my district wouldn't touch that stuff. Even if they did, it would blow over. People don't elect politicians on their moral behavior anymore, if they ever did."

Diana Ringer nodded vigorously. "That's what I told Senator Wisnewski, but she wouldn't listen. She was so mad at the males in the health care committee for not passing her bill as she wrote it that she was out for revenge."

"That's right." St. Clair nodded. "She played dirty politics with senators and assemblymen who knew how to handle it. Then she started pushing around someone who couldn't fight back. She manipulated and lied to the person until that person killed her."

"Nobody killed the old bitch," said Chadwick. "She overdosed on her cigarettes. Served her right. She should have stopped smoking years ago."

"You're partly right," said St. Clair. "Senator Wisnewski died of nicotine overdose, but it wasn't an accident. I talked long-distance to some drug company chemists. They became nearly hysterical when they heard that a State Board of Health official had said a state senator died from nicotine patches. They said the nicotine dose on patches is carefully calibrated and only prescribed jointly with an addiction counselor who watches the person's other intakes of nicotine, like cigarettes. Even if people using nicotine patches continued smoking, they wouldn't die of nicotine overdose because they'd start vomiting, which would make them stop either the smoking or the patches. The vomiting is terrible. It happened to me, right on the senate floor. That's when I figured out how the nicotine was administered."

"She didn't smoke it?"

"Somebody added nicotine to her gum. A trained chemist obtained nicotine fluid by some means—either distilled from cigarettes or stolen from a research lab—and probably injected it into her gum with a syringe. The senator put a piece in her mouth before the senate hearing."

"How do you know?" demanded Chadwick.

"I saw her," said Glover. "I said something about it at the Nurses' Association dinner, a while before I got sick and was carried off to the hospital."

The security guard stepped forward. "She was chewing gum," he said. "She always put a piece of nicotine gum in her mouth right before committee hearing. She said it kept her awake. She and I even laughed about it that day, but I forgot."

Rhonda Schmidt nodded. "She was supposed to stop when she started with the nicotine patches, but she didn't.

I was telling somebody about it last week. I can't remember who."

St. Clair nodded. "The person you told was the same person who heard Senator Glover ask me at the senate hearing if Senator Wisnewski could have choked on something, the same person who heard Senator Glover at the Nurses' Association dinner say that Irene was chewing gum."

Senator Glover looked pale. She looked at Beverly Rubenstock. "You heard me," she said.

Rhonda nodded. "And you were in the room when I said it. It's your office; you're in and out all the time."

Chadwick pointed at Rubenstock. "You did it. Irene made you go along with her stupid blackmail scheme, then she wouldn't vote for your abortion-on-demand clause. So you poisoned her."

Senator Rubenstock glared at Senator Clark. "Optometrists know their way around a lab. You were lying when you said that morals charges wouldn't affect you. Two-thirds of your vote comes from fundamentalist churches. They wouldn't like what Irene was planning to send to their pastors. You were toast."

Wilk interrupted. "Beverly, you could easily have poisoned her. You were a high school chemistry teacher. You could order nicotine through a supply house, or distill it out of cigarettes in a chemistry lab. When Irene went further than you wanted, you poisoned her. You lived together; it would be easy."

"Wait!" called out Diana Ringer. "Senator Rubenstock was poisoned, too."

Wilk waved off the objection. "Overdosed herself on her own quinidine to make Irene's poisoning look accidental. Then she figured out that Renata knew what she was doing and tossed strychnine into Renata's food at the Nurses' Association dinner."

McNulty shook his head. "Beverly didn't poison anybody. She's too logical."

Rubenstock closed her eyes. "I had a failure of logic, I'm afraid, Mark. I let Irene talk me into going too far. I let her pressure people too much. Maxene was right when she said that if you pressure people too much, something explodes. But believe me, I don't know who poisoned Irene, or Renata, or Maxene. I didn't do it, and I most certainly didn't poison myself."

St. Clair nodded. "Beverly and Irene were both poisoned by the same person. They were given an overdose of their own medicine because it was supposed to look accidental. It worked, briefly. The investigation was closed. But the poisoner couldn't stop because too many people knew about the chewing gum and would start to connect the gum to the convulsions and figure out who had to have put nicotine in the gum. Renata knew and Rhonda also knew. That's when they got poisoned."

"I wasn't poisoned," said Rhonda.

"Your candy dish was poisoned. The person realized that sooner or later both of you would connect the gum to the convulsions. I took a piece of the candy and got sick when I was on the senate floor."

Rhonda's jaw dropped. "You mean that whole basket was poison candy?"

"The police lab will tell us. The nicotine only made me sick, but it would have affected you much more seriously, since you already have a high nicotine level from smoking."

Grabowski held up a hand. "It's true that whoever did this knew their way around a lab, and Senator Rubenstock did teach high school chemistry. Beverly was accused of something more—of phoning the State Board of Health and telling them to close the case."

Rubenstock raised her dark eyebrows. "Of course I didn't do this, either."

"You're right. This is when the poisoner made the fatal mistake. Senators' voices are recorded every day during session on radio or television. I played all the senators' voices to the man who took the call that Senator Rubenstock supposedly made. He couldn't identify her as the caller."

McNulty frowned. "Sketchy evidence. Matching a telephone voice from memory is nearly impossible."

"Besides, a senator could have forced a staff member to make the call," said Diana.

"True." Grabowski nodded. "But I played Ivan a tape of the real caller making a speech at a dinner two days before. Senator St. Clair told me where to get the tape. Ivan recognized her immediately."

The senators looked at each other and at the people sitting in the audience. Finally Diana spoke.

"There's only one person left who had lab experience, gives speeches, and was present each time the senators were poisoned."

She looked at the woman sitting next to her, the nurse-lobbyist, Karen Wolfson.

Rhonda gasped. She pointed a chubby finger at Karen Wolfson. "You're the one I told that Irene was chewing gum! And you gave me that candy!"

Karen folded her arms. "Irene lied to me. I went along with her stinking scheme so that she would push through the physical therapist clause and the nurse-prescribing clause in the health care bill. Then at the last minute, she bargained them away in favor of an abortion-on-demand clause that Senator Rubenstock told her to put in. Senator Rubenstock knew that I had to produce or I would lose my clients, but she didn't care any more than Senator Wisnewski did. Women should stand together. They shouldn't stab each other in the back."

McNulty grabbed his hair. "Don't confess! Say nothing! Grabowski, read her her rights before she utters another syllable if you want this to go to a conviction."

Karen was standing now, shouting. "Irene said she was a feminist, but she lied. She said she cared about people's health, but she sat there smoking and wouldn't give any health professionals a chance, except doctors. She was bought off by the American Medical Association, just like the Republicans."

Grabowski and a uniformed policeman were already

hurrying over, Grabowski yanking a copy of the Miranda Rights out of his wallet, the policeman pulling out a set of handcuffs.

# CHAPTER

## 22

FOR ONCE IN their existence, the Senate Health Care Committee sat in silence for longer than it took one of them to draw a breath and start arguing again. They watched Grabowski and the uniformed policeman escort Karen Wolfson out the door. Then Senator Glover put her head down on the table and began to weep.

"I knew the poisoner was either her or Beverly as soon as I collapsed at that dinner," she sobbed. "I thought I was a goner. If that ambulance team hadn't got there so fast, I'd be dead."

"Don't forget Dr. St. Clair's excellent medical care," said Senator Rubenstock.

"And her logical mind," added McNulty. "I'm impressed. How did you figure out it was Karen Wolfson?"

"Partly process of elimination and partly logistics. She had an appointment with Senator Wisnewski just before the senator died, and she was present at each poisoning. When Senator Glover told the ambulance medics that she didn't want her two friends to ride in the ambulance, I realized that Renata suspected either Senator Rubenstock or Karen Wolfson. So Grabowski played voice tapes for Ivan."

"Lucky he recognized the voice," said McNulty.

"Actually, he didn't," said St. Clair. "That was bluff."

McNulty shook his head. "Did he get a search warrant for Karen's apartment?"

St. Clair nodded. "They didn't find any poison, but they found the apparatus she used to scrape nicotine off the patches. Apparently that's what she injected into Senator

Wisnewski's gum. She must have given her a pack of gum before the hearing."

"Did they also find the evidence envelope that was stolen from your car?" asked Rubenstock, gesturing toward the policewoman, who was still holding the manila envelope.

Assemblyman Birnbaum cleared his throat. "Can't we forget about that envelope?"

"Don't be a wimp, Birnbaum," called out Chadwick.

Wilk cleared his throat. "I'll speak to Detective Grabowski about this envelope matter. I'm certain we can come to an understanding."

McNulty laughed.

Diana was frowning. "Why was Senator Glover poisoned by strychnine?"

"That's easy," said McNulty. "Renata doesn't take any prescription drug she could accidentally abuse. Hard to fatally overdose on vitamins."

Glover had dried her eyes. "Was the strychnine in my vitamins, like Beverly thought?"

"I don't think so," said St. Clair. "The police lab didn't find any in the rest of the vitamins they tested, but I don't know if they tested all twenty-five bottles. I think she put some in her after-dinner coffee cup and switched cups with you when she heard you mention the gum chewing. You were all sitting at the head table."

"But why did she do it?" demanded Kay. "She had a great career; lobbyists make a ton of money."

McNulty shook his head. "She was a woman in a traditionally man's job—an uphill battle all the way. A lobbyist's job is persuasion, and when a lobbyist's clients lose faith, they move quickly to another lobbyist. Karen's background was nursing, and her clients were nurses, physical therapists, other health care people. Karen's only way to keep her clients happy was to get them what they wanted from the health care bill. Which meant sucking up to Senator Wisnewski."

Wilk turned around to look at McNulty. "How do you know so much about lobbyists? You won't even let them in your office."

McNulty yawned. "Lobbyists are a big part of politics, and it pays to know about who they are and what they're up to."

Rubenstock nodded. "This session there were only two clauses in the health care bill where Karen could produce results for her clients—allowing nurses to prescribe and allowing physical therapists to diagnose certain ailments. To get these for her clients, Karen went along with Irene's idiotic blackmailing scheme by going to the parties and being the actual bait for drunken senators."

"How do you know?" demanded Wilk, his face red.

Rubenstock laughed. "I was at the parties, too. You don't think I saw what was going on?"

St. Clair continued. "Karen was doing it for herself, too. Her chances for success were being destroyed by the Republicans and by Senator Wilk, who opposed both those clauses. Senator Wilk also promised state money to Catholic hospitals and universities, which I found out from my hospital administrator and from the vice chancellor of Marquette. Senator Wilk needed the Catholic vote to win his next campaign, so he was also going to vote down Beverly's state-funded family planning clause. Beverly kept him from killing that by agreeing to vote against the physical therapists. Karen was getting torpedoed from all sides. When Irene told her she was going to vote against the two clauses, she handed her a package of gum."

Senator Glover shuddered. "I can't believe someone would kill just for politics."

"She didn't mean to, I believe," said St. Clair. "She just wanted certain people out of the way when the bill went to the senate for final vote."

"Is that why she wrote me those threatening letters?" asked Rubenstock.

Evelyn Brown laughed. Assemblyman Birnbaum flushed. "Let's forget about those letters. But tell me where did you find the manila envelope, Maxene?" asked Birnbaum.

"Grabowski found it along with Senator Wisnewski's missing briefcase. They were in the safe with the liquor in the office of Senator Wilk, just like Senator Glover thought."

# CHAPTER

## 23

ST. CLAIR AND Grabowski were tucked into the pillows of St. Clair's soft chintz couch in front of a crackling fire in St. Clair's apartment, drinking hot toddies and watching the snow pile up on the window ledges. Outside, the streetlights caught the falling snow.

On a crisp fall day months before, they had rented a U-Haul and driven to an apple orchard, where they piled the U-Haul full of split apple logs from the pruned trees. They had stacked the sweet-smelling wood in the back of St. Clair's garage, and in the blue dusk, had carried a load upstairs to build a fire in the fireplace and watch the blue flames curl around the logs. They had fallen asleep curled up together on the couch, with just the sound of the softly crackling fire. The same blue flames were crackling now.

The phone rang.

St. Clair groaned. "Tell the person I have double ear infections and I can't put a phone even near them."

Grabowski picked up the phone from the side table and grunted a hello. "She's deathly ill," he told the caller. "She's in bed and will be there until Monday morning." Then he took the phone off the hook.

"It was Rhonda Schmidt. There's a lobbyist fund-raiser Sunday night. It's vital you attend. The new Nurses' Association lobbyist will be there and particularly wants to meet you."

"Temporary senators don't attend fund-raisers," said St. Clair. "That's a law I passed."

"I thought you were starting to like politics." Grabowski passed over her hot toddy and took a long drink of his.

"I am. Especially now that Senator Wilk is back in the hospital with more bowel surgery and Renata Glover is chair of the Health Care Committee. Rumor says Wilk is getting himself transferred to the Transportation Committee."

"How's the health care bill?"

"It passed the senate complete with nurse prescription clause and physical therapist diagnosing clause. The lobbyist for the AMA is in the hospital with a bleeding ulcer. The state-funded abortion-on-demand clause failed, but Birnbaum has a similar bill coming from the assembly, and Senator Rubenstock and Senator Glover are jointly sponsoring it in the senate. They're currently fighting the feminist backlash. Senator Rubenstock gave a speech in caucus yesterday on postfeminism."

Grabowski groaned. "Give me a break. The word 'feminism' is giving me a headache."

"Well, go back into your bastion of machoism down there at police headquarters and find out what life is like without independent women."

"Take it easy, Red. I'll make you a deal. Marry me and I'll become a life member of NOW."

St. Clair smiled and stroked the gray streaks in his curly black hair. "If we get married, the first thing we do is repair the fireplace in that sweet little bungalow of yours."

Grabowski rolled over and looked up at her. "You actually want to live in my dump?"

"I'm fond of the lake across the street and the seagulls. I'm even fond of the banging shutters and the leaky roof."

"You could change your whole life at once," Grabowski suggested. "You could get married, move to the South Side, quit St. Agnes' ER, and run for the senate. I'll be your campaign manager, even if you are a feminist."

St. Clair smiled. "Kay has already offered. But I told her, not a chance. Politics is fun, but I'll be glad to get off the phone."

# Janet McGiffin

## Published by Fawcett Books.
## Available in your local bookstore.

URSULA K. LE GUIN

THE
Other Wind

ACE BOOKS, NEW YORK

THE OTHER WIND

An Ace Book / published by arrangement with
Harcourt, Inc.

PRINTING HISTORY
Harcourt, Inc. hardcover edition / September 2001
Ace trade paperback edition / January 2003
Ace mass-market edition / October 2003

ISBN: 0-441-01125-X

ACE®
Ace Books are published by The Berkley Publishing Group,
a division of Penguin Group (USA) Inc.,
375 Hudson Street, New York, New York 10014.
ACE and the "A" design
are trademarks belonging to Penguin Group (USA) Inc.

PRINTED IN THE UNITED STATES OF AMERICA

10  9  8  7  6  5  4  3  2  1